CW00406400

Rude
Mechanicals

RUDE
MECHANICALS

Sue Prideaux

An *Abacus* Book

First published in Great Britain in 1997
by Abacus

A CIP catalogue record for this book
is available from the British Library.

ISBN 0 349 10941 9

Typeset by M Rules in Melior
Printed and bound in Great Britain by
Clays Ltd, St Ives plc

Abacus
A Division of
Little, Brown and Company (UK)
Brettenham House
Lancaster Place
London WC2E 7EN

To Michael

CHAPTER ONE

It wasn't that he couldn't say no to his wife. The truth was his manners were so perfect they threatened his direct impulses with total extinction.

Take their first Christmas together, newly wed. She'd given him a reading lamp, tied it with a tinsel bow and plugged it in behind his chair.

'The *Sunday Times* survey says it's the best. It's Japanese-designed.'

He could believe her. Its searchlight beam would have lit up the furthest corners of Changi's compound. Under her avid eyes he read for half an hour, by which time his ear was cooking nicely and dyslexia had broken out on the blazing white page. He switched off the new possession and closed his aching eyes.

'Tired?'

'Meaty.' He indicated the book, fortuitously not a Dick Francis. 'Brain food.'

A week or so later he changed chairs. Solicitously, the lamp moved after him. That was when Peter gave up the pleasure of losing himself for hours in other people's words. The Japanese reading lamp had turned him into an original thinker. Only on bad days did he think about the question of where good manners ended and compromise began.

Two boys were born in quick succession. She'd wanted to call them Dominic and Benedict.

'But nobody's ever been called that.'

'What do you mean nobody?' Lucy knew exactly her huge capacity for blackmail in the maternity nightgown that buttoned down the front.

'It's just not a Skeffington name. Nobody in the family . . .'

'Who cares? Stuffy family. They're beautiful names, listen to the melody. Dom-i-nic, Ben-e-dict,' she set them to the tune of 'Frère Jacques'. 'I love them. Let's be the first.'

They were the first.

His mother enjoyed an assumed incomprehension.

'Heavens! I'd no idea your Lucy had a thing about the monastic orders. It'll be Francis next, I suppose. Rather a drippy name I've always thought. We'll have to hope for a girl. Even poor Clare's better than drippy Francis.'

No sooner had he finished defending the names' beautiful musicality than they were cut off staccato: Dom and Ben.

'Dom and Ben,' he hummed, 'flowerpot men.'

But names, what were names? He threw himself into the nursery years. They stretched in his memory: seamless, frictionless, broad sweeps of dimpled domestic bliss. Even sour retrospect could find no flaw. The young family turned inward on itself, utterly self-absorbed, landlocked in an entrancement. Nannies were the only foreign encroachment. Invited into this closed hermetic circle, the nannies enjoyed the status of occupational soldiers: courted, needed, yet the focus of wild resentment. Poor girls; they never stood a chance. Florence Nightingale herself wouldn't have been good enough to look after the boys. The succession of noisy firings and anxious hirings provided dramatic counterpoint to days that might otherwise have seemed, frankly, dull.

Nursery years moved imperceptibly into drawing-room years. Invisibly, involuntarily, Lucy and Peter slipped into a new stage of mummies and daddies. Lucy exaggerated feather-headed charm; he assumed paternal gravitas. Tension was introduced, a little iron crept into the backbone of the otherwise too-cheerful marriage.

Peter stuck an inadequate label on to the next stage. The guinea pig years he called them and was guilty of a great understatement.

Had he forgotten that with young childhood his sons had turned his home into a snorting, buzzing, clippety-clop vivarium? Keythorpe Grange oozed caterpillars, marmosets, gerbils, stick insects, terrapins. The living toys each enjoyed a brief obsession. Each was forgotten suddenly or, worse, dwindlingly. Tearful little funerals at first, slow processions up to the animal graveyard. Later a casual fling on the compost or the bonfire heap.

He could remember a shoal of tiny sharks enjoying a brief imitation Caribbean in a tank on a windowsill and disappearing mysteriously one by one. The cat accused and only months later, during the spring clean, skeletons found behind the tank. His heart contracted in horrified compassion. He loathed the fish but his family had a duty to sustain even their dull little lives.

'Lucy darling, didn't you bother to find out that sharks can jump? You should have put a pane of glass over the tank.'

''Course I knew. It said so in the book. But it was a terrible bore to lift up every feeding time.'

Neither the boys nor their mother paused a second to mourn the many and varied deaths. On they tore through mini-crocodiles and a wormery – 'so educational' – headlong into hatching silkworms in the airing cupboard. Fondly he hoped that generations of future archaeologists would concoct great theories on the balminess of Sussex in the late twentieth century, as they unearthed the exotic skeletons. Of all the outlandish pets it was the less-than-electrifying guinea pigs that gave their name to his sons' boyhood years. The guinea pigs, Longhaired Peruvians by breed, were also brothers and they were very like his sons. The little mammals – rodents? – fused and became inseparable from his recollection of the boys in those running and squeaking years. Memory muddled their parallel cutting of teeth, growing of balls, extravagant physical growth and cautious approach to intellectual development.

The two little animals had a limited repertoire but within it tremendous powers of expression. Fear, disapproval or anger made them flatten snakily. 'Tick,' they said.

'Yuk,' said the boys in similar mood.

In pleasure the little animals closed their eyes, rounded their bodies and sang. 'Purr,' said a happy guinea pig.

'Yum,' said a happy primary school brother.

A few years later in cool punk clothes under twin shocks of surprising platinum hair: 'Great/Drag.'

'Purr/Tick.'

Imitating bisexual rock stars next, tossing louche scarves and tottering on silver platform boots (mercifully a brief stage, this). 'Dee-vaine/Not quaite naice.'

Their mother understood the boys' devices. Her growing up had also been all style. Their father was uncomprehending. She might have explained the utter harmlessness of earrings, quiffs and carefully cultivated moronism; instead she stepped up her own skittishness. There was a certain larky triumph in being an honorary teenager; youth might be catching through youthful attitudes. She gave him no way out of the ponderous disapproving role he had only assumed in the first place as a game.

The teenage boys viewed their father through a haze of astonished boredom much as they had, as small boys, viewed a pet after the first fascination. He, in turn, found a defence in distancing himself even further. He took to thinking in terms of a foreign tribe: 'Two of the Peruvians need more bran. The other two need batteries for their Walkmans.'

It gave the boys a bearable comic-strip quality. He stopped bothering to remember their ages. Often he jumbled their names, called one by the other, confusing Ben with Dom.

The little animal brothers went to the guinea piggy heaven (he buried them hurriedly, furtively and alone, obscurely ashamed). Now they were dead there was no more amusement to be gained from pretending his sons were honorary guinea pigs of the Longhaired Peruvian tribe. His flash-and-blood sons were two capable City tyros now with two new words: 'Profitable/Wipe it.'

It seemed less credible than ever that they should be his mortal legacy. Longhaired Peruvians no longer, they needed a new name. Like naming a baby, the renaming of his grown sons had not been simple. The obvious name was slow to come but when it came it was perfect. They were the Polyphemans: outsize, dull and limited of vision. Now he could deal with them again.

And now it was time to join them for breakfast.

CHAPTER TWO

They were five for Sunday breakfast: the family unit and
Zanna Eggar, daughter of the local garage proprietor and
egoist *par excellence*. All but Peter wore fawn elasticated
jodhpurs and the righteous faces of those who have taken
excessive exercise unreasonably early. Ben and Dom had
grown up in jodhpurs; it puzzled Peter how these days they
wore them with the air of merchant bankers at a masquerade.

'Good ride?'

'Mm,' said his wife, which was a syllable more than his
sons.

The hungry riders were digging into all sorts of things
under chafing dishes. Lucy's vision of domestic comfort
currently favoured Edwardian splendour: a heavy, undomestic atmosphere, silver domes over the sausages and
huge fanned napkins. Happily she didn't dress to match.
She'd changed since bridal days of course: an element of
dignity had crept in, but not a whiff of Edwardiana, thank
God. Her hair was a little less golden now and certainly
more organised. He was pleased she didn't ride in a hair-
net, hideous contraptions, ultimate turn-off. She piled her
long hair in restful heaviness on her head. There was a line
across her forehead where the riding hat had pressed.
Discretion had got the better part of make-up with the passage of the years: her lips were large, firm, and shapely; she
accentuated the slight almond shape of her eyes. The set of

her features might be called commanding: her nose had fined, the bone noticeably pressing against the thin skin of the bridge. In conversation she would give her whole attention, like a myopic reading a face. While reading, her lips and eyes would stay quite still and expressionless until the speaker had finished. Only when the sentence or question had run its full course and she had taken on the speaking role would her face become animated in answer. This unconscious trick of hers flustered many into foolishness. Some were frightened of her. In their courting days Peter had found her apparent unresponsiveness utterly challenging and seductive. He still did.

'You're taking Muckraker to Longchamp,' Zanna Eggar accused. He wondered why she sounded so angry about it.

'Well, I think it's rather ambitious, I doubt the horse is worth the airfare,' he started cautiously – there were reefs to negotiate here – 'but my wife . . .'

'She says I can't go.' Zanna clattered her fork noisily on to the eggy plate. She scowled, patted her pocketless jodhpurs, scowled some more at being cigaretteless and then decided to suck her thumb instead.

Zanna came to the grange on the coattails of Lucy and her horses. Lucy liked the girl, despite her youth and conspicuous beauty. Zanna was always ready to have fun, and never too busy to help with the horses. She fitted in all sorts of extra work: worming and poulticing were undertaken with a Pollyanna cheerfulness. How surprised the fifteen-year-old's parents would have been at all this unprompted cheer from their youngest.

'But surely you can't spare the time off school to go to a horse race?' Peter hoped. 'Aren't you doing exams?'

'Oh that.' She practised her hair-tossing. 'I can spare a weekend. Besides, the coursework's easy. I do want to go,' Zanna wheedled, 'and I do all this riding out for you with no pay or nothing.'

Zanna's voice was goodish and, Peter noted, getting

better every time she came up to the Grange. Imitation came easily to her, more easily than logic and deduction. As a result her pronunciation ran ahead of her grammar, which still had a naïve quality.

Peter disliked this girl with her gunboat diplomacy. It aggravated him to find Zanna Eggar at his breakfast table more often than not these days. Eggars and Skeffingtons had lived in the same village for the last hundred years without ever feeling the need to eat breakfast together. The two families had always felt perfectly comfortable with each other. Mutual society flourished in due season and within certain well-understood limits. The men stood together among the reeds at the edge of the village pond shooting wild duck, or leant companionably on stalls, conducting entirely predictable conversations about crop yields and the price of fatstock. The equivalent female occasions took place among the sheaves at harvest festival, and in hedgerows at sloe-picking time. Generations of Eggar women had helped clean the Skeffington house. In that capacity it was perfectly proper they should take elevenses at the kitchen table with or without the Mrs Skeffington of the day, but this breakfasting *en famille*, this was something else altogether. Village considerations apart, the last thing Peter needed was another hormone-rich teenager imported into the house just when his sons were over their silliest phase. He might at least be spared smouldering sex first thing.

Little Zanna Eggar couldn't help it of course. Like a saint in a window she was surrounded by a great nimbus. It just happened that she glowed not with holiness, but sexiness. Whatever she said, or saw, or touched, had to travel through this extra outer envelope, this musky complication. Everything was completely personal for the girl, or completely meaningless. Abstract, intellectual or formal concepts might be moonspeak; indeed, so self-absorbed was she that not even gossip appealed.

But this Paris trip was different, something she took seriously. Zanna had never been abroad in her life, and she'd commit murder to go. Foreign travel was a great and important item in her curriculum. Nothing to do with the old saw about travel broadening the mind; she would have recoiled in horror at the picture of her beauty thrown out of proportion by bulging brains and expanding widths of forehead. Nor yet was she drawn to Paris by the lure of all that shopping. She wanted to fly to Paris because if she did that she'd be like supermodels and other people in magazines.

Peter hadn't a clue who was being vamped over breakfast: himself? One or other Polypheman? Which one was she after, Ben or Dom? Were all three at it, gangbanging like rattlesnakes? He put up his paper: a defence of sorts though maybe a crucifix would be more effective. Or a silver bullet: that'd do the trick. He grinned suddenly, mystifying Lucy, but she was pleased to see him happy, whatever the reason, so she poured him more hot coffee.

'Thanks, darling.' Lu could sort out this girl and horse business.

'A weekend in Longchamp can't muck up my exams,' Zanna told the room in general. 'Riding out for you for free of charge every morning before school's much more likely to blow it.'

Not yet a tactician, Zanna had left her jugular exposed.

Peter imitated the lion: 'I seem to remember you begged to be allowed to help exercise. There's really no need. We can manage perfectly well if it bores you.'

Zanna's full lip trembled and her eyes almost managed tears. She looked over at Lucy in case the pathetic brimming had passed her by.

'Honestly, darling, don't be unkind to the girl, she's had a tough morning. 'Course you can come.' Lucy's voice had softened for the girl, but she added on a more practical note, 'We can't do without her. No one else can keep Muckraker quiet on aeroplanes.'

At once the teenager was transformed. Out came the thumb, and in went eggs and bacon.

Peter looked at his watch. Twenty to ten, time to draw stumps. 'I'd better be getting ready for church.'

Nobody moved. There wasn't even a little guilty shuffling. There was the next lot of riding to be done, and everyone knew that horses had never been able to exercise themselves.

Tweed-jacketed, content to be alone, the squire of Pendbury strode down the village street. Downhill to church, uphill back home. Keythorpe Grange lay at the top of things in more ways than one.

The village of Pendbury had not existed at all until some enterprising Victorian had thought to cut a railway line through what had till then been native forest. The village had sprung instant and full arm'd from an 1870s sowing of dragon's teeth. It had enjoyed inventing a long and colourful past for itself ever since.

Local legend spoke of The Forest very much with capital letters, conjuring impressively yet vaguely a medieval royal hunting ground. Falconry was modestly but proudly implied, embroidered surcoats, picnics in flower-studded glades after the noble chase. Somewhere along the line these medieval romances had achieved the status of fact. First one of the Henrys had hunted here; soon an Edward or two had come to join him; finally and inevitably Pendbury Forest had become the favourite arena of Bess herself to hunt both harts and Cecils. Fond fantasy. The native habitat of spiked gorse, hooked brambles, and adder-harbouring bracken would have given those royal steeds (magnificently caparisoned in gay chequerboard silks) a hard job to penetrate and return in good decorative order.

A triumvirate of large houses was the great cornerstone of the Victorian village. Built in competition between the three big families, it ran the gamut of building styles. Any student of architecture too impoverished to travel the world might take in almost all its historical development for the price of a ticket to Pendbury.

Beginning at the monastic centuries, Norman and Gothic jostled at the Brook House where mullioning and leading proliferated on carved foliate capitals and iron-studded doorways of horror-story proportions. These days the Brook House was an asylum housing young criminals.

Wildbeam Park, the second great house of the village, demonstrated in stone Victoria's wide trade connections from sea to shining sea. Nabob's Mughal (expurgated of lewd sculpture) wove seamlessly into Arabian minaret and chinoiserie conceits. It boasted a Tudor-oriental long gallery, manically polychromatic. Someone had once counted the hundreds of thousands of brick and flint strips arranged in crossbars, lozenges, chessboards and various other patterns. Wildbeam Park was now a country hotel advertised expensively on American TV.

Peter was proud that Keythorpe remained a family home. In building, the original Skeffington had corseted himself tightly within the general area of the French baroque. Remarkably majestic, the house was mainly pink and white in colour with ferruled pilasters. The skyline was enlivened by barleytwist chimneys. Over the windows things got quite out of hand with broken pediments richly ornamented with balls, vases and cherubs, heraldic and military emblems, scenes and cartouches, flags and palms, crests and grotesque masks. There was a garden pavilion with a wonderfully coloured series of glazed tile tableaux.

One could entirely understand why Lucy Skeffington had been drawn to become mistress of this house. One could also entirely understand why much of her life was spent moving furniture.

Until the wars the families in these three large architectural vanities had vied in opulence and in the magnificence of their charitable gestures. This competition sprouted a rich harvest of solid brick-built symbols of benevolence throughout the village: rows of almshouses, ranks of workers' cottages. There was a village green with an unnecessary pump ornately porched, carved with rhymed uplifting sentiment.

The church had been built on generous mini-cathedral proportions to suit an age when a huge servant class could be pressed into pew-duty. Peter was no philistine. He knew St Guthlac's was no beauty but his heart lifted seeing the old monster this morning. Against a fine autumn-blue sky piled high with silvery clouds the building looked almost handsome. The west door was open and the coldwater smell of unused air struck stale in his cold nostrils after the invigorating walk.

His mother was already in their pew. She liked to be in her place well before the performance began. That way she'd overhear maximum gossip.

A small-boned, fragile-looking woman, Honor Skeffington was in fact very tough. Nothing about her was as advertised on the outside. 'Poor Honor,' her friends had said, 'she'll never survive as a widow. Talk about clinging vines . . .'

Honor adored widowhood. The vine could transfer its support perfectly well to its son for the tiresome things; the amusing could be enjoyed unhampered, without a husband to consider.

She also adored being old. She loved the deference accorded to age, the wisdom read into any banality she cared to utter. She enjoyed the assumption that the old were so busy making their reservation with St Peter that they could always be trusted to eschew mischief. People expected you to stick rigidly to honour and truth.

Honor cared nothing for heaven – a superstition – an invention for the weak-headed who couldn't face up to the concept of the full stop. Not a believer in God, she'd hardly missed a Sunday's church in all her seventy-odd years.

She enjoyed the power conferred by her age and social position in the village. She also knew this power would vanish instantly should she let herself go in any way: imprecision in speech, behaviour, dress. She took great care to preserve the perfect conventional appearance while working away at plots and schemes, some innocent, some not, to provide amusement for herself.

This Sunday service was the vehicle of a current mini-plot, with the vicar as dupe.

A second man lived in the vicarage. All Pendbury believed the two men lovers. It was the special reason they felt quite justified in mischievous defiance and sabotage of their priest.

All Pendbury, in this instance, happened to be mistaken. Contiguity in time and place had brought the two men together, not sex.

Father Terence would have been pained and surprised had he known the village opinion. He had taken a vow of celibacy and had adhered to it. In truth it suited him, asceticism being his grand title for a nature very sparse in lusts and longings. The temptations of the flesh did not torture him, they were just strong enough to tweak a teensy bit from time to time.

If you were to take up holy orders it must be a great help to look like some half-starved early martyr. Thin-cheeked, pale-skinned and hollow-eyed, Father Terence was a walking reproach to those Christians foolish enough to waste their time in eating and drinking. Habitually he would feed himself on whatever prepackaged meal came first out of the freezer and he would read the heating up instructions before bothering to find out the title on the packet.

'I only eat to keep body and soul together,' was a favourite saying. It about encompassed his understanding of the human soul.

Ashley was the second inhabitant of the vicarage, presently fumbling at St Guthlac's organ. Unlike the vicar,

Ashley enjoyed his food but he was happy to offer up his bodily comfort for his friend. Ashley ate well only when he and the vicar were invited out together. He lived as his friend lived and was grateful both for the companionship and for the deprivations which made him feel happy, and even a little holy by proxy.

Something had gone badly wrong at poor Ashley's birth and he had as a result grown up small, twisted and bent. His pregnant mother had been reading the book at that time taking the world by storm, even to her outpost of limited literacy. All her long girth-increasing months she'd struggled in heroic tongue-mumbling toil with those hundreds of pages that made up *Gone with the Wind*. The baby must be christened Ashley (she liked him so much better than that nasty Rhett). Bitterly she watched her little Ashley grow, so obviously the opposite of his glorious golden prototype, and never forgave him.

Ashley and Terence had known each other all their lives. Their two families had lived in the same long row of back-to-backs in a dale not far outside Manchester. As boys the two of them had attended the same rudimentary schools where they had both been scorned, but Ashley had been marginally more scorned than Terence, who'd joined with glee in the general bullying of the little crooked boy.

Ashley was no more loved at home, where his parents cared so deeply about the neighbours they almost had him adopted. The scheme didn't work. They were poor and didn't know how to go about it the right way.

Like many misfits, Ashley sought comfort in the animal world. As a boy there had been the usual collection of small wriggling things in jam jars and matchboxes. What singled out Ashley's little menagerie from those of his back-street playfellows was that each cherished animal would be disabled in some way. The worm would still be writhing despite a terminally squashed end, the beetle would be missing a few legs. All his adopted pets were on an inevitable road to a dolorous end. This was how it had to be for Ashley. Had his parents had the money or the kindness to give him, say, a healthy bouncing puppy of his very own, he would have been deeply baffled.

Ashley spent the minimum time in the educational system. Terence went on to theological college, where it was his turn to be truly at the bottom of the heap, and to discover that theology students were no less cruel than any others.

His teachers guessed that his ambition to enter the priesthood was grounded in a wish to better himself socially. They were ninety-nine per cent certain he'd no vocation. There remained the one per cent. Who were they to deny a genuine vocation? Besides, there was a lamentable shrinkage recently in the number of young men rising to the challenge of surviving cheerfully on the small clerical stipend. The powers that be swallowed hard and Terence Corbishly was duly priested. There was no question of Ashley finding a job, of course.

'Not really well enough . . . you know . . .' his mother whispered. A lot of whispering went on in that house.

Eventually Ashley's ghastly childhood ended. He rose to man's estate, if not man's stature, and then he did something heroic that no one ever gave him credit for. In fact his great achievement brought him only ridicule and calumny: he established a modus vivendi independent of his parents, doing a useful job and following his calling. His job was looking after the priest, his calling was looking after animals, and his independence lay in the miracle of managing to live on the small invalidity benefits that came his way.

Ashley was a great convenience to the man of God. He saved him the cost of a cleaner in church and in the vicarage. He cooked of course, and shopped and washed, and did those things. Ashley had made himself adequate at the keyboard too, so long as he was not flustered.

Unfortunately it took little to fluster the poor, timorous little man. Frequently his fingers would get all crooked and knotted and very disobedient, and when that happened the priest set his jaw and concentrated on how much his friend was saving the parish in organ fees.

This was the two men's third parish together, the suffragan bishop moving the priest always quickly on: movement that the priest mistook for progress.

'It's a small, settled community,' the bishop briefed his representative. 'Pendbury tithes well. Needs no radical surgery. Hatch, match and despatch with elegance and you'll be a great success. By the way, don't neglect the Skeffington family, they're generous benefactors.'

Eager to please, Terence had called on Peter Skeffington's mother, old Honor Skeffington, within a day of taking up residence. He had given much thought to the time of his call, and rang her bell at five-thirty precisely, a suitable time for parish calls: sociable, but not on the scrounge for tea, and no embarrassment to the lady of the house; ladies could be very embarrassed if they were caught peeling potatoes. He had not thought to telephone first.

The priest couldn't have chosen a worse moment. Five-thirty was the dividing line in Honor's diary, the exact place where the thickly pencilled paper turned white every day because nothing should interfere with the private pleasure of the first gin in front of the favourite soap opera.

He would never have guessed he was interrupting. The old lady made him elaborately welcome with strange-tasting green tea and dry cake from the tin. Then she plied him with questions, and Father Terence blossomed: he'd found the perfect listener. She had asked him what plans he had for the parish, and the priest didn't hold back. He described with enthusiasm his intention to wring the tepid Anglicanism out of his parishioners' milky hearts, and place there instead a thoroughly modern impulse towards extempore prayer, a guitar group and an undying hatred for the movement towards women priests. But these were large issues; first he would start by bringing the sleepy village bang up to date with the very latest form of service.

As soon as she'd shut the door on him, Honor got on to the telephone.

'We have to call him "Father", though he couldn't father a goat,' she told all her friends. 'Says he's going to "draw out our fervency". I can't wait. And the other one who lives with him, the little one, he calls his partner, just like they do in the *Telegraph* Aids obituaries.'

She'd gone to his first service agog to see Pendbury fervent, and taken her prayer book as usual. It hadn't been planned, just happened really, that she'd carried on with the old form of service while he read his new playschool version out of the little yellow pamphlet.

'The Lord be with you.'

'And also with you,' the little pamphlet said.

Honor from habit said, 'And with thy spirit.' Honor had a voice trained to ring out over the hunting field. The rest of the congregation followed her lead as usual.

After the service he told her kindly, enunciating clearly: 'We'll have to get you a special large print edition for you to read the correct form of words.'

She gestured with her prayer book. 'What has suddenly made these incorrect after four hundred years, I wonder?'

Coffee mornings in Pendbury that week had a different flavour. You couldn't be seen without a prayer book, it was the fashion object in the handbag. Cranmer was the man of the moment, Conservation of our Literary Heritage the cause, and suddenly everyone became a bit of an expert.

Churchgoing till now had been a calm business. A sort of after-life insurance policy really. You insured for things going wrong down here, paid your regular dues; why not tuck this prudent insertion into the last pocket of your efficient filing system just in case? Why not go on a Sunday?

Now, with buggers in the vicarage, religion had become a burning topic.

'Morning, Mother. Hope you're going to stop your nonsense this morning.'

Peter slipped into the pew beside old Honor just a moment before the choir started to process. He always timed his entry to spare himself as much as possible of Ashley Crowther's organ fantaisie introductions.

Today Ashley's fingers were making a mess of 'Sheep may Safely'. He couldn't for the life of him understand why. It had worked so well in rehearsal. The priest shot a look filled with rebuke from vestry door to organ, a public look, dissociating himself from this musical incompetence. Ashley's eyes fell to his knotted knuckles in shame. He bit his lip. This was but the beginning of the service. To calm the terror that his fingers would grow ever more prankish, Ashley would repeat his soothing word. Often it had the power to compose him.

'Utensil,' he said. It had a beauty, a musicality, an ability to absorb his mind completely in its different sounds. 'Utensil, utensil.'

Father Terence processed in behind the choir, a small and unimpressive figure given to holding his arms huddled across himself in an attitude of skinny, cold lack of confidence.

He found comfort in tucking each of his hands into the wide bell of the opposite sleeve. With his sloping shoulders and habitual green cassock it gave him the perfect triangular shape of a Christmas tree with a face instead of a fairy on top.

He turned to face his congregation, and bungled the opening sentence with a mumbling delivery: 'It has been granted to us that for the sake of Christ we should not only believe in Him, but also suffer for His sake.'

Taking up his position at the crossing he prepared for a

little suffering. The priest lifted up his hands wide to the takeoff position, saying, 'The Lord be with you.' He dropped his pebble into the still water of the congregation, and waited.

'And with thy spirit.' Honor Skeffington led the rebels.

'And also with you. Mother, behave!' her son beside her boomed.

It was to be another Sunday shouting match.

Open conflict during the service was certainly good for attendance figures. People who had not set foot inside a church since their christening suddenly developed devout and regular habits. Never in any previous parish had Father Terence been blessed with such crammed pews. There was a frisson in openly defying your pastor, a feeling of being in the shocking vanguard of things.

'Let us offer one another a sign of peace.'

He set off down the body of the church, seeking hands to shake like a politician seeking babies to kiss. Honor in the front pew kept her hands to herself and fixed him with her basilisk stare. Her blue eyes floated on a teary rim. They drained his courage. He went back to his place and, as soon as he had his flock's heads safely bowed in the pre-Eucharistic prayer, he lifted his own head to beam a quick burst of throat cancer at the old lady. No, not cancer, Lord, better change that to non-malignant nodules on the vocal chords. Nevertheless, not my will but Thine be done.

The closing hymn; Ashley was doing well now (utensil, utensil). The priest composed his face into approval and turned it to the exact angle so the organist could see his profile, though he would not give him the full reward of a direct smile on account of the earlier botching.

Father Terence processed down the aisle in the wake of the choir. Goodbye-and-handshake time.

At theological college his most repeated fantasy had been the one about standing at the church door after the service. He had imagined himself smiling graciously at the centre of a mobbing circle of warm hands and warmer glances, bathing in compliments on his sermon. Under a very pretty porch he would be conducting a weekly cross between a theological seminar, an MP's surgery, and a magazine problem page. There's be lots of invitations too: dinners at big houses, tea and lesser meals of that sort in humbler homes. Oh how the student priest had looked forward to the weekly dismissal.

And now he'd do anything to avoid it. Being put in Coventry by the mob as they jostled towards the door, his outstretched hand ignored, had come as a genuine and bruising humiliation.

'Good morning, vicar.' Honor Skeffington twisted the knife. How he hated to be called vicar. 'Always a stimulating service.'

'See you for lunch.' Peter shook the vicar's hand emphatically. 'Twelve-thirty will be fine.'

He saw his mother to her car, held open the door until she'd settled in the driver's seat.

'You'll have a gay lunch party,' she said.

'Poor fellow, somebody's got to be kind.' But he couldn't see the party going with a swing.

She smiled sublimely, fiddling with her dashboard instruments.

'I think I'm winning, you know.' With a great lurch she aimed the car for home.

Peter preferred to walk. Uphill, back to his wife.

The riders had not changed their clothes. They were in the rose-chintzed drawing room when Peter reached home. One of his sons was in the father's favourite armchair and showed no sign of moving. Boredom hung in the air, palpable. Across the large room Zanna Eggar was sprawling, tummy-down, on the cushioned windowseat, one muddy riding boot on the pink and white chintz cushion, one describing circles in the air, waving for attention. She was the only one not reading a newspaper and she looked disgruntled. There was nothing to do after the fashion pages and it was no fun to be in a room where people were just reading the paper. She greeted Peter like the relief of Mafeking.

There was no further need to vamp him, not now she'd her ticket to Longchamp, but his entrance into the static room gave her a chance to satisfy her endless craving to have some effect upon her surroundings.

'Have you ever had a Mule's Hind Leg?' She sat up suddenly, rubber-jointed as a yogi.

Was this the first line of a joke? One of those schoolgirl traps that made you foolish whether you said yes or no? Just back from church, he'd better stick to the truth.

'Err . . . no.'

'Great!' Zanna leapt up, crossing the room in a great drama of movement. Drinks were kept in a rather good Georgian corner cupboard. The energetic girl flung open the doors and leant on them, swinging them in a fanning motion while she catalogued her needs. Peter found the movement intensely irritating. He glanced at Lucy. She smiled brightly back, knowing he'd be minding about the hinges. Too bad. Served him right, inviting the vicar to lunch.

'Gin,' said Lucy Skeffington, 'it certainly starts with gin.'

'Gin.' Zanna fanned the doors. 'Well, we've got that. And Benedictine, wasn't it, Dom? Your father's never had one of these, come on, stir your stumps. Don't just sit there reading the City shares. You said yourself it's one of the great drinks of the world. You can't die without having an MHL. Help me make it. Oh, yes, d'you remember, Lucy, did the barman use any apricot brandy? I'm sure he said maple syrup. I wonder if you've got maple syrup in the kitchen?'

It was something to do. Zanna had galvanised the room. The other three who'd met this Mule's Hind Leg at the Savoy last week clustered round, joined in the shaking of the cocktail shaker, the selection of glasses, the measuring of measures. They thoroughly enjoyed arguing mixtures and giving their opinions on progressive tastings. Zanna had achieved perpetual sound and motion, a united purpose with herself at the controls.

Peter meanwhile had slipped into his own chair and regained his own paper.

Maple syrup. Mrs Occhi was sent for; she kept the real thing in the larder for pancakes. But still the cocktail did not taste quite right. Maybe it needed just a squeeze of this, or maybe just a whisper of that. Mrs Occhi droned back and forth while Zanna sampled every new addition but nothing could make it *exactly* as it had been last week at the Savoy.

'I should have stuck to a Bloody in the first place.' Zanna emptied her glass and the remaining contents of the cocktail shaker into the winter-flowering camellia that stood in a large and valuable Chinese cachepot in the centre of a pretty Pembroke table. The camellia was a handsome and unusual plant, crowded with single pink flowers, as though a cloud of winter butterflies had flown into the room and settled along the branches.

'That'll make it grow like smoke,' the girl giggled.

Lucy gave a little frown. People like the Eggars never knew when they were going too far. She hoped the alcohol would not kill the plant, which was pretty, matched the chintz and was useful in the house those difficult winter months when chrysanths screamed with pink. Beside these household considerations, Lucy knew that the plant was precious to Peter, one of his best greenhouse babes. Zanna must learn that though she was useful in the household she was not, nor ever would be, assimilated. The minute she interfered with established structures, with permanent and central features, such as, for instance, the status quo between husband and wife, she must go, however great her talents in the stable. On this point Lucy was quite clear. She frowned. A few split droplets of Mule's Hind Leg lay dewy on the polished mahogany. Zanna wiped at them with her finger, converting the cool pearls into a sticky smudge. She licked her finger and winked at the boys.

Lucy said, 'I expect your parents will be wanting you home now,' which was as close as she could get to apologising to Peter in public. She put out her hand to stroke his tweed sleeve, but it was going to take a great deal more than a stroked sleeve to pacify Peter. He might be known county-wide as a mild-mannered, cheerful, reasonable sort of a chap, one of the more unlikely candidates for homicide, but just now he was labouring against a very real urge to strangle Zanna Eggar. His very fingers were curling. He didn't want to kill her because she was common, which she certainly was, and conniving and transparent with it; nor because her rampant vamping was unrestful on a Sunday morning; nor even because her gymnastics would quite soon split the door of his nice corner cupboard. The capital offence was drowning his camellia in Mule's Hind Leg. Peter had an almost religious respect for plants.

It had to do with his profession as land agent. Historically a sleepy backwater for the dimwitted country boy, the early years of his career hadn't overstretched his intellect. Just in the years when he might have become bored, or even contented to let his brain atrophy into a country corduroy brownish fog, the hot debate between conservation and progress had come into sharp focus. It became an issue for knives and skulduggery, spilling on to front pages and prime time. All unplanned, Peter's career-timing had been impeccable. Just at the moment when experts were wanted, he was an expert, practised and competent. He was trained in assessing environmental impact. He had no trouble recommending the route for the bypass, the siting of the superstore; cheerfully he took decisions that would alter the look of the country for decades to come. He enjoyed playing Solomon in local politics; he'd long since lost his awe of government ministers.

Commercially he swam dangerous waters full of sharks

and pirates, waters where his old-fashioned virtues – probity, balance, industry – had a value beyond price. He was successful at what he did. Had he not inherited Keythorpe, he might have bought just such another estate with his own earned money. As it was, he had managed to rescue his patrimony from the disastrous muddle his widowed mother had made of it before she hung it round his neck: no mean achievement.

Peter Skeffington had become an authority. He had also become a passionate man, though had you said so to his wife she would have shrugged her pretty shoulders lightly, and maybe given a small rueful smile, implying that she knew better though she was far too loyal a wife to say so. She would also be careful to conceal any trace of real regret for the strong intangible that had been very real between them, but unaccountably, mystifyingly, had disappeared somewhere along the line.

He had, in fact, always been passionate. All his life he'd been passionate about the mystical union existing between Skeffington man and Skeffington property: house, chattels, land. Keythorpe wasn't Chatsworth, but that was no handicap in his eyes.

For many years he had also been passionate about his Lucy. He was as puzzled as she how passion could be eroded by the million drips of everyday bromides: overtiredness, children, nannies running in and out at unpredictable times, the mismatching of his and Lucy's timetables and desires. The daily divides started at dawn. He got up with the first fingers of the sun, to walk his land slowly, marking each day what needed to be done. His dawdle, she called it, finding it impossibly chilling, and useless in terms of exercise. She soon stopped walking with him, preferring to get her blood moving by riding a bicycle without wheels while reading a book, or rowing a boat without a bottom across mile after nautical mile of dressing-room carpet. She adored huge trashy novels. She read late and slept on into the mornings. He worked late hours; he was often away overnight on business.

The mechanics of the dwindling of passion are hardly so exceptional as to need detailing. Suffice it to say that Peter's passion these days was rechannelled in two main directions. The first was the question of the Brook House, the gothicky-crockety mansion in the village that had been turned into a home for delinquent children; and a shame and a scandal and a running sore it was in his opinion. A large body of villagers objected to the Brook House on NIMBY grounds, terrified of all those dangerous teenagers polluting their green and tidy land. Peter was not of their number. He objected to it on different grounds. He was appalled that in his small village a grimly cruel Victorian asylum regime should be allowed to flourish behind high walls because of the imprecision of the Mental Health Act. He would be visiting the Brook House later this afternoon on his self-imposed weekly task of keeping an eye on what he considered a dangerous situation.

But first he would have time to take the alcohol-sodden camellia out to the flower room, ease it out of its pot, wash the roots and pot it up again in fresh compost. The flowers would drop of course, they'd have to wait another year for flowers, but at least he could save the plant.

Zanna Eggar, little gumboil.

Plants were his second passion. A passion triggered by a crook at the time when the boys were punk and Lucy had chosen to side with youth, and Peter was lonely. He had been working on a large and very profitable development where, strangely, much hinged on a scheduled mulberry tree. The crook had been tied up by the Ministry in what the Ministry devoutly hoped was a Gordian knot: they'd given the crook the green light to develop providing that the mulberry, which would have to be felled, could be replaced by one of its own bloodline.

Peter was called in by the crook for a fee that would

retile the south face of Keythorpe's roof. 'Save my deal, Pete; find me a young Mountain Jennings' (wink) 'mulberry.'

Not one to fudge a brief, even a brief from a low fellow, Peter had trotted off to Kew prepared for failure and boredom. He'd never liked mulberry trees, dull things, their fruits both sickly and pippy. In Kew's library he read the history attached to the tree and was unexpectedly moved; it was dramatic, romantic, touching, fresh as a Verdi opera. The story started with a Chinese princess so in love she risked the executioner's sword to take the first silkworms out of the Forbidden Kingdom, hiding them in her high hairdo while slaves carried her over the border into Persia. Thus, through love, China's ancient silk monopoly was broken. Six hundred years more history, and silk and mulberries were on King James' mind. (Ah! here was Mountain Jennings. He was gardener to the king.) James wanted to establish a silk industry in England, so he decreed that six hundred red mulberries should be planted and – wisest fool in Christendom that he was – he got it wrong. Silkworms like white mulberries, not red. England's silk trade was strangled at birth.

This sharp dart of history pierced Peter's imagination. All these people, countries, times, events, long-dead and invisible, led in a dead-straight line to the tree: a tree he had all his life found unremarkable, even rather disliked. It frightened him, this abyss of his own ignorance. What other footsteps of history was he ignoring?

The following year Lucy suspected him of adultery. In fact he was doing overtime in the library at Kew. It had become an obsession.

On Lucy's dressing table there was face cream made from aloes. Aloes? That called for a further trip to Kew.

Captain Hawkins . . . slave trade . . . East India Company . . . Hawkins' cargo of hot scratchy English linsey-woolsey cloth bought by the Mughal court (what on earth would they do with it in that heat?) . . . swapped for a huge cargo of aloes . . . enough to solve all Europe's constipation at a blow and soften its skin for generations.

Onwards ranged Peter's interest. Outward went the circles. Darwin and Banks, he read their very longhand; the faded ink-strokes opened new worlds, isolating Peter Skeffington dangerously, rendering the past more real than the present. Joseph Banks . . . James Cook . . . Charles Darwin . . . The *Beagle* voyage, the *Endeavour* . . . Primrose picked in Tierra del Fuego . . . moment of electrical connection: *'Old man, I say, an English primrose here in this godforsaken place.'* Springboard connection made to a keystone law of creation: geographical distribution. All that through a primrose, a flower that Peter Skeffington had seen every spring of his life and never given any special significance. Such purblind ignorance! Once started, his pursuit set up circles that spread wider and wider through time and space. Taking Joseph Banks a little further: Banks supplied Coleridge with Indian hemp . . Coleridge and Wedgwood binged on Banks' hemp to cheer themselves up. Three great peaks of eighteenth-century England: romantic poet, botanist explorer and entrepreneur (if you took Wedgwood's trade connections, the linkages became quite dizzying: dinner services for Catherine the Great, china for Napoleon to eat off in exile on Elba). Wedgwood and Coleridge mixed Banks' hemp with opium and henbane . . . Bad thing to do . . Conspicuously uncheering drug-trip . . . Maybe the henbane made for the failure to cheer?

Out went the circles, out and out, endless. It gave Peter a curious perspective on the world. Each growing thing he saw was not so much alive in its own right as vividly populated by ghosts and the echoes of foreign lands; each with its own distinct connected points of people, place and time. The number of plants in this world being, if not infinite, then almost so; the number of social, historical, economic, and geographical intersections had a bewildering complexity. It was a network, once glimpsed in his mind, that made him long to turn it into a grammar covering the world, accounting for history. Occasionally he would get almost mystic flashes of the pattern complete. More often he would find himself fogged in the cloud of unknowing, overcome by the unmanageable overpopulation in the files where he was trying to record the entire picture of the world's plant connections. He needed a computer of unimaginable proportions.

Peter pretended to himself that he was content with his self-perceived role of connector-historian. There was no room today for an innovator, he told himself. The lost valleys had all been found. It would be dotty even to dream of being another Banks or Darwin.

And yet at nighttime, his mind uncorseted, his reason unfettered by reasonableness, he'd often dream of discovering a yet-undiscovered law. He would wake up from these dreams with bliss-dimmed eyes, seeing his life exalted, the world made meaningful through each blade of grass. After his dream he would take his routine morning walk exactly the same as usual, except his body would be as light and transparent as a wraith. But by the time he had come back to Keythorpe for breakfast the mystic had bled out of him, to be replaced by the leaden *drip drip* of the probable. If he'd turned to look he might have seen small pools of abandoned hope in the dark trail his stout boots had drawn through the dew-frosted grass. But as it was, by the time he'd finished his daily round and was sitting down to breakfast, the dream had faded quite away. He was once more Reasonable Peter, the man whose waking ambitions were confined to retracing steps, content to relive other people's great moments.

He had a journey planned. Leaving Lucy and her matching luggage behind, he would retread the Silk Route alone, take pleasure in walking that long ribbon of history. And this was why he wanted to strangle Zanna. The plant she'd murdered by alcoholic poisoning was rare. Samurai played a part, and Benedictine missionaries, Chinese sea pirates and Napoleon's banker; it had a long and important history in Peter's perception of things.

Lucy joined him in the green-and-white-tiled flower room where he was busy over the sink teasing out the roots of the plant. Her conscience was, if not smiting her, then certainly tickling her gently. She gathered up the fallen flowers from the grooved wooden draining board.

'The garage classes never know where to draw the line,' she observed.

'I can't think why you keep her around, Lu.'

''Course you can. She's wildly useful with the horses. And you know my little strategy. While she's here on my invitation the boys couldn't be less interested. On the other hand, if they thought they'd discovered her for themselves she'd be preggers in no time and we'd be marching up the aisle behind her and Ben, or Dom. It'd be too frightful to have the mad Bible-basher as an in-law. Eggar's garage is no substitute for park gates, either.'

'Even the boys wouldn't be that stupid.'

'She might be that clever, though.'

'Heigh ho.' Peter had completed the repotting. 'Lunch I suppose. Ma was at it again this morning in church. What shall we find to talk to tiny Father Terry about? I've a feeling he'd curl up and die if I gave him the apology direct on Ma's behalf. Besides, it wouldn't do much good coming from me and her carrying on. Couldn't you fix it so she behaves, Luce? It's so rude . . .'

'Honor's a law unto herself. You know she is. Quite capable of deciding to tease worse by doing it all in Latin. Besides, it's only a little mischief. Does no harm.'

The sun must have come out from behind a cloud. Suddenly it shone through the window, a wedge of radiant light encompassing the figure of Peter standing with the denuded bush. Lucy remembered she was still holding the broken flowers. Gingerly, as though she were afraid of breaking them to pieces, she put them in the waste bucket.

The news that the priest and his friend were coming to lunch had a quite electrical effect on the Polyphemans.

'Bummer.'

'Downer.'

They leapt up with great energy from deep cushions and declared that London called. Urgent bizzo. Pressing engagement with the telly in the London flat.

'But, darlings,' Lucy coaxed, 'it's toffee pudding.'

'Doggy bags?' came the hopeful suggestion.

Peter had to admit the boys had a point. The luncheon party at Keythorpe Grange was as ghastly as everyone (except the priest) had anticipated. Peter picked a topic, the priest and his little friend rushed at it pell-mell, ran out of road, pulled up short and ended in silence. Hardly, then, a table at which unfolded a wild, surprising intellectual landscape. Lucy abstained from words, contenting herself with looking more beautiful than ever, and smiling ambiguously and benevolently in the manner of the Mona Lisa. She missed no opportunity to ply her guests with food and drink in a way that was unnervingly redolent of stuffing a Strasbourg goose.

Peter was unexpectedly attacked with strong waves of lust for his wife and his mind started threading through possibilities of reasons why all that had been so promising between them for years had taken this unaccountable direction into armed neutrality. He had a great yen to throw out the priest, carry his wife up to bed and spend all afternoon and all night too, if need be, fucking her into the way they were before.

To quell his huge erection, he thought of the afternoon before him. How might he bring forward his plan to reform the horrid institution that was the Brook House? It seemed that anyone who set up a private home to look after troublesome citizens of any kind – the old, the indigent, the over-spirited child – might exercise any amount of unsupervised power behind closed doors. What's more they were even paid a *per capita* grant by the state so to do. Peter sighed.

Lucy brightened at the sigh. It gave her an excuse. 'I think,' she leant forward towards the priest, fixing him with her lovely eyes, 'my husband's had a hard week, you know. It might be best if . . . so lovely to have you both . . .' Now she was on her feet.

She and Peter made sure to stand waving at the door right until the unimpressive couple had disappeared round the bend of the drive behind the cedar.

'Darling,' she said playfully, 'that was the most boring Sunday lunch I've ever spent. Without exception. You are deep in debt. You owe me fids and fids. I shall have no scruple in co-opting you on to my most boring committee.'

'I could put a bottle of the widow in the fridge for tonight? Some reparation?' ·

Or I could take you up to bed and screw you rotten.

But he couldn't. He had his duty to do at the Brook House. Besides, now she was standing beside him so upright and impeccable, so very much what he had made her: Mistress of Keythorpe Grange, *Grande dame*, upper-class DSO and bar, he was quite incapable of the masterful scenario that had seemed so simple at the lunch table.

'I'd better be getting on, I suppose.'

'Not before you've put that bottle in the fridge.'

'No indeed.'

CHAPTER THREE

Zanna Eggar did not go straight home after she'd been dismissed from Keythorpe Grange. Once she knew she was out of sight she dodged round the dense shrubbery that hid the base of the big cedar tree and jumped up, swinging into its lowest branches, pulling her legs up to follow like a caterpillar's questing tail. A little short of the very top she sat astride her branch and bottom-shuffled out as far as she dared. She wished for more wind; it was like a roller-coaster when the branches, blew. Pendbury was short of physical thrills: a gallop on Lucy's thoroughbreds, a stomach-swooping ride in Lucy's cedar tree.

Zanna was probably looking at the best view of Pendbury village there was to be had, but she didn't climb the tree for landscape appreciation. Her attention was all on the house she'd so recently been dismissed from. Her angle of vision showed her the neat dovetailing system of ridges and valleys on the roof and how they had been planned for the perfectly efficient dispersal of rainwater. The cleverness of this passed her by. Her attention was all on the windows and the segments of rooms she could see through them: floors and walls and doors. Ceilings were cut off but that didn't matter; people didn't walk or sit or sleep on ceilings. She couldn't see anyone just now, the drawing room faced another way, but just to look in on the empty rooms was a pleasing invasion. Ben or Dom might come and take a pee in that loo. She'd like to see that. Peter and Lucy might have a sudden urgent compulsion to make love on that big bed.

She imagined she was a mermaid looking down at a miniature subaqueous world; the cedar branches were her green slabs of ocean. The village looked like toy town and as usual nothing was happening, Pendbury was dead.

Zanna was a harsh judge: there wouldn't be much activity in the streets of the liveliest town in England on a Sunday lunchtime in October.

Beneath the tree, where the treasure chest ought to be resting on the ocean bed underneath the mermaid, a rabbit was scuffing at the lawn. Hastily Zanna tore at a cedar cone. Shaped like a large egg, grey, and tenaciously attached to its mother branch, the cone had to be twisted and torn before it came off. The aromatic resin stuck to her fingers. Zanna frowned at the gummy mess and tried to wipe her fingers clean on her jumper but that only picked up fluff. She hated to look messy and scraped the gum-fluff off with her teeth, daintily spitting out each scraping. Now she was clean. Taking careful aim she let go the cone to drop on the browsing rabbit. From this height it should kill it.

The missile landed wide of its target. The stupid bunny gave one or two non-urgent rocking-horse hops inanely this way and that, then it got on with the next bit of grass. If her father wouldn't let her go to Paris she'd murder him, kill him like this with a stone from high up. No – a water-bomb like at school. That'd be better. Water was undetectable. She fell to dreaming how she could get high enough above her dad.

If Zanna had paid attention she would have seen the activity going on in the bedrooms while she was conducting her rehearsal for homicide, but the rabbit had made her miss Dom and Ben scrabbling clothes into their smart initialled grips as fast as they could, before putting as much of the M23 as possible between them and the lunch party.

Zanna watched parents and sons enact restrained farewells at the front door. With the parents safely indoors the show was over. No point in staying here to watch the mouldy priest arrive.

She'd be up at the Grange again tomorrow morning. Lucy'd need her for early stables as usual. She'd have forgotten all about the stupid plant thing by then.

There were blackberries to pick in the hedges on the way home; the first signs of autumn were in the trees. The hand-shaped leaves of horse chestnut had brittle brown outlines as though they'd been scorched. The first ripe conkers, run over on the road, lay spilling their crushed white kernels.

The street that ran the length of the village widened for a green space around the pond where the mallards showed their own signs of the winter coming – the drakes' vivid bottle-green heads had faded now to their fainter winter colour. The mendicant flock paddled towards Zanna, crushing the leaves and misty pink flowers of the water mint as they walked towards her with their own peculiar duckish awkwardness. The pressure of their paddled feet released the mint's wet, sharp toothpaste smell. They walked behind her gabbling and fussing for a short space but turned back when Zanna gave them no notice. She had always had a great contempt for these wild creatures who sold their freedom for handfuls of crumbled bread.

The village green curved round the pond. Inevitably there was a thoroughly beamed pub called the Royal Oak. There was also a tea room, a hairdresser and three antique shops. Pendbury was a village that traded in pretty luxuries. It had long stopped thinking in terms of self-sufficiency and usefulness.

One of the antique shops interested Zanna. This was the one that might suddenly sprout a huge ship's figurehead for sale, or the hindquarters of a marble horse. The other two shops were pale cowards in comparison, full of highly polished safe investments.

Nick Mercer lived in the dashing shop. He was in the same class as Zanna at school. She looked into the Mercers' wide glass window, hoping to see Nick or his father Roger. The two men lived with little differentiation between their home and the shop; sometimes Nick's father, wanting a change from the humdrum living quarters on the first floor, would decide to eat or sleep among the exotic pieces, and then it became like a stage with real people to watch. This idiosyncrasy of his father had deeply embarrassed Nick and his mother, indeed it had been a large factor in driving the mother to leave her marriage and her son. She had not enjoyed sleeping the night in the public eye, however grand the four-poster bed. Nick had been teased about his father's odd habits at school. Now just sixteen, Nick was doing his best to grow into an imitation of his father. He kept a neurotic eye on public opinion while labouring hard to be judged raffishly indifferent.

Nick Mercer had been in love with Zanna for precisely the last two terms at school. She, on the other hand, had secretly worshipped him the previous year and endured all manner of frightening ordeals for his sake. Nick's sudden and very visible volte-face had worked like a magic potion, turning her longing to instant and utter contempt. The son no longer held any romantic interest for her; she really fancied his dad, though.

She peered in the window hoping to see the older man but she saw only the son doing his homework. He raised his head to smile and his hand to wave but she pretended she had not seen, turned quickly away and carried on towards her home.

The Eggar place in village hierarchy was precisely defined, its outward and visible sign Eggar's garage on the outer reaches of the village beyond the duck pond. Here a modest fifties four-up-three-down housed the compact family. It was a remarkable house to find in Pendbury these days because it was entirely innocent of gentrifications; it had never even sprouted a Georgian bow window. All the drab paucity of fifties vernacular stood quite undisguised among the jumble of petrol pumps and invalid autos that made up the business end of things. The family still lived cramped over the shop in the ugly house Tom Eggar's father had put up in 1958.

Certainly not beautiful, the house was also uncomfortable: water condensed on the metal window frames; thin walls and plyboard doors encouraged draughty rattles and the rusticated granite inglenooks were the despair of Tom's magazine-reading womenfolk. To Zanna her home was wormwood and gall. She knew she was made for better things than dying cars and pebbledash. To Tom it was home, right and unalterable; modernisations and 'improvements' were probably devilish and certainly extravagant, though he could well afford them.

Tom Eggar was a very rich man, a fact unknown to his women and unguessed at even at the pub. Had his matronage known the truth there would have been an orgy of spending on a lottery-spree scale. But his women didn't know about Tom's net worth, nobody did. That was what he really loved: being rich and nobody knowing. Like Superman he preserved a humble façade as a kind of gloat against his private possibilities. Always he measured his present substance against his origins, for the son of the Skeffington chauffeur dreamt a dream: one day he'd overtake the Skeffington acreage.

Tom's money came from the garage, and it came in a good steady stream. Eggar's garage had fallen behind the times (hand-operated pumps were good enough for his father . . .) but it was the only one in the village, so there had never been the need to spend out on frippery forecourts and neon come-hithers. Tom had an unshakable faith that land was the only unhazardous investment; whenever a parcel of land came up for sale round about, be it a small scrubby corner or a large fertile field, Tom would buy it anonymously for cash (he never borrowed from the bank, having a biblical horror of the yoke of usury). This land Tom was simply happy to possess, to walk over knowing it was his. It was not his plan to sow thickly with houses and bungalows, and reap profits an hundredfold. That would have declared his hand.

Tom Eggar was a firm, churchgoing Christian and, as he understood it, an exemplary husband and father. Tom would have smiled quietly in superior scorn if it had been suggested to him that there was anything amiss with keeping his wife and family completely ignorant of their financial position. His women had no business with money; anxiously he shielded them from its polluting influence. Wife and two daughters were given allowances carefully increased by a small amount every year but as they had started from an unrealistically low base nobody ever had enough, and as a result elaborate swindles were resorted to. Tom's scrupulously gallant and Christian interpretation of domestic duty led directly to lying, cheating, and sticky fingers in the till.

The biblical naming of the Eggar womenfolk was no coincidence. Tom's wife Mary begat Martha (the nearest Tom ever got to a joke). She also begat Susanna (as in the Elders) whose subsequent snappy shortening to Zanna was entirely the child's own work – and probably the devil's as well.

Zanna's elder sister Martha had married Arthur. Tom had always held the pagan name against his son-in-law. In due course two little girls were born. Martha and Arthur had longed for a Samantha and a little Nicole. Old father Tom pulled together his great eyebrows at such heathenish prospects. Wordless, he thrust the dreary fifties family onomasticon at his daughter: *Proper Names from Bible Times*. It was stuffed full of Leahs and Judahs. Salome and Jezebel were pretty, though. Martha and Arthur settled happily on them.

This was the cast list for the family lunch lying in wait for Zanna. Certainly she deserved marks for courage as she scrunched up the cinder path, ducked under the flopping strands of the carousel washing line (empty in honour of the Sabbath) and kicked open the door to her home with some bravado and also with some fear. Skipping both church and Sunday lunch was a left-and-right in sin.

'Withhold not correction from they child; for if thou beatest him with the rod he shall not die. Thou shalt beat him with the rod and shall deliver his soul from hell.' Tom Eggar was a Bible literalist. Whether or not he was a sadist, whether he got physical pleasure from the act, remained opaque. It was his plain duty to God to keep his womenfolk in their proper place.

Zanna, his favourite, seemed to need an inordinate lot of beating. He'd not had half the trouble with her elder sister. Plump Martha would never dream of missing church. She'd always be there in good time for every meal as well. Not a clever child, nobody could accuse her of that, Martha, bless her, had gone through school just right, popular with her little band of friends and never any worry to her parents.

Martha had always been close to her mother. They had shared the feminine things which made Mrs Eggar feel that she was reliving her girlhood not through her daughter but with her. In Martha's girlhood she was recreating a more perfect one for herself. Martha had the facts of life clearly and rather disgustingly explained to her because her mother had gleaned them all lopsided, and as a result had spent the years between the ages of ten and fourteen thinking that she must be pregnant from sitting on an uncle's knee at Christmas. Mother and daughter together explored fashions and diets, worshipped the same screen idols and started a joint scrapbook whose ambition was to illustrate every item of clothing worn by the Princess of Wales. Martha wearied of the scrapbook long before her mother: Mrs Eggar was still cutting and pasting to this day; Martha simply liked to be shown the book from time to time but the actual doing was rather hard work.

Zanna came in on the family seated at the gate-legged oak table. Her brother-in-law looked up. Normally the butt and scapegoat himself, he greeted her entrance with a jubilant wink. Thanks, said the wink, you've let me off the hook. Arthur's eyes were his best feature. They were big and round and blue and blank under a Neanderthal brow from which lots of orange springy hair fought an endless battle with styling gel. The heavy gold ring on the stubby-sausage finger matched the spirit of his wife Martha's diamanté suite and the whole flight of jewelled butterflies in Jezebel's and Salome's hair.

All looked up at Zanna in her heretical jodhpurs, expecting the paterfamilias to bar her from lunch on the spot and book her into the 'snug' after lunch for a spot of corporal punishment.

But old Tom was playing a different game today. Tom knew as well as anybody that an important part of tyranny is unpredictability. He simply went on with the matter in hand: the chewing of beef with his long yellow teeth, and nodded his head at the empty place where the two little girls Salome and Jezebel sat in silent rebellion against the piles of healthful cabbage on their plates. Old Tom chomped on. Apart from the noises of mastication, cutlery on china and occasionally the odd swallow of water the table was in utter silence.

Mary Eggar took the arrival of her younger daughter as an opportunity to jump up. A stout small figure, Mary was not fat in a bulgy way but solid and distended as though pumped up to her limit under the flowered housedress.

Her eyes had a long way to peer out at the world through deep-set fatty slits. She'd kept the dinner plain for the little girls. Well they wouldn't go for anything wildly erotic, would they? A nice plain roast with a jelly like a castle to follow. She'd get it now and clear away the cabbagey plates while Tom's mind was on something else. Zanna did look great in them tight jodhpurs; like that Jilly Cooper cover. You wanted a steady hand with a jelly castle. The little castrations had come lovely out of the mould today. It was the refineries that made a difference. Tom must have noticed them. He was in a good mood today, it must be the refineries. If she gave Zanna the jelly now, she could have her meat and gravy afterwards. That'd be best. They'd all be finished at the same time for Tom's grace over the empty plates at the end of the meal. Yes, that would be best.

'For what we have received . . .' rumbled the grim sexagenarian. The extraordinary had been accomplished. Sunday lunch had passed chez Eggar without dispute or violence.

'You been up the Grange?' her mother asked Zanna, though she knew full well. Her daughter merely nodded while chewing her tepid beef. The women were in the kitchen now, washing and clearing. It was a moment of peace, one that Mary Eggar looked forward to from week to week. Herself and her daughters in the kitchen, her son-in-law settled in front of the football with a pack of Benson and Hedges and the two little sugarplumps making good the cabbage-gaps left in their stomachs with Smarties, Lion bars, Kit Kat and Twix.

Unspoken questions hung in the kitchen, palpable as the condensation on the windows: what of Dad? What of Tom? Why this ominous mildness? Where was the thunderbolt, the rebuke and the reproof?

He had his reasons. He was turning them over in his mind as he adhered to his unbreakable Sunday habit of an afternoon walk. Along with the reasons bobbed the carnally arousing picture of his younger daughter flaunting her nether limbs in those skintight occasions of sin.

A creature of habit, Tom liked to divide the Lord's day equally between his two manias: the Lord and his (Tom's) land. Church in the morning, and in the afternoon an inspection of the security-blanket of useless land he had accumulated. He'd walk over it leisurely, sticking to the footpaths as though he'd no more right to be there than the next man. And all the time he would be thinking, 'Mine, mine, mine.'

There was a small spinney that Tom did not yet own and it irritated him. Gasson's Spinney made a peninsula between two parcels of Tom's land. If it could be acquired they'd run in together, making it neater, all the same colour on the map. This little rogue spinney had been growing in Tom's mind as Sunday after Sunday he brooded on the untidy stupidity of its existence. The problem was of course that it belonged to Peter Skeffington, and he'd no need to sell at all.

Tom smiled. He would leave his daughter free to mix and mingle with those Skeffingtons and their heathenish unsabbatarian ways. Women couldn't help falling into sin. It was the way of the Lord. Sooner or later someone would step out of line, the squire himself maybe, or one of the lads, it didn't matter which. And when they did Tom would be there to strike with all the strength and all the fury of the avenging angel. No sin would escape his pure all-seeing eye; nay nor sinner neither. His daughter's swelling fork pressing against the stretched breeches . . . There would be a solution to the acquisition of Gasson's Spinney. Quite soon, he'd wager. But old Tom could wait his time; he was a patient man.

CHAPTER FOUR

Old Tom was probably not aware that he was whistling 'Colonel Bogey' as he loped across the bright autumn countryside. Over the woods and lanes and open fields hung an air of last-gasp beauty. Soon dun winter would descend but meanwhile the oak leaves showed every shade of saffron and mustard against a fast-moving mackerel-clouded sky. A cluster of enormous oaks was alive with rooks; further away and darker were firs and rhododendrons. The skinny old man wore Sunday-grey, long old-fashioned garments that flapped as he walked. His loping stride ate up the footpath round the edge of the fields where Skeffington winter wheat was pushing up through fresh dark brown Skeffington earth. The beauty of the scene left him indifferent, he'd other things to look for than beauty. As his feet trod Skeffington land so his jealous eye sought Skeffington things, missing no detail concerning agriculture, husbandry, or human activity. The Skeffington cock pheasants were well-grown this year, their tails a good length. They would make fine shooting and better eating. He would send that fool Arthur out with the gun; one or two would find their way into the Eggar family pot. The larch in the Skeffington spinney he coveted, Gasson's Spinney, were in need of thinning. They needed clearing round. The death-herb some called nightshade was strangling their lower growth. The spinney needed going through; his fingers curled as though they were holding a brash-hook. There was a good hundred pounds or so in the thinnings if they were caught in time. If he could only get his hands on the land by Easter.

A figure came on to the scene. Tom's foxy eyes narrowed. Hello.

Young Peter Skeffington making his way . . . Tom checked his watch . . . three on the dot. Young Skeffington would be on his way to the Brook House. Tom's eyes followed the upright tweed-clad figure swinging its arms as the man walked vigorously and quickly up the sunken lane. Where the lane plunged into the trees the figure was lost only to re-emerge on the next grey serpentine curve before once more plunging out of sight, this time into the dark fir plantation surrounding the Brook House. Through the thin tops of the firs stuck the house's gothicky-crockety chimneypots, their frivolous form causing old Tom to mutter with dark disapprobation some words about gaudery show. He paused a moment, poking at Peter Skeffington's winter wheat with his toe, dislodging two or three plantlets from the soil and relishing something in an obscure, dark corner of his mind. When he carried on he was still whistling the same old 'Colonel Bogey' but now he had differently angled thoughts in his head. Because he'd actually seen Peter Skeffington, the man now occupied an even more prominent part in Tom's musings than before. The old man bared his teeth in a grin expression of optimism and good cheer, though from the outside it made him look like nothing so much as a death's-head.

Peter was unaware that Tom Eggar was watching him. If he'd known he'd have tipped his hat and mimed a well-mannered 'Good afternoon' across the distance between them. But he looked only ahead. A brisk quarter-hour's walk had taken him from home away from the direction of the church and the village green. Here the lane became sunken between oppressive banks of fir trees so thick that nothing grew in the gloom beneath their heavy branches. The sunken land led to a gate that bristled with iron spikes and saw with electric eyes. There was a key in his pocket, a plastic card that he knew to show up to the camera cunningly masquerading as a bird box in a large and branchy holly. The gate swung open to let him in and he was walking under a flaking painted notice: The Brook House, it said, Carolina Foundation for Special Children.

Their specialness was not particularised.

This sometime Carolina (now defunct) who had given her name to the foundation was a native of Hamburg. A rich spinster with romantic leanings, she had once been attacked in a small way in her home town. Thereafter she decided to dedicate the rest of her life and her considerable funds to this exciting event. A home was to be founded for young attackers (male).

The Brook House was for sale very cheaply in 1953, about the time Tom Eggar's father was rising to his zenith and exactly two years before Honor Skeffington was to give birth to a son and call him Peter.

The Brook House reminded Carolina of home (Bavarian Ludwig had always been a hero), and she settled in Sussex gathering her young offenders about her. The institution quickly acquired the reputation of a Bluebeard's castle run by a sadomasochistic witch. Carolina from Hamburg was much talked about in Pendbury but very seldom seen, and then only at a great distance in the back seat of a black Mercedes Benz, a car of mystical rarity in Britain at the time on account of its impressive price and recent Nazi association.

She was useful to the Pendbury mothers: 'Carolina will get you' became a saying, just as 'Boney will get you' had been a hundred and fifty years before. A whole generation of Pendburyites were subdued by the threat.

In the fullness of time she died, leaving a great deal of

money tied to a very complicated document designed to ensure the continuation of the Foundation for ever and ever, amen. The ever-impoverished local authority blessed its luck and piled in the delinquents who would be fed and clothed for years at very little expense to the state. Once a year the place was officially inspected and never found wanting. Between these inspections it could carry on exactly as it pleased. It was governed by a disinterested board of remote dignitaries keen on a quiet life. The governors in turn appointed a 'guardian' to run the place (head sounded too schooly and governor smacked of prison).

The guardian of the Brook House occupied a position of some considerable power and little accountability. Unless actually caught *in flagrante* doing something quite impossible to explain, the guardian had the opportunity to indulge every pet theory on punishment, forgiveness and rehabilitation. Over the years the theories had followed fashion: curative massages with body oils (a very tactile guardian, this), biofeedback machines and dervish dancing. Marvellously powerful ley lines had been discovered to connect Pendbury direct to Glastonbury Tor; tapping their energy entailed a mixture of shoeless orienteering and open-air bondage. Theories flourished and had their day until a bungled search for alpha-rhythms led to a fairly serious electrical accident. Time to call in a new guardian, one with both feet on the ground. Jimmy Stonor fitted the bill. Currently he filled the post and Peter was on his way to the weekly meeting with him.

Up at the Brook House, this Sunday morning had dawned just the same as any other, for the regime at the Brook House made no concessions to Sunday. The rising bell went at six-thirty, though the sun wouldn't be above the horizon for thirty minutes yet and there was certainly no reasonable point in lengthening the cold dark day; there was nothing for the boys to do but fill the weary hours with pointless toil.

Raught, the prefect, snapped on the light and paced the passageway between the black-painted iron beds flicking to left and right with a long wet towel, making it crack like a whip. As he went down the dormitory the boys rose up either side of him in a frightened bow-wave. Today everybody was awake, there was no victim still lying deeply asleep. Nobody would be in for the special towelling today.

Danny was up by the time the prefect passed his bed. In the unheated dormitory the little boy's bare feet were feeling the unwaxed softness of floorboards swelled with autumn damp. His eyes had not yet entered the day; they remained unfocused, part of them still in the land of sleep while his hands followed their morning routine straightening regulation hair and regulation pyjamas.

'Crack.' The prefect's towel caught hard, stinging Danny's shoulder and his neck. A corner of it had got into his eye. His eyeball felt as if it were torn. Danny put his hand up to it but the liquid he wiped on the back of his hand was tears, not blood. Blinking, the little boy didn't dare draw attention to himself. A handkerchief would have been as provocative as a white flag. He carried on blind the scramble into slippers and managed to keep his place in the rush to the cold basins. You had to wear your slippers or you got punishments. Sometimes they put dead spiders in them or pissed in them, and sometimes worse. It was all blurry out of his left eye now and felt like a long raw graze. It wasn't fair of Raught to do that. You were only meant to get towelled if you hadn't got up.

Small for his age, Danny jockeyed for position to piss and facewash. It didn't do to fall behind. He wasn't badly placed in the boy-jostle back to the beds to dress. Okay so far. Mr Skeffington would be coming today. Danny's mind left the morning race, one thin sock an empty cone of air on the end of his foot. His small face lost the hard, pinched look it had assumed on rising – it softened and went blank as his thoughts travelled. Today he had something to look forward to. There were things he wanted to ask Mr Skeffington. Things he'd thought about and saved all week. Thinking about them made him dawdle. The boy was late. Latecomers obviously didn't want any breakfast so they were stood against the wall looking outward. That way they could see the food as well as smell it.

While the small, flop-haired boy was standing there in the victim's place his face had a placid, dreamy, almost happy look that was infuriating to the prefect Raught and the guardian Jimmy Stonor at their egg and bacon. The unperturbed boy goaded them to imagining how they might punish him further. In truth this was no silent insubordination; Danny had not that degree of guile in him. He smiled because he had gone back to a dream, retreated into his private world, the world that made nothing else matter. He'd forgotten Raught the prefect and the towelling. He'd forgotten cold and injustice and undeserved punishments and cruelty: these things had paled into shadows. His eyes had passed straight through the dreary walls of the institutional dining room and into another world. A world where it was three o'clock in the afternoon and Mr Skeffington was arriving for his Sunday visit. How could he manage to talk alone with Mr Skeffington this afternoon without being caught and punished? So far they'd come close to being caught but they'd always managed. If he was caught it'd be lockup. It'd be worth it though, if he had the time with Mr Skeffington first. He dared a glance up at the wall clock: seven ten. Eight hours to keep out of Raught's way and punishments.

Gate negotiated, Peter started up the rutted and puddled asphalt. A dripping evergreen rhododendron jungle pushed in towards the centre of the drive. Nettles flourished on banks pockmarked by rabbit warrens. This lamentable drive offended Peter's professional eye and as he walked he calculated exactly how much money the drive wanted spending on it. This mental arithmetic was automatic and occupied him not at all, being merely a professional tic and a way of suppressing his real concern: would Danny be here today? He looked about for the small companion who might appear and keep him trotting company up the drive. For some reason it was important their meetings should seem coincidental; Peter had once thanked him for coming and there had been a welter of embarrassment. Ah! There he was, not so far ahead, a meagre figure scrambling towards him through a spotted laurel. Peter was glad.

'Hello, Danny,' he said, and smiled.

The boy was very small for his age; nearer a ten- than a twelve-year-old. He'd a starveling's body and the unhealthy skin of a town child. Peter suspected the Brook House diet. The flop of badly cut hair was light brown and some was standing up still where he had slept on it (Peter strangled at birth a fatherly urge to smooth). The wedge-shaped face was pale, pinched and permanently set in defence. On their meetings the man would wait for the moment when the worldweariness would drain out of the boy's eyes. Then into them would seep the sleepy self-absorbed look of one newly out of the egg. Peter found the transition unbearably moving.

'What've you done to your eye?'

He broke a rule, touched the boy. Put his hand under the bony chin, holding the face up to see it clearly in a patch of sun. The lashes glinted gold where the sun caught them, the blue-grey mosaic iris was fathomless. In the inner corner the clear white was splashed with bright blood, a scarlet patch that had nowhere to go.

Not an atom changed physically in the eye he was scrutinising and yet the boy's whole expression changed. Once more he was the little tough.

'My eye? Nothing.'

'Hmm. It looks as though a little blood vessel's burst. If it doesn't affect your vision I expect it's nothing to worry about but it might be best to see the doctor just in case.'

Peter might have been speaking a foreign language. The Brook House was not a place where you saw doctors ever, let alone 'just in case'. Mr Stonor gave out medicines, and you had to be very ill to want to see him. The boy had jerked his head away so Mr Skeffington shouldn't see the tears. Peter could see he was on the point of running away. He felt in the pocket of his tweed jacket.

'Look,' he said, 'I've brought a Brimfield lens. It shows how a dragonfly sees the world.'

The retreating boy turned. Peter held out the instrument, a small thing like half an opera glass with an eyepiece and a lens of faceted glass.

'Hold it up to your eye. Catch the light.'

Danny snatched ungracefully, and was absorbed.

'How do they know they see like that?' Danny asked, handing it back.

Things were always handed back. It was axiomatic that the man would never bring presents; any sort of special treatment only brought punishments. Nor might they ever be seen together. If a branch cracked lightly under one of the numerous rabbits Danny would be off into the bushes as quick as a rabbit himself.

'I don't know, Danny. I suppose they reconstruct the eye in glass on a larger scale.'

'They'd have to cut it up first. Ashley'd go mad. He hates anything done to animals. D'you think it's right cutting them up?'

'Vivisection?' The boy was full of surprises. 'Yes, I suppose I do think it's right. I'm squeamish about it though. I must say I'd never like to do it myself but there's no doubt it does advance learning. Medicine and such wouldn't be where it is today.'

Peter always made a point of answering as fully as he possibly could. The walk together up the drive was always too short for the number of questions that would be crammed on top of one another higgledy-piggledy, no logic in their sequence but as they rose to the top of the list in the boy's mind.

'You know the rainfall cycle you was telling me about last week?'

They'd fallen into step as they forgot themselves in talk. Their heads were inclined towards each other and they were too absorbed to notice the broken arches of rainbow where the sun was refracted in the wet rhododendron leaves.

'I remember.'

'Well, what I don't get is this. The sun takes up all that water from the sea, right? Then why doesn't the rain come down salty?'

The boy had spent some time during the intervening week with his tongue out making absolutely certain before risking asking this question. It had got him some extra teasing, but his need for knowledge had outweighed his fear. He had been nervous of coming back a second week to ask Mr Skeffington such a daft-sounding question.

'Good point. It's a long time since I was taught about it myself. Let's think.' Peter started to explain and as he explained there was a heaviness around his heart. The boy had such a curious, lively mind, it poked in the oddest corners: exactly the corners that interested Peter. He recognised the endless quest for knowledge, just like his own. He could not help contrasting Danny with his two complacent, incurious sons who now seemed determined to live in an ever-narrowing world. It was monstrous the boy should be shut up here and nobody bothering with a proper education. Sometimes, if there were no pressing questions, he would tell Danny the stories of the plants they passed on their walk up the drive; from the way the boy listened he too was entranced by the secret history hidden in leaf and branch.

Danny was on the retreat now. The skinny figure was scrambling through a bush, taking a roundabout route so no

one should know where he'd come from. He'd see him
later but they wouldn't be able to talk. Like secret lovers
they'd have to pretend to be strangers. Absurd.

'I'll see you later,' Peter called. 'You'll be at the gardening club?'

There was no reply. He might just as well have asked the
rhododendrons. Peter continued the cheerless path alone.
Now for his little weekly stint in purgatory, his little
weekly session with the guardian.

Jimmy Stonor, guardian of the Brook House, liked to frame
himself in the gargoyled portico when expecting visitors.
He stood there today in his invariable uniform redolent of
the sea. He wore a blazer with lots of anchor-embossed buttons and below the Plimsoll line were corduroy bags and
sandals; atop all this was a beard, grizzled but with some
memories of auburn about it and glasses which magnified
his glaucous eyes alarmingly to those looking in. By many
little hints and roundabout references he liked to imply
that he was a naval man – the sort of cove not altogether
steady on his pins off the briny.

The lengthening haircut was only one of many things
about Jimmy Stonor that would never have been tolerated
in the Senior Service.

'Welcome aboard!' the jolly sea dog boomed out heartily.

With stage politeness he opened the heavy iron-studded
door to bow Peter through, let the visitor walk before then
suddenly darted on ahead to hold the next door open for
him. This erratic progress went on through the many doors
required by fire regulation to chop up the length of passage
leading to the guardian's study.

God, Peter hated the smell and the atmosphere of these
passages: cold, poverty, dirt, the odd boy on fatigues scrubbing floors on his knees.

He was ushered with much ceremony into the inner
sanctum, the study, a warm fug of a room smelling too

much of pipe smoke. It always made Peter's stomach queasy. The room was host to every masculine cliché: buttoned leather, golf clubs, ashtrays with steering wheels in the middle, a telescope on tripod legs that looked out through the bay window on to the wide landscape of the Downs. There was also a plaster bust of Nelson looking gritty with his empty sleeve pinned up to his epaulette. The remaining eye had been painted an impossible turquoise blue. It gave the head a dissolute, leering look.

Peter winked at old Horatio to give himself courage. He needed all the courage he could muster in this joke room. He should have found it funny, all this bonhomie laid on with a trowel, but he never did. Repeatedly, illogically, he found it sinister. His business here today was touchy. It always was. The minute he displeased Jimmy Stonor he could be slung out and refused admittance ever after. These forays of his into the Brook House were not unlike the forays of his plant-hunter heroes: he was invading a dangerous kingdom as a spy and a thief while covering his tracks with an innocent purpose.

The Brook House concerned Peter. It gave him the distinct impression of a bad scandal on his doorstep waiting to happen, a problem needing a radical solution. His first choice would have been a hand grenade. Failing that, a seat on the governing body. He tried. But that placid body knew the danger of infiltration. The governors, who made a point of not looking into things too closely, were nevertheless vaguely aware of books ill-balanced, expenses unquestioned and skeletons safely locked away in cupboards. They enjoyed the status quo and looked forward to a rosy *far niente* future. Peter was comprehensively blocked. It was not his nature to be defeated so he looked for a back way in and, before long, he found a way through Jimmy Stonor.

The guardian might be a knave but he was no fool. He knew he was at the helm of a ship going through pretty choppy waters; the Brook House was far from snug in port yet awhile. The electrical scandal preceding him had brought unwelcome publicity that had only been calmed by the sacking of his predecessor. Jimmy was in place but not in full command; the uneasy governing body poked and pried too much for his liking. He'd need to make his mark before he could sink back into the paid inertia that was his ambition.

Stonor's absolutely correct instinct was that in order to keep his governors happy he must introduce a wide spectrum of wholesome clubs and hobbies for the boys – a long list of titles to impress them and make them feel that their latest guardian was working energetically to foster that team spirit without which *mens sana* could not possibly flourish. Showily he called in experts and semi-experts to get the activities going, but Stonor's cunning was not as great as he thought it to be. By this short-term pacification of his government he was letting his kingdom be invaded. Unintentionally he'd created the opening Peter wanted. Peter invaded the Brook House under the aegis of the limply titled gardening club. Once in he made absolutely certain of its success. Other clubs and societies came and went, distracting Stonor's attention from the fact that Peter was digging himself in.

The gardening club was a childishly simple scheme based on the idea of getting the Brook House's redundant kitchen garden working profitably again. It made use of the boys' labour, Peter's expertise, and a small amount of his money to get the scheme off the ground.

By happy fluke the boys' delinquency worked to their profit. Lest they run dangerously amok they were strictly confined within the corsets of organic husbandry. Pesticides, fungicides and artificial fertiliser were strictly forbidden. Wholesome dung supplied free from the Skeffington horses ensured high yields of totally organic produce. Local health food shops fought to buy the stuff. To ensure the profits didn't disappear straight into Stonor's pockets Peter had taken on the role of wholesale green-grocer. The boys were paid on a profit-sharing basis and as a result the gardening club flourished mightily. The boys didn't get paid for any of the other activities.

The gardening club impressed the governors. Sociologists and educationalists were starting to notice it, rival institutions were coming on study visits. In short it was the means whereby Brook House was acquiring a reputation in the world of rehabilitation, and this reputation was a great feather in Jimmy Stonor's cap. Now Stonor wanted all the money and all the glory for himself; he wanted to off-load Peter.

Peter had no interest in the glory; he was anxious to keep the money for the boys and more anxious still to keep his weekly foothold in this place.

'It will be simpler if we reorder from the seed merchants in my name this year.' The unstraightforward sailor burned sincerity through intensely magnified eyes. 'Kind, most kind of you in the past to put it in with your order from the Grange and preferential rates for the larger quantities but I think that we should do our own bookwork now. Sail our own ship! It would make a great difference if the boys knew we had the rudder between our own teeth.'

'I hope you'll still allow me to come up every week; I'd like to help in any small way I can.'

'No, no!' a violent shower of spittle. 'Time to paddle our own canoe. You gave us a fair wind to see us out of harbour and we salute you for that. You may rest assured I shall propose a formal vote of thanks in the annual report. You primed the pump. Now you must leave our feeble hands to nurture the little seed – ha! *Little seed*, that's good. I shall put that in too. But to be serious for a moment, the little plant is sturdy and healthy. It is up to us to nourish it with love. Nothing,' his voice slowed and deepened to telly-evangelist treacle, 'nothing grows without love.' Six eyes beamed sincerely at Peter through the prism'd bifocals.

'Shame,' Peter replied as he rubbed his chin, 'it'll be difficult for you without the tractor.' The Skeffington tractor was lent part-time every year for the vital jobs of ploughing and rolling. 'You know how the insurance demands my supervision on the spot.'

Jimmy took out his little spike. He scraped the bowl of his pipe, knocked it, looked deeply into his oilskin tobacco pouch as though for an answer, but the answer wasn't there. The tractor was vital to operations.

'Tell you what, Jimmy. Why don't I just come up every week as usual but leave all the organising and all the paperwork to you? You'd do me a favour taking it off my shoulders.'

The pipe billowed joyously. The arrangement called for a tot of grog. The best of good friends went outside together to see to the latest session of the gardening club, Peter preceded by many bows and courtesies.

The traditional Victorian walled acre of kitchen garden was on a slightly sloping south-facing site, placed as that generation always knew how to place things, to take best advantage of the sun and to let the frost roll down and away off the cultivated ground. The high brick walls were in some state of picturesque disrepair; here and there the stone coping was missing, allowing the rain to run down and turn the brickwork green and the lime mortar to crumble and cease to hold. Swifts and housemartins had nested messily in the wall's fissures. They wheeled about in great numbers over the kitchen garden, swooping and twittering, restless for change at this season.

Peaches, almonds, apricots and figs had been fan-trained against the walls and it was these bushes that caused three or four boys today to be busy about wheelbarrows and buckets of cement. They were repairing the wall to hold vine eyes and horizontal wall wires; the fruiting trees should once more be organised into bearing prolifically.

'Building skills,' the guardian noted with satisfaction. 'Job training.'

This scene in the garden lifted Peter's heart; he was not a man to congratulate himself on his own achievements, so his own part in the creation of the scene was forgotten in his impartial satisfaction at what he saw. The figures in their timeless setting, going about their timeless tasks, looked exactly like a miniature from any medieval monkish manuscript, give or take blue jeans for leather breeches and the bright green tractor, Peter's passport, ploughing a very straight furrow for next year's leeks.

He couldn't see Danny anywhere. He looked for him, anxious about the eye, but it was impossible. The boys in their uniform of jeans and grey jumpers were difficult to identify as they squatted and knelt to work the earth, or bent over their spades and forks.

The garden was divided in quarters by gravelled paths. At the centrepoint where the paths crossed at right angles was a round stone basin. Some of the boys were sitting on its rim, a loose group comprising little Ashley Crowther's birdwatching club. Peter's recent lunch guest looked up and his face took on the closed and frightened look it always wore when the guardian was in the vicinity. Peter made a point of smiling and waving; Ashley returned the wave with a small uncertain gesture. When he got closer Peter would make a point of saying how much he'd enjoyed having him to lunch.

Stonor was now seigneurial. Wherever the guardian went the boys stopped working instantly, straightened up, called him sir and semi-saluted: a royal progress with Peter to show off to.

'Steady as she goes,' Stonor jollied along a barrow-wheeler.

'Sir.' The boy stood to attention.

This was the month for planting out the tough little blue spring cabbages. Three or four boys were busy about the job. Clumsy teenage hands were dibbing holes exactly ten inches apart, gentling roots no thicker than threads into the beautifully raked seedbed. Danny was one of the group; he was holding the line so the row should be soldier-straight. The boy squatted on the edge of the gravel path pulling his line taut, frowning slightly against the sun. His mouth was open and his tongue between his teeth in concentration. The little boy was so engrossed in his task that he'd not noticed the approaching party. He didn't hear Stonor's 'Gangway!'

Jimmy Stonor's foot shot out, clearing the path before him by a good strong kick. Danny toppled forward into the seedbed which he and the other boys had spent most of the day watering and raking to make smooth and even. The boys' care had given the earth a good adhesive quality.

'Stand up, boy. You're no good on the ground. Stand up, can't you? Mr Skeffington is here to inspect your work. Look lively.'

Danny stood up obediently. His face and front and clothes were covered in fine particles of moist soil. He'd soil in his hair, his mouth, his ears; his eyes were blinking it away. His hands didn't go up in the natural gesture to wipe his face but remained at his side as he stood ramrod stiff to attention, facing the guardian. Peter's hand went to his pocket for a handkerchief.

Jimmy Stonor poked the blinking boy. 'Playing mud pies, eh? Call that a seedbed?' He bent over to plant his big foot square on the mud and leave a deep print. 'Not good enough, is it?'

Danny tried to say no sir but his mouth was full of soil. He dribbled. Stonor giggled. The other boys in the group set up a giggle in sycophantic echo.

'Go in and clean yourself up. Have a bath,' Peter said, 'and bathe your eyes. Soil will do you no good in them.'

But this made Stonor furious. He rounded on his guest. Boys bathed at bathtime and no other. This afternoon was gardening time and if the little fool was dumb enough to fall into the mud he'd only himself to blame. Every single one of those cabbage plants must be in by sundown or there'd be a waste of good plants.

Danny had already picked up the four-pronged fork and was plunging it into the ground, doing his unseeing best to work at restoring the soil to its previous smooth, even state. The boy's activity was pathetic.

Peter had never felt so completely helpless. He despised himself at this moment, knowing he must endure more of this, as much as Stonor wanted to dish out. It was at this moment that a thought which had been knocking at the door of his consciousness for some time burst through and came rushing in. He would do something about this place. It wasn't enough merely to keep a watching brief and acquiesce with public opinion that these days saw the Brook House (through – and here was irony – through the club he had created) as some sort of model penitentiary. Peter's instincts told him another story. He'd get to grips with it, sort it out and get Danny to a safer place.

But meanwhile.

'After you.' The guardian bowed him on and Peter continued making small talk while keeping hold in his mind of the small flame. Control was all, and remembering the greater game.

They were approaching the axial centre, the crossing of the paths at the central circular pool. Here sat little Ashley Crowther slumped like a half-filled sack on twisted legs. Ashley felt the cold. From October to May his thin nose was the only strong colour in a waxen face under a shock of black hair. Huddled in his anorak, he was at the centre of the medieval-looking group distributed round the curved stone rim.

Ashley was one of Jimmy Stonor's little band of experts called in to impress his board of governors. He had in fact invited Pendbury's priest to start the birdwatching club.

Father Terence himself had been Jimmy's first choice: status attached to having a priest; but Father Terence was interested neither in birds nor in the welfare of souls at Brook House. The boys didn't come to church, *ergo* they were none of his concern. The priest had volunteered Ashley in his stead. Ashley had been scared of running a club all by himself. A club to do with birds had been doubly daunting. While loving animals in general he'd never made a special study of birds, maybe because their capacity for flight removed them from the worst excesses of man's inhumanity to his fellow creatures. The boys soon caught Ashley's lack of interest. The whole birdwatching thing would have fizzled out sooner were it not for Ashley's perennial obsession with the pity and the terror of man's inhuman cruelty to animals. This so horrified the pitiful man that he could never keep his mind away from it for long. Vivisection, factory farming, trapping and hunting, genetic engineering, laboratory experiments, abominable behaviour to domestic pets; Ashley burned with miserable horror at them all, the sort of horror that could not leave well alone but must always be at the forefront of a mind tortured by a conscience compelled to take on sin for the whole of humanity. It was inevitable that the birdwatching club should metamorphose into a weekly platform for his cause. By informing the boys what went on out in the real world he hoped to convert them into soldiers for the cause of animal welfare. The boys always listened quietly and politely – at least to his face. They had a morbid avidity for Ashley's stories. Mistaking their salacious and ghoulish interest for shared sympathy, he went on reporting new cases to them every week. Now he was telling them about the parabiosis experiments written up in last week's RSPCA journal: 'They take two live rats, cut them in half and sew up the two halves but that is not the end of it. If they do manage to survive, and some do, they suffocate them.'

The boys exchanged delighted grimaces, one mimed the cutting and sewing. The guardian approached. As one they jumped up from the well's rim to stand and salute Jimmy Stonor. Ashley looked up in gentle doubt. How much had the guardian heard? He'd not noticed the approach. Like Peter he treasured his time here; he felt of value to the boys, and the boys of value to his cause. He knew he existed on the knife-edge of expulsion. He was frightened of the guardian, felt more crippled in his presence, became stupider. He knew his physique maddened the guardian and he was right. Stonor's instincts ran to purity, perfection and master race. Had the Brook House been co-ed Jimmy Stonor might have dabbled in genetics and breeding pro-grammes.

'Well, young man.' The benevolent old salt made to cuff the crookback matily on the shoulder but the naval arm stopped just short of touching the repellent lump. 'Godbothering my boys? Converting the heathen?'

'No.' A despairing squeak.

Jimmy sniffed his favourite scent: uneasy victim.

'What were you up to, then?'

Before he could answer a fast fleet of swifts flew down over the cloud-reflecting pool in a precision flypast, almost a bombing mission. They flew so low they skimmed the insects off the surface water but never a wingtip got wet.

It was a little-known fact that Jimmy Stonor was fright-ened of birds. The closeness of these swifts made him duck and flinch. The unexpected sight of the guardian showing fear gave Ashley a moment of courage, leading him to do a most uncharacteristic thing: to come out with a bald, bold statement.

'I was thinking of sounding out the boys to see if any of them might like to join the church choir. With your per-mission, guardian.'

The flash of fear on Jimmy Stonor's face, the intimation of vulnerability, had led to this unprecedented audacity;

but even before Ashley had finished his sentence the guardian's expression had reverted to its characteristic stony brutishness. Ashley clapped his hand to his mouth, his body miming the unconscious desire to stuff the words back unsaid. There would be consequences. Stonor in his bullying fury was liable to expel him from the garden as pitilessly as the avenging angel with the flaming sword had expelled Adam from the garden of Eden. It would be a great deprivation. These weekly visits to the Brook House were very precious to him; the lack of them would leave an ache in his soul. No more chats with the dear boys. Exile, solitude, disgrace. 'Please, Lord,' Ashley prayed wistfully with tears in his eyes, bowing his head, waiting for the torrent of foul language and abuse to break over him, 'help me, somehow.'

It was a strange animal characteristic of Stonor's, one that was recognised by all the inmates of Brook House, that when he was about to deal a blow he would swell up like a toad about to spit venom or a fighting cock about to strike.

Peter also recognised the sign. Intervention was called for.

'What an absolutely marvellous idea.' Peter said. 'I was just thinking in church this morning how ragged the choir was sounding. Most of the voices are well past their sell-by date. A strong group of young voices would be balm to the ears. Make a huge difference to the attitude of the village towards the Brook House too, I shouldn't wonder. I think it might do a lot of good all round if you could swing it to get a choir of your lads down to the church every Sunday.'

'We could certainly do with a strong group to lead the singing,' Ashley ventured.

The toad was less pumped up, several degrees smaller than the dangerous over-inflated stage. He stopped looking at Ashley in that terrifying way. He forgot to go a-bullying. An uncharacteristic expression knotted his brows: the guardian was thinking. Something was emerging from this conversation that was even more tempting than Ashley's cringing victim figure, if only he could think it out clearly. Stonor stood, a hulk becalmed against the mossy well, his mind sailing creakily through waters new to him.

The church? Every Sunday? A muscle twitched on Jimmy's cheek. For all that he was nominally spiritual as well as temporal guardian of the Brook House, the church was a foreign land. Moral welfare was part of his brief. The words 'religious instruction' were in his contract and they weren't words that had ever caused him a moment's twinge. He presented himself to his nodding complaisant board of governors as a believing man, and he believed he was telling the truth as he said it. Believing in what was not so clear. As far as he was concerned spirituality was entirely divorced from discipline, intellect, and established religion. It had everything to do with the muddleheaded exaltation induced by the sheer number and distance of the stars seen through his telescope, the sound of a brass band in the open air, and the awesomely amazing facts on nature programmes.

But the church. St Guthlac's every Sunday? Not a starter . . .

. . . On the other hand.

Still he remained motionless by the well. Peter and Ashley were just as still; polite and passive as courtiers in their suspense. What was going on in Jimmy's thick impenetrable mind behind the thick impenetrable glasses?

In fact he was watching a film unreel in his head. A bright, highly coloured film, silent but none the worse for that when at the centre of it was himself clad in shining raiment, a figure demurely but powerfully resembling Charlton Heston in a bible epic, a Moses in sandals, a Noah militant at the head of a crocodile of white-surpliced boys processing two by two into church. The procession reached a gold lamé altar. The congregation shuddered with expectation. Down came Stonor's arm. Up lifted the boys' voices in soaring doxologies.

'Yes,' he rumbled, to his audience's surprise. (The board of governors had just nipped in to the front pew to join the swelling congregation.) 'Maybe it's not such a bad idea at that. I would be willing to discuss it in principle if a meeting could bet set up with the padre.'

Peter and Ashley exchanged astonished glances.

'Bless you,' said Ashley quietly, giving Peter a small, singularly sweet smile.

Peter motioned for the little man to make himself scarce while the going was good. And while it was good he'd capitalise himself on Stonor's new sunny twist of humour.

'That boy who fell in the mud,' Peter began. 'I think it might be a good idea to get him seen to, old man. I noticed he'd an eye inflamed.'

Jimmy stared hard with a quarterdeck eye towards the plot where the boy was labouring.

The picture had all the ingredients of Arcadia but none of the flavour. A child in a sun-dappled garden. A robin bobbing at the child's feet, making quick darts to peck for the grubs and eggs and worms as the earth was disturbed by the child's attempted recreation of the seedbed. The Arcadian picture even had a wholesome smell: loam, ferns and decaying leaves wafted on the air of autumn. The scratch of the rake followed the moist sparkle of the watering can; but it was futile labour. There was desperateness about the boy's actions. His clothes were streaked and caked from where he'd been sprawled in the mud. The earth itself refused to cooperate with his task. Already too heavy and damp, it had been compressed too densely where the boy had been thrown down on to it. All Danny's careful attention was only making it worse. The group of boys watching his frantic activity stood with the still expectation of a Greek chorus waiting for an inevitable outcome that would not be cheerful.

'Raught,' Jimmy bellowed.

His favourite came running. 'Sir?'

Stonor had gone a little way off, and was speaking softly. Peter couldn't hear what he was saying to the boy. Dark-haired, thin, blue-eyed, Raught stood like a streetfighter on the balls of his feet, ready to lunge in whatever direction was needed, stiletto in hand. Peter studied the boy. Older than Danny by a few years, and sharper by a lifetime. Handsome in his way; not the way Peter liked. A little breeze shuddered through the garden, billowing in the dry autumn grass, lifting a lock of Raught's dark hair and setting it back again in a different place, but the boy might not even have noticed so still did he remain, so entirely focused on Stonor, his master. His eyes flickered once towards Peter during Stonor's instructions. The meeting of their eyes was like a physical blow. Peter flinched from them as from an abyss. Later he couldn't believe himself. He thought he must have imagined the terror that took hold of him. But later still that night he met those eyes in a sleeping dream, cried out and woke up abruptly, sweating.

'Yes, sir.' Raught's voice was neutral. 'I'll see to it.'

Raught strutted cockily down the broad path towards Danny, and said something to make the little boy straighten up. Danny came to him. The mud on his clothes was paler at the edges where it was drying. His face was unreadable. The older boy put his hand on his shoulder and led him in this way out of the gate, out of Peter's sight. It should have been a good moment. Peter ought to be feeling triumphant. Danny was to be cared for; surely this was victory? Why did the retreating backview of the two boys make him feel so wretched, so utterly forlorn?

CHAPTER FIVE

Honor Skeffington was preparing to entertain the newborn choir to tea. She was accordingly embarking on a young person's tea party in the only way she knew how: the way her mother had trained her, the between-the-world-wars way. Much silver was involved, and pomp and circumstance. The silver service was too heavy for her frail old arms these days but Martha Eggar (sister of zippy Zanna) had great hammy limbs. The young mother was as strong as a carthorse. She could lift the teapot, carry china, shift furniture, and probably carry a grand piano in one hand while dancing a hornpipe, though Honor wasn't so sure of the hornpipe. It would require a certain lightness of foot not obviously apparent. Honor suspected hairy fetlocks tucked into those hideous white shoes she came to work in and called her trainers. Honor speculated what Amazonian sport she might be training for: shot-put possibly, or maybe a little light tossing of the caber hither and yon.

Martha came up to 'do' for Honor. The job put her on a par with Lucy's cleaner who was top dog in the hierarchy of village cleaning ladies. This honour must have counted for much in Martha's eyes to make up for the job. Honor was not unkind, she'd simply never caught up with the friendly customs of modern employment. Working for her was almost indistinguishable from slavery, but for Martha, veteran of the royal scrapbook, big house glory more than made up.

'We must find the quoits!'

The old lady's anxious concern was that the mice hadn't got at the rings of rope since their last outing. She also worried that the Souza marches might have warped. Martha Eggar was sent up ladders and into corners to look for these things between preparing food and drink. Robust sandwiches were on the menu: meat paste and anchovy paste, strong flavours suitable for young persons. Then cake, and games on the lawn. Honor's quarters didn't run to a lawn, but that wasn't a thing to stand in her way. She'd commandeered her son's for the afternoon.

Space had once flowed vast and free through Honor's life. When she was mistress of the Grange she'd never given a thought to the fact that six men could march down the staircase abreast and wheel in formation, if they so desired, at the half-landing.

Her life as her son's pensioner was confined to a self-contained angle of the house where her three or four adjoining rooms were filled and crammed. She didn't miss the space in the big house. Nor did she miss her things, having, to her daughter-in-law's chagrin, brought all she wanted with her and crammed them into her few rooms. As a result her part of the Grange was quite different to Peter and Lucy's: much thicker in texture. Each jostling object added its own character. The fruitwood furniture was sweet with lavender wax, thanks to the elbow-grease administered by the resentful Martha; the silver and ormolu smelt tinny with metal polish and the window-panes and chandeliers (Honor had made a point of keeping hold of the chandeliers) smelt hotly peardroppy from the meths that made Martha feel quite giddy while rubbing it in. All these atmospheres and smells mingled like the smells of people in a crowd. Honor's own atmosphere knitted it all together with gin, Chanel No. 5, face powder, and agreeable cooking. Close your eyes and you'd still know you were in the midst of a rich, plushy, contentedly self-indulgent life.

Lucy found her mother-in-law's rooms a trifle dowdy, certainly overcrowded, full of good objects that had no room to breathe. They'd look much better in her own part of the Grange.

Honor looked forward to Lucy's visits. They were not as frequent as might have been expected from a daughter-in-law living through a connecting door; Honor pretended to mind more than she actually did. Lucy's visits might have been more frequent if Honor had not always taken the opportunity to draw her daughter-in-law's attention to some piece of furniture and talk up its provenance and saleroom value to the skies. Lucy knew she was meant to feel covetous, and sometimes she did. She no more liked the twinge of envy than the fact that Honor was playing such an obvious and puerile game.

Honor had other pleasures, too, in these small quarters; small pleasures but considerable when set in the diminished context of an old woman's life. It was no loss of dignity to live warm and snug like a snail tight in its shell when you had entered dowagerhood. Occasional vulgarity was also perfectly all right. At last she could enjoy certain lifelong cravings she knew were appallingly vulgar: a perfectly huge TV, a Teasmaid, and plastic flowers in her vases.

'Peonies in October? Honor, you've really gone over the top.' The glaring globes wouldn't fool a soul: months out of season and velvet-bloomed with dust.

Lucy's mind returned next door where immaculate lilies had taken the place of the poisoned camellia on the piano. The appearance of things was vital to Lucy. As a result she had a great talent for accurate visualisation. Seeing these ghastly peonies called up the satisfactory picture of opulent straight-stemmed porcelain-white Madonna lilies whose reflexed petals exactly matched the glistening white of the cachepot they stood in.

'I never have to pick new. Admit you're jealous, Lucy! Think of the time I save. No slimy stems or disgusting smelly green water. You can't be expected to arrange flowers after seventy. Now there's something for you to look forward to in your dotage, Lucy dear.'

'If it's a bore, darling, I'll come and do them for you every week. Or Mrs Occhi? She's awfully good.'

'I'd feel I was in the grave already with someone coming to do the flowers once a week. Clinical. Besides, our tastes are different. You're so frightfully unrobust with your whites and creams. They used to be terribly nouveau: *style Syrie Maugham*. Only the other arrivistes wanted to copy her in my day.'

Lucy bent down to hide that she was cross. It wasn't fair, the old could always make you feel vulgar whatever you did or didn't do. Honor made her feel vulgar just by being vigorous and blood-filled and not in her seventies. She straightened the tassels on the rug, combing through them with her fingers.

'Thank you, darling. Always so tidy. Actually I'm quite surprised you came through to join me this afternoon. Choirboys and tea parties. Not really your sort of thing.'

'Didn't think it was yours either at the moment. Aren't you at war with the vicar?'

'War?'

'A fiver you didn't invite him today.'

Peace had broken out between mother and daughter-in-law.

Sometimes in his mind Peter likened their behaviour to a pair of rival pheasants; on first meeting they always had to fight about little scraps of territory, lifting their tails and pretend-pecking at each other's ground. The ritual took about ten minutes, after which they could glide into perfectly happy co-existence. They were extremely fond of each other, a fact they would admit to in a tight corner.

'I did invite the vicar actually but you can keep your fiver. It would have been hopelessly improper not to invite him. We are after all enrobing the choir. A church occasion, I couldn't not invite Our Father.'

'Is he coming?'

'Well actually, no. Nor his little catamite.'

'Oh do tell, Honor. I only came because I thought you were up to something.'

'Not very much actually. Harmless fun. Just enough to keep an old woman amused.'

Lucy stroked a jade crab on one of the many occasional tables. She had only to wait. Honor's well-known attitude to secrets was that they were pointless if nobody knew them.

'It just struck me,' the old woman began, 'that if I took this new choir under my wing – Martha, have you polished the muffin dishes? – I don't see why I shouldn't get them on my side in church. We'd drown the others out and I'd have won the Prayer Book War. That's all. Not very much, I told you. Innocuous stuff.'

'Do you think that'll get rid of the vicar?'

'Well, it must be a possibility. I should imagine even a funny little father might feel strongly enough to resign over that sort of thing, and then we could get a proper Christian back in the vicarage.'

'So that's why you're making such a fuss of the boys and their dreadful admiral fellow.'

'Well, yes.'

'Now, Lucy, your turn. I never expected you to turn up today, and I won't believe you've merely come do-gooding.'

'Yes and no. Nothing exciting. I'm curious that's all. You could call it dipping my toe into the water. The Brook House takes up more and more of Peter's time. It might be time to take a wifely interest.'

'Very creditable, darling, but awfully boring. I'd hoped

you might have conceived a mad passion for the admiral fellow.'

'Beards. Disgusting.'

'Quite foul. I remember Edward the Seventh tried to kiss me once. I wouldn't let him. Oh no. That awful foul smelly—'

'Honor, he couldn't possibly. You weren't even born.'

Caught in the lie, Honor hardly checked. 'The Duke of Windsor then, or Clarence, I can't be expected to remember which. Those royals were all interchangeable – ghastly beards to a man.'

Some shoplift in old age. Honor Skeffington told stories about herself and royals. Most people believed her. Most were awestruck by her accounts of a past thickly studded with crowned heads and royal incidents more numerous than currants in a bun. Honor backed up her claims with signed photographs in crown-ornamented frames; some had genuinely been given, and some picked up in junk shops. Royal jostled royal on every flat plane of her many pieces of glassily polished furniture. Lucy looked forward to the day when the old woman was checkmated by some-one who really *had* been there holding Wallis's hand as dear Edward made his speech, but history's witnesses were being safely gathered in. Maybe the old fraud would get away with her stories.

Honor was not twisting any knives when she suggested that Lucy might be set on the seduction of Jimmy Stonor. It was no rebuke, no sidelong reference to past flings. Honor had almost always been a faithful wife, Lucy likewise. Lucy knew that Honor's reference to conquest was an oblique comment on the younger woman's dress, and in truth she was done up rather grand for today's tea party in pink silk she'd optimistically bought for a winner's enclosure, but then Lucy always overdressed. She often wore pink. It suited her vision of herself: feminine, positive, pretty. Honor thought Lucy's style too gussied up; the older

70

woman favoured a quieter style. She wore a coat-and-skirt of blue-grey tweed, cut by Hardy Amies a hundred years ago, and a precise coiffure. It was part of Martha's duties to set the thinning hair in rollers and frizz it out about her employer's head.

There was an additional purpose to Lucy's dazzling turnout today, one she'd no intention of confiding to Honor. Pink silk was to play a part in softening up the guardian of the Brook House. Lucy was after information from him. She'd noticed that Peter was changed whenever he came home from the place; he would have a quiet, happy certainty about him. He'd go there after lunch each Sunday and not come back till dusk. In the summer when the days were longer he'd stay there till nine or ten at night supposedly helping with the kitchen garden. On his return from the Brook House he would be tiresomely self-contained, out of reach. She had marked down the weekly visits to the Brook House as a weekly item in the progressive slippage between herself and Peter. His eyes had a distant look on coming back from the place. He spoke faster. Lucy remembered these signs from courtship days; she could only suppose he was in love.

For some years now she had felt a bewildering loss of control over her marriage. Peter had been slipping out of her reach. She had been out of tune with the frequencies of slow change taking place. Like a will-o'-the-wisp the change was ungraspable, misleading. Time had hidden from her eyes the process by which he had grown, not different, but differently to her so that it was marked how much more absent he was when present in body. An imposing quality had crept into Peter while she wasn't noticing. She couldn't remember when they'd last made love and it wasn't for want of her buying expensive negligées and drifting about in open invitation. To go further than that was not her style. Pride prevented. Besides, she felt shy of his new self-contained rigorousness.

71

This tea party today presented her with the opportunity to find out in an entirely natural context exactly what her husband was up to. She'd cosy up to Jimmy Stonor – a man she avoided like the plague in the normal run of things – and extract precise information on cooks, matrons and any other female accessories he kept up at the Brook House. For all she knew the place might be stuffed with nubile carers hellbent on stealing her husband away.

Jimmy Stonor brought the boys on the very dot of four so as not to miss a minute. First he cast anchor in the middle of the room and stood like the Duke of Edinburgh, legs apart, hands clasped behind his back, opening his pores in case he could catch aristocracy from this rare exposure to it. Taking up a large percentage of the space in the old lady's close-crowded drawing room, he was persuaded into her solidest chair, where he lolled about exerting a terrible strain on its thin-ankled rosewood legs. Impervious to his hostess's worry he rocked comfortably, his bulk acting incidentally as efficient firescreen to most of the room. Soon the light incense smell from burning apple boughs was quite eclipsed by Three Anchors rough rubbed shag.

Some fifteen Brook House boys had been judged of decent enough voice to make the choir. An advertisement in the diocesan magazine for cassocks, ruffs and cottas had borne fruit: one church's redundancy was another one's economical robing. There were vestments in plenty. With some small patching and altering they would do.

The patching and altering would be done by Martha at a later date when she was less busy with trays. The measuring of each robe on each boy was Lucy's job and the justification for her presence at the tea party. She made space for her scissors and dressmaker's tape among a crowd of royal personages and *objets de vertu*. With pins in her mouth she measured, tucked, eased and shortened in an out-of-the-way corner. Always efficient, she soon devised a system. Taking one boy at a time, she marked the ruff to size for later sewing. The short white cottas needed no alteration, they could be quite approximate in length. The heavy sea-blue robes were the garments requiring precision. Each boy slipped the blue robe over his head. Standing, she put the tape at the nape of his neck; the boy then had to put up a hand to catch the top of the tape while she stretched it down the length of his back, kneeling finally to mark the hemline with pins.

Her industry was an island of stillness in a room taken over by cakes, ale and music. Honor's tea party was a roaring success. The boys moved in and out of doors completely taken up in the innocent entertainments of another age: leapfrog, three-legged races and pin the tail on the donkey. One by one the boys would be called in to stand tailor's dummy to Lucy's seamstress.

It was the turn of a very small boy: feet of hem to take up on this one. The little chorister was showing aptitude for his trade, swaying in an irritating way in time to the music.

'Do you think you could possibly stand still?'

Obviously he wasn't listening. His eyes had that faraway look she'd found so maddening in Dom and Ben when they were small. Where did little boys' minds go? This one would have to be hemmed by guess and by God.

'Okay. You're done.'

The little boy just stood looking idiotic.

'Scram, Danny.' A taller boy had more effect than she did.

'I thought he'd be there all day,' she said. 'Is he a little . . .'

'Doolally. Yeah. Danny's not all there.'

'Have I done you yet? What's your name?' She had her pen and scrap of paper to pin to each boy's robe.

'Raught.'

He was the first boy she'd noticed as an individual. She thought he must have some Irish about him for the blue of his eyes and the black of his hair. He was thin with growing and his hands had the large knuckles of adolescence. This coltish nubbliness was the only remnant of childishness about the boy. His blue eyes were fascinatingly flat; as windows to the soul they revealed about as much as a pair of Raybans.

He made a better clotheshorse than his predecessor. She couldn't complain that he didn't stand still but the very stillness made her uneasy. A stupid picture came into her mind: Raught above her holding a pub player's dart elegantly between finger and thumb, pointing downwards. The O of finger and thumb opened, dropping the dart to stick, flight upwards, in her back. There was nothing of the soft romance of Cupid in the image. Her top vertebra itched. She knew it was neurotic but she had to look up. Raught was just transferring a gold and enamel egg from the table's rich surface cargo to his pocket. Seeing Lucy's eye shift he bent his knees so that he could bend down to stroke the little treasure along her cheek in a strange, quick and disturbing gesture, before putting it back casually as though it had always been his intention to restore it to its proper place. Her gaze was fixed, astonished. Looking down into her eyes he gave her his most intense smile, a moment of solar radiance, Jove from on high. Shaking her head she looked down towards the hem, the business of the day. She was peculiarly aware of his feet. Turning back to her pinnings, she felt foolish kneeling there and altogether uneasy.

A high voice piped above the general racket: 'Is that yer 'usband, madam?'

One of the boys was pointing to an old photograph, one of Honor's flotsam of memories. Unusually this one was not in court dress, nor was there a gold crown branded into the leather frame.

'No,' said Honor. 'This is a photograph of a very great and famous man. I have known a great many famous and interesting men. This was an explorer, and if you don't know about him you should. I shall tell you.'

She picked up the frame and held it high so the boys should see the illustration to the coming story. It was a face that showed both intellectual imperative and obvious physical toughness. It sat like an eagle among popinjays, this hard face among the flock of soft-faced majesty. Heavy-lidded eyes stared uncompromising. There was some of the look about him of old Tolstoy, during that obstinately political period when the novelist swore there was most mental satisfaction in scything a field.

'See the signature.' The liver-spotted hand traced the faded blue-black ink. 'Roald Amundsen. He was a great admirer of mine.'

Lucy's head jerked up. Until she heard the name, Honor's hostess chat had been washing over Lucy, a back-ground babble weaving in and out of the Souza marches. Now she paid attention to every word. Honor had certainly never met Roald Amundsen. What was she up to now?

The explorer had been a boyhood hero for Ben, or was it Dom? Either way the worshipping boy had cut the picture out of a *National Geographic* and presented it to his grand-mother. New enough in grandmotherly lustre, Honor had done the right thing; Roald had joined the distinguished gallery of black and white royal 'friends'.

'He was the first man in the world to discover the Northwest Passage,' (some sniggering) 'and he discovered the South Pole. He was quite devoted to me. When Roald Amundsen was training for his polar expeditions he took his dog sledges across the wastes of Russia bordering Norway. He was Norwegian, you see, but his own country was too mountainous to be useful. He needed long ice plains to practise on for the Pole.' Honor paused before her next whopper: 'The Czar, king of all the Russias, was an old family friend.'

Lucy jerked on the hem.

'You will also see the Czar's photograph on the table. His imperial fur farms were up there in the North where Amundsen was training. He presented Amundsen with a bundle of the best sables, the ones only the royal family were allowed to wear. Roald Amundsen, being madly in love with me at the time, sent the furs to me. Sable is the king of furs, and this was the king of sables, worth a king's ransom. Martha!'

Martha's red fat-lobed ears had been captivated. She had never heard anything so romantic.

'Martha.'

'Yes, madam?' For once she gave the title willingly.

'Go up to the linen press on the landing and fetch the sables: third drawer down wrapped in blue silk. I should like these boys to see a piece of living history.'

What would the Eggar girl bring down? Lucy had stopped pinning altogether.

The sables descended the staircase. The blue silk was reverently unwrapped, and a throat-gagging naphthalic smell rose from crystalline white mothballs. The dust from the disturbed article danced like a crowd of gnats in a shaft of winter sunshine. Honor laid the fur across her arm and Lucy recognised her mother-in-law's mink: Harrods fur department, vintage circa 1950.

The Brook House boys didn't even pretend interest but Honor had a devoted audience of two: Martha and the guardian were dazzled. That they were mingling with such people! They gathered round to admire the light golden-brown colour. They wondered at the glassy gloss, and imitated Honor's stroking movement. It was softer and warmer than anything they had ever felt, and Honor held it up to the late sun so they should always know imperial sables from the other kind.

'Only the imperial furs glint with a little rainbow on each hair,' she told them didactically.

'Just like Jez after a new shampoo.'

What was a Jez, Honor wondered, and how could it be made into a coat?

Martha bathed her ruddy cheeks in softness. If only her Arthur could see her now.

Lucy was fighting a terrible impulse to giggle. She pretended total absorption in the hemming. So astounded was she by Honor's story she'd even forgotten it was Raught still standing above her until the guardian called out, 'Avast there, Raught!'

Jimmy's feeling of self-importance had been growing with every minute of the afternoon. It made him ever more nautical. Had he a hook he would have brandished it.

'Cast off,' he cried, 'and I'll belay alongside ye! I'll be next for the galligaskins, fair lady! Measure me up! Measure me up!'

'I've finished with you now,' she told Raught. 'Just pin your name and put it on the pile.'

R-a-u-g-h-t. Letter for letter she read the strange boy's name. During the rest of the afternoon she was aware exactly where in the room the boy was to be found.

'Mr Stonor.' She sat back on her heels looking up at him. 'I'd no idea you were going to join the choir. Do you sing bass or baritone, I wonder? Now if you could just?'

But he couldn't.

The old seadog's arthriticky shoulder joints prevented him reaching over to secure the tape at the back of his neck. With a little shuffling an alteration was made to the arrangements so Lucy knelt in front of him to measure the length down the front.

Grasping the tape to his breastbone the guardian looked down through those thick lenses that made his eyes leap so much more alarmingly close to you than the rest of his face. Through those lenses he saw the top of Lucy's blonde head as she knelt at his feet. Jimmy Stonor was struck with desire. This was quite new to him. Maybe the stroking of the soft fur had prepared the ground, woken an unaccustomed sensuality in his calloused heart. Maybe he had sensed and caught some infectious whiff of that odd tension between Raught and Lucy. Maybe he was turned on by Big House glamour. Whatever the root cause, the accurate fact was that for the first time in many years priapic movement was provoked by three-dimensional flesh-and-blood, by a girl who was not colour-printed on a page.

Pornography nestled in various corners about the guardian's study. Not desperate stuff. Just the magazines that newsagents kept on the top shelf against dwarfs and tots. Those girls with their flawless peach tan bodies, enormous bosoms and down-home biographical notes were exactly what Jimmy Stonor could cope with in terms of sexual demand. They satisfied him.

Now a real-life fleshly woman knelt before him and he looked down on thick wavy golden hair moving at the level of his thighs and genitals. A startling connection was made. Certain favourite photographs sprang to mind.

'If you could come back to the Brook House, dear lady,' he said thickly and quickly, 'we could have a drink in my study.'

She tilted her face to smile up at him. 'I should like that very much.'

'Ah.'

Lucy had hardly thought it would be so easy. Nor had the guardian. Much to his disappointment she cut the drink in his study, saying she'd prefer a tour of Jimmy's land-locked ship. He could have done with less conversation in her – and less movement too as she strode about energetically opening doors, looking into things and enquiring into this corner and that. What physical energy that woman had. If only it could be diverted into the original purpose. She was bound to be thirsty after all this; they'd end the tour in his study. They'd have the drink on the leather sofa. That would be the tour de force, as it were.

Heart's pang. What if she didn't like rum?

Lucy's lightning tour showed her one or two depressing scrubwomen but no one who could possibly catch Peter's eye. When she'd scoured the last ashy grate for a skulking Cinderella she left, crashing her gears. God it had been an endless afternoon, and fruitless.

But Jimmy was not of the same opinion. Alone in his study he basked in her afterglow, intoxicated with that swimming exaltation he was accustomed to finding only in the bottom of the ship's decanter.

'Raught.'

'Yes, sir.'

'See to it I'm not bothered this evening. Take charge of the ship.'

The guardian would devote the rest of his day to private duties in his study, leaving Raught to do whatever his heart desired.

CHAPTER SIX

At the vicarage the invitation to the enrobing party had all the effect Honor had hoped for. If only she could have been there to watch Father Terence swoop on her envelope, the only white in a cloned crowd of flimsy brown. Feeling the smooth fat letter, the priest came as near as he could to sensual pleasure. Stylish blue-black inkstrokes: something exceptional. The bishop's palace? Had Ashley not been in the room he might have held it up to his nose to sniff for incense. At last he could prolong the possibilities no further. Now was the delicious moment with the paperknife; still all things were possible, every lovely daydream opportunity stretched before him.

Then he read the words: 'Mrs Honor Skeffington requests the pleasure . . .' They curdled his expectations. His normally waxen cheeks suffused with a dull, angry red.

'To tea? With that Herodias?'

Ashley's name was also on the card; wobbling, meandering, fainting almost away then coming back stronger in the old-fashioned script, but there undoubtedly.

There existed an unlikely friendship between Ashley and old Honor. Grand she might be; nobody could say she was not a snob but she was not exclusively snobbish. She'd found Ashley one day nosing around the animal graves in the far reaches of the garden. Following the fashion of their generation, the original Skeffingtons had seen fit to make their pets' final resting place into a garden feature, semi-whimsical, semi-lugubrious in character. A small glade had been artfully turned into a romantick wilderness with winding paths, funerary urns, a rough grotto and obelisks, each with an inscription incised.

Thus: 'Peto. A brave and dashing Labrador', 'Agatha. A pretty Jersey Cow whose cream was never surpassed'.

It was probably the animal-infused dreamlike setting that had liberated Ashley from his customary shy fears. The two of them had immediately got talking and become firm friends. She was one of the few people with whom he could feel unselfconscious. He could be himself with old Mrs Skeffington. The running feud between her and the priest caused him much distress. Every night on his knees he prayed for its resolution.

'I might just look in on the tea party,' he ventured timidly, concluding that she might be hurt if they both refused. Besides, tea at the Grange was not offered every day. It would be a great treat, something to look forward to. He didn't receive many invitations.

'Haven't you learnt anything yet? You're only invited to this sort of thing as an accessory. Like a wife. People feel they have to ask you if they ask me. She'd be most put out if you turned up and I didn't.'

'But the choir was my idea,' Ashley was bold enough to whisper in his husk of a voice, 'they might particularly have asked . . . I'm sort of godfather in a . . .' but soon he abandoned his small attempt at independent flight. And so the afternoon of the tea party found both men in the vicarage study.

A poky room on the north side of the house, it always struck chill. These early October days were bringing unpredictable fluctuations of temperature. Some mornings there were frosts. Some days the sun never came out at all, soggy, saturated days when it was difficult to keep warm indoors. The vicarage central heating held out as long as possible in autumn: mortification was so good for the flesh, and bills so bad.

There was a small fire in the study's utilitarian Baxi grate: some few anthracite eggs glowed pinkish-grey and gave out more fume than heat. In the corner furthest from the fire was Ashley's desk, a flimsy card table with one leg short enough to wobble even under his feather-weight elbow. Ashley was writing up his weekly Animal Inspection Diary for the RSPCA. The noise of his fluent pen moving so busily across the paper maddened the priest. Ashley stole small glances at his friend intermittently; he saw a fidgeting and sucking of pencils and general caricaturing of the reluctant student.

Father Terence's desk was made of teak-look melamine and simulated leather, with drawers down both sides. It was almost on top of the fire and was also subject to the temptation of the only window in the room. He must put up with a small but distracting segment of swaying beech branch, an angle of green-lichened garden shed and, if he altered his neck position just a little, a wedge of village street, just four or five steps of passing pedestrian. The sun had come out. The priest could see it bringing out strong colours where it struck the shoulders of people's jackets and coats. A fine day for the tea party.

The metal-framed window that gave this limited view had drops of condensation dawdling down the smeary panes. They'd be getting those black mould spots soon. Terence turned back to his desktop. Ashley saw the movement back to work with relief; he knew his friend was brooding on this afternoon's happenings up at the Grange.

Terence picked up his pen and wrote one sentence: Ashley wipe w's. Fungicide? Anti-mould? Ask at Do-It-All.

The aide-memoire brought his eyes and his attention down to his neglected work. The document he was finding such difficulty in addressing was as old as St Guthlac's, a church inventory filled by priest after priest, a study in the degeneration of longhand over the century. As present incumbent it was his duty to check and update it. He struggled to identify one fair linen cloth from another, but his heart was not in it. There was a syborium that simply wouldn't come to light. He'd been trying to find it for weeks. Was it for this he had been ordained?

12. Schedule of Church Plate. (Assistance in filling up this schedule can be obtained from the Diocesan Bishop's Advisory Committee or the Local Archaeological Society)

His eye kept wandering down the columns, irresistibly drawn to the 'Tulip-shaped chalice decorated by small moulding with slender stem, three rings containing diamonds. On bowl coat of arms surmounted by mitre and "Honi soit qui mal y pense".' In the last column relevant to this entry, the one headed 'Where kept and whether in a moveable safe or a safe attached and fixed in a wall' he read 'Bank'. No later entry described its sale.

His mind fell to dreaming of jewelled communions, his own pale hands graceful round the stem. He put them now in the position they would assume in holding the cup and thought how well the diamonds would look sparkling through his white fingers. He dreamt diamonds and a choir, glamour and enchantment sufficient to bewitch even his disorderly congregation and ensure his own popularity. Oh! How he longed for popularity.

'Life is always an exile of course, for the truly great,' he would tell Ashley when congregations were being more than usually uncooperative. Apartness he knew to be his noble burden, assumed with the office. God had chosen to set him above the community, a height from which he could only condescend. On the other hand he might be able to combine apartness with popularity if he could manage to bring these two new magnificent ornaments, the choir and the jewelled cup, to St Guthlac's.

The choir was very exciting and very threatening. He must make sure that he and Ashley kept the upper hand. The two of them against that fearful Stonor. Ashley could always be relied on to back him up. He must not forget that he himself was, after all, the incumbent. The priest changed his hands from the chalice position to palm-pressing prayer. He'd ask for strength to withstand the guardian and he'd slip in a little one for the recovery of the chalice from the bank. But he neglected his prayers, falling instead to the contemplation of the beauty of his own hands, mirror-echoed in the classic devotional position. Where was today's Dürer?

Either side of the flattened hands his eyes caught the papery shake of the beech branch against the window. Some first few leaves were starting to fall.

A. sweep up. Besom where? he added to his list and doodled a heavily Koh-i-noored chalice.

Seeing that his friend hadn't settled properly, Ashley went soft-footed to the kitchen. Terence liked a cup of tea. It often settled him.

The kitchen was as meagre as the study. The kettle was of thin aluminium, dented, with a little cap over the spout to whistle when it boiled. Just such were starting to be restored to period kitchens by the National Trust. He took the flimsy thing over to the sink to fill it with the right amount of water for two cups. A fat housefly was dying in the shallow stainless steel sink. First on its back then right way up it whirled about on the metal surface describing circles and spirals like an ice skater. Death had already come to its wings: they could flap but not fly. The legs scrabbled frantically which made for the eddying move-ments. Ashley stood still, kettle in hand, all compassion. He'd not think to swat it, even to put it out of its misery. Never knowingly had Ashley killed a living creature. Now he stood reverent vigil at this housefly's deathbed because no creature should die alone, unobserved. The smallest passing should be dignified by another's respectful companionship.

Soon there was less movement. The continuous buzzsaw noises of flailing legs on metal sink had changed to short rattling bursts. Fewer legs moved, then fewer, at last just one or two twitches. Silence. All had been quiet for the required length of time. He said the Nunc Dimittis: 'Lord, now lettest Thou Thy servant depart in peace according to Thy word . . .' He shifted his condolent gaze from the creature, and filled the kettle carefully so no water from the tap should wash the inert body down the sink. Then he put the kettle on the gas, returned to the sink and, very carefully, so as to do no damage, lifted the dead fly and took it in his hand to the door which led outside. He did not put it on the narrow brick path where it might be trodden by the milkman, but chose a little sour earth in which some rusty hollyhocks were resigning their own lives to the season. A pecking bird might find it there, or the fly take its proper place in nature's quiet cycle of decay.

Ashley went in again to the thin whistle of the tinny kettle. He took some trouble to arrange the tray nicely with a cloth and slipped it on to a corner of his friend's paper-strewn desk. The tea was consumed; still the fidgeting continued.

'I could do with some air,' Ashley said tentatively. The priest not immediately squashing the idea gave him courage to continue. 'It's a pity to waste the last of these glorious autumn afternoons. You never know how many more there'll be.'

'I could spare half an hour, I suppose.' Terence could use a walk. He needed Ashley close as a glove for the coming power struggle with Jimmy Stonor.

'Let us walk.' The priest tossed back his head in sprightly mood and smiled a rare smile. 'Forgive me. I did not thank you properly for that excellent cup of tea. Most refreshing. Now I should like us to go out and refresh our souls. Let us worship together at God's own cathedral!'

'Shall we go up to the reservoir?' Ashley suggested. He hoped it was not guileful but he had given some thought in advance to where they might go. From the vicarage you could walk to the reservoir without Keythorpe Grange coming into sight. If Terence did not see the house he might not remember about the choir-enrobing going on there at this very moment.

It was a characteristic of the vicarage household that it always took ages to leave or get back in. Terence and Ashley were pernickety about scarves and socks and boots. Then there was all the locking up to do, and the going back and double-checking, and making sure the temperamental answerphone was on for business.

The reservoir was on the small hill overlooking the village. Hardly an out-and-out beauty spot, it was much loved by coarse fishermen. Green umbrellas proliferated at weekends, and courting couples at stealthier times. Today was a brisk blustery day of late dogwalkers.

'I went to the afternoon surgery to check on the poor abused pussycat,' Ashley began. 'There are signs of *gross* cruelty. The vet says it looks as if it's been used as a football. The crushed paw will never be any good and the anal area is crawling with maggots.'

This was Ashley's idea of therapy, a diversion for his friend's thoughts. Whatever happened, Terence must not be allowed to brood on the painful party. He would like to know about the poor pussycat. What people didn't know about they couldn't do anything about.

Terence had his own reactions to Ashley's endless stories; he didn't feel sick, as many people did. Nor did he get a prurient thrill like the boys at the Brook House. The stories bored and irritated Terence. At first they had revolted him, but he'd heard so many living-corpse tales over the years that even the most sickening left him unmoved by pity or even disgust.

He'd let Ashley run on a little now, humour him, invest the next ten – no maybe not so much – the next *five* minutes, in the rock-solid anti-Stonor alliance. He'd tolerate Ashley running on.

'I'm planning an all-out investigation to track down the owner. We'll get him by hook or by crook. I'm worried about the new housing estate, you know. Those people go out to work all day, even the wives, and you hear the dogs howling. I'm sure they leave them alone all day. There's one particularly bothering me. Tomorrow I thought I'd spoon dog food through the letter box to the poor lonely mite. Oh that reminds me, I was ringing round the supermarkets to see where I could get the cheapest tins. Were there any messages on the answering machine?'

Ashley had said the wrong thing. The telephone was a sorer point than most. Terence's previous parishes had not run to answerphones but here in prosperous Pendbury it was part of vicarage furnishings. Terence loved the machine in the same way he loved the arrival of the post twice a day. Hope sprang eternal. However often disappointed, still he hoped and expected every post to deliver summons to violent promotion, or public clamour for his complete sermons in book form. The post came only twice a day, but the telephone machine increased the fairy-godmother possibilities by many many times. First thing indoors he'd rush to press playback. Invariably the tape ran to yards of animal messages (the price of dog food was a recent raw case in point). Ashley got more messages than the unpopular priest himself. This hit a nerve.

'I thought you were going to get the RSPCA to pay for a separate line. The diocese really cannot go on bearing the cost, you know.'

'I asked but they say they can't fund me. Oh do look at that poor Canada goose. I don't like the way it's waggling its head at all. These fishermen will continue to murder birds with their terrible lead weights, however often we spread the word. It's not as if I'm on the staff, you see. Only an extra-vigilant member of the public.'

'I think you'll find the goose is struggling to swallow that rather large crust,' said Father Terence, whose vastly superior eyesight was only one of the many advantages he possessed over his handicapped friend. 'Shame about the telephone, I'll see if I can wangle your calls for the next month, Ash, but after that maybe you could instal your own answering machine on a separate line. It's meant for my business. People could be trying to get through to me. Distressed parishioners must come first. Shall we sit?' There was a slatted wooden bench beside the path.

Twilight had flattened the water into a pewter glass under a pewter sky. A vaporous mist was reforming the reservoir's limits; small winds shivered its surface from time to time. Magpies were cackling in the woods nearby, disturbed by the occasional dogwalker. Hawthorn berries spattered the bare-twigged hedgerows like drops of pigeon's blood.

The wooden seat didn't even bow under the small weight of the two friends, two narrow wraiths in similar anoraks, shadows in a deepening dusk. Ashley's head was up in case he saw an owl. Father Terence was bowed, a habit he had fallen into. It looked holier.

'What is it you're worried about?' Ashley could be more direct here in the dark and the open air.

Terence cleared his throat and began statesmanlike in measured tones: 'I have great expectations of the choir.'

'I'm really excited too.'

'But now at this very minute they are all taking tea with that terrible woman. She's got to them first and even now as we speak she will be filling their ears with poison about me and my new form of service. What if they all roar out the King James words in church? What shall I do?'

'But they're only laymen. Nobody can tell you what to do in your own church.'

Ashley could not understand that this was a problem for Terence. He had perfect faith in his friend. All their time together that faith had never wavered but always grown.

Terence's unkindnesses to his friend were never seen as such, but as the broader wisdom of a greater man, a man of vision. Ashley had no pretension to vision, nor any ambition on his own account. He was a man of inner thoughts and words and mantras: utensil, Nunc Dimittis. 'They also serve who only stand and wait' was a text he blessed; it might have been written specially for him, composed in order to give his life meaning. There were those like Father Terence who needed to be waited on and there were those like himself expressly made for the purpose. Truly the Creator was all-anticipating.

One of Ashley's favourite figures in church history was Cardinal Newman; favourite on his own account but also because Ashley saw much of his friend Terence in Newman. He liked to read how the cardinal progressed through the trials of his life overcoming great struggles and always his faithful friend Ambrose St John was at his side – an ideal, if lesser, friend treading the same *via dolorosa* a step or so behind the great man. The two men's platonic path had been punctuated beautifully by mutual gifts of inscribed psalters. Ambrose had died first. Ashley would do likewise because of his disabilities. The account of how the soon-to-be-sainted cardinal had been dragged sobbing and keening from the grave of his friend was deeply moving.

'You'll get the better of the guardian,' Ashley said with absolute faith, 'especially if you've prayed.'

There were times when Ashley's faith flattered Terence, and times when it irritated. 'Thanks for your support, Ash. We'd best be on our way. I must go up to the Brook House now to hear how the tea-meeting went. Wish me luck.'

'I shall go back to St Guthlac's and pray for your needs . . .' A sudden curdled screech came from out of the wood. It was plainly animal and, as such, was the only possible thing that could have drawn Ashley's attention at this moment. He started up, ungainly over the rough tussocky grass.

'A trap!' he cried. 'Those woods are notorious.'

Father Terence remained seated, his body twisted round to watch the crookedly galloping shadow melting into the misty margins of the wood.

And this was his armour against Jimmy Stonor?

The priest had no paper about him. Besides, it was too dark to write. Mentally he added a third note to the list: Ash. Own telephone. Own bills. Tomorrow first thing.

In the afterglow of Lucy's visit Jimmy had forgotten all about his later appointment with the sky pilot. It came as a rude interruption. Too late to conceal the brimming schooner.

'Padre!' The guardian's breath was hot and spirituous. 'You've already met the leader of your choir then?'

Raught's handsomeness in tandem with Stonor's forcefulness struck Terence dumb.

The polished boy put out his hand. 'We didn't shake at the door, sir, knowing it was not my place, but if there's anything you need, your reverence, you've only to snap your fingers.'

Intoxicating stuff.

Raught followed his words by making himself conspicuous with doing nothing. His passive presence hung pregnant in the study. If only Terence could think of something he urgently needed. But he couldn't. While Terence felt dumb and stupid, the boy dawdled easily at the telescope. It was far too dark now to see anything through its curious eye, no stars even, with such thick cloud over. Stonor, an undomestic man, hadn't got round to drawing the curtains. Odd moths were clinging like lovers to the lit-up windowpane.

'I'll be getting the boys to bed for you then, sir?'

'Cast off, lad.'

Humming 'Danny Boy' Raught left the study to practise discipline unsupervised through the dark dormitories.

Jimmy was drunk enough on various things to go in fighting. 'What would my rank be then?'

'Rank?'

'I'd want to be musical director at the very least.'

'My organist occupies that post,' Terence improvised.

'Choral director then.'

Musical director, choral director. How good these names would look printed in the parish magazine.

'I'm a plain man and I'll put things plainly. I want to be answerable direct to you, padre. I won't kow-tow to that bloody cripple, if you'll pardon my French. I know he plays the organ in church. But that's my considered position.'

'Of course, guardian, of course,' absently. And then with more attention, 'What did you . . . at the tea party, did you discuss the responses?'

Jimmy looked blank.

'At the tea party today?'

Jimmy thought he vaguely remembered what responses were but he wouldn't like to risk a keelhauling on it. 'We'd other things to talk about,' he said loftily. 'Rough outlines, broad principles.' He illustrated the broadness of the principles by a gesture that just happened to have the rum bottle at the limit of its outward sweep. Glug glug. 'Lucy and Honor and me didn't bother with details.'

'Guardian, you do understand that the parish sticks rigidly to Series Two. You'd sing the responses?'

'If that's the job, padre, if that's the job.'

There was a little silence before Jimmy went in again. 'I could only bring them down to the village for the Sunday service. Practices and things up here, yes? Christ knows they're difficult to control in a fenced environment. I'm the one who carries the can if a lad jumps ship.'

'Our organist,' Father Terence began and then he remembered, 'our musical director could come up. I should imagine you have a piano about the place. For morning prayers?'

There hadn't been morning prayers at the Brook House for a very long time. But there was bound to be a piano about the place. He'd set the boys on a search party, comb the piggeries.

'No problem. They'll need a conductor in the church or they'll be ragged as hell.'

Now Jimmy was at the very nub and crux of the matter: conducting the choir.

Perceived as the most glamorous job in the world, as well as the easiest: a little airy-fairy waving; all three men wanted the job of conductor.

Ashley took it for granted that the job would be his. It was usual; the organist conducted in lots of churches.

Initially Father Terence had also put himself at the centre of glorious Bernard Haitink fantasies. Then he reviewed the service in detail, and his own part in it. Regretfully he realised there were too many crucial moments when music was still going on but the priest needed both hands for other things: receiving the collection, administering the Host. There was no way round it. Reluctantly he had to let go of the idea.

Now Stonor leant forward confidentially. 'My last ship I was considered quite a fair conductor. We had a tiptop marching band.'

'An accomplished conductor in our midst!' Terence bowed his head in reverent thanks. 'Truly He moves a mysterious way His wonders to perform.'

CHAPTER SEVEN

Peter Skeffington was at his desk. This was unusual for a Tuesday morning, but not absolutely exceptional. He was busy writing, but not, Lucy saw, filling in those endless multicoloured file cards on plants. She wondered what he was at; it must be something more absorbing than monthly bills. He hadn't noticed her coming into the room.

Her husband had kept his looks and his figure; his straight broad-shouldered back looked well-proportioned in the Chippendale chair with the tapestry seat. Peter's desk was a thing of ritual, almost a museum. The inkwell presented to his father on coming of age, the blotter with the Eton fleur-de-lys, the paperknife willed from a god-father (he was the only person she knew who still used a paperknife, tearing with one vigorous and effective gesture). Lastly there was an ashtray made by Dom in prep school pottery (Peter had never smoked).

Her husband's back view was neat. She'd hate a husband who overflowed. Thinking of overflowing she slipped in a quick exercise, the one against double chins, lifting her tongue to the roof of her mouth and keeping it there to a count of ten. The better one, the one where you made a face like a Chinese dragon with your tongue shot out and your eyes starting, was not for company, even with its back turned.

Unaware of the facial gymnast behind him, Peter struggled on with his letter. Composition usually came easy, but this letter was a bugger. He was writing to that shadowy body, the governing board of the Brook House and suggesting with tact and what he hoped was a note of absolutely uncritical enthusiasm that a rather more energetic pursuit of organised education might be of benefit to the boys as well as to the ever-growing reputation of the Brook House. He, Peter, might consider funding a scholarship for the purpose. He had an eye on a boy who struck him as unusually gifted. Special lessons might be in order to develop an exceptional talent.

'Blah blah. Bollocks bollocks,' he exclaimed, thinking he was alone in the room. Behind him Lucy grinned. Passion; high feelings; this boded well. He passed his hand over his eyes. Sod the flannel. After the scene in the garden he desperately wanted to get Danny away from the place. How far could he go and not be counterproductive to the boy? Why not just apply for custody of the boy and be done with it? His pen hovered. How to suggest Danny might be better off outside the asylum without casting slurs on their governorship? How to paint a vivid picture of himself as a warm, caring human being who loved nothing so much as the welfare of little boys without raising the spectre of paedophilia?

He shifted in his seat, discontented with his own lack of inventiveness, and became aware of his wife, crisp in emerald.

'You're looking pretty today, darling.'

'I'm going shopping. I've nothing to wear for Paris.'

He looked blank.

'Oh, Peter, don't tell me you've forgotten. It's this weekend. We're taking the horse. You're coming. We'll stay on after the others. Hole up at the Georges Cinq. What do you say to a second honeymoon?'

She leant forward to put her cheek against the top of his

head. Her forearms rested light on his shoulders. Her eyes
fell to the desktop but Peter had already shuffled bits of
paper. A catalogue presented her with its innocuous face:
'Fletchers of Fochaber,' she read, 'suppliers of forestry
goods to the Royal Estates.' Oh for x-ray eyes to read the
longhand draft beneath the catalogue!

'The *cèpes* will be in season. We'll eat so well.'

'Sorry, darling, I can't come.'

''Course you can, sweetie. There's nothing that can't be
cancelled. Come for little Lu.'

'Not possible, even for little Lu. I've got things organised
that can't be changed.'

'You are a bore.' Her earlier surge of affection broke on
the shore of irritation and was dispersed. In its place
another wave broke, a wave of a thousand niggling resent-
ments. 'It's that dreary Brook House, I suppose. I don't see
why you have to go there every single weekend. Why can't
you put me in front of those delinquents for once?'

'It's not them. I'd made arra—'

'I really can't manage the boys and the horse and Zanna
Eggar all on my own. You must come. Anyway I want you
to be there, I'm going to win. You never take an interest.'

He got up from the desk and put his arms around her.
'I've forty cedar trees arriving bare-rooted. They're on the
lorry from Scotland, I can't stop them. We'll have to get
them in, the frosts are unpredictable.'

'Anyone can plant trees, you don't need to be there.'

The timed arrival of the trees was no coincidence at all.
The weekend in Paris would be hell. It might have been a
recipe concocted by a vengeful God with a specific grudge
against Peter: take one mediocre horse, one overoptimistic
Lucy, one oversexed Zanna Eggar and two overexcited
Polyphemans. Stand back for fallout.

'Other people cannot plant trees,' he said firmly.
'Nothing's worse than a bungled avenue. They have to be
on the exact line and the exact distance apart, inch-perfect.

It's a precision exercise. You know what the men are like unsupervised: it's "there or thereabouts".' He drew her over to the window. 'Look, darling,' he coaxed, 'what a difference it'll make. How pretty it'll look; imagine a long green *allée* of downswept branches marching up the hill. People will photograph it for books.'

'We could close it with a statue at the top.'

'Well . . .' God preserve us from statues.

'I'll go to Sotheby's. They have the best garden statuary sales. And peacocks. Avenues always need peacocks. Darling!' She faked an impulsive impromptu hug. 'You're going to Essex today, aren't you?'

'That's right. I'm inspecting some plantations. The grant from the Forestry Commission . . .'

'They've peacocks at Audley End. You could dot in and buy me some chicks.'

'You'd hate them, Lu. They scream worse than tomcats. Whistler kept peacocks when he lived in Cheyne Walk. They made such a noise there's a bye-law to this day forbidding peafowl throughout the length and breadth of the Royal Borough of Kensington and Chelsea.'

Why must he always be teaching her things? If she'd wanted to be educated she'd have married a schoolmaster. 'We'll cut their vocal chords,' she said to amuse him. 'Or buy dumb ones. There must be dumb ones. Like there are people.'

But he wasn't listening. He'd drifted far out again on that unreachable frequency.

Lucy's peacock notion had brought pictures to Peter's mind. He was remembering descriptions of peacocks roosting in cedars in the snow-swept Atlas Mountains: Darius, Xerxes, Alexander. Then later, that account of Genghis Khan's journey – what a vivid account – he could smell the snow as the Mongol horde poured into the civilised world and found themselves starving in the mountain passes. With nothing to eat or drink they'd opened their mares' veins to drink the hot blood, then stopped them up again by some technique unknown today. And people called them savages! The hungry mares had stood quite docile, the eyewitness account had said, only pawing at the snow to get at the grass beneath for food. And then as they started to eat, the peacocks in the trees had screeched. The mares had never heard such a thing before. Terrified, they'd panicked and scattered. It had caused much trouble to the exhausted warriors to find them and round them up again.

All those eyes, Darius, Xerxes, Alexander, Genghis, they'd all looked and seen the bird's long tail curled in a line of beauty against the blue-green pile of fragrant needles. At once Peter longed to reunite the bird and cedar tree for his own eyes. The cedar had come to England the year Laud was beheaded . . . the web of history, ah the web of history. The specimen at Keythorpe was hardly antique, no older than the house in fact, but its hundred-year-old branches were strong enough to take a whole flock, if he wished.

'Darling. I'll do it.' He gave her shoulder a squeeze. 'I'll find the most beautiful one I can at Audley End. Will it make up a bit for Paris?'

She became kittenish in gratitude. Overacting maybe? She wanted him to know she was pleased but oh how difficult it was when self-consciousness extinguished her natural impulses.

Peter had meant to talk to Lucy before writing to the governors of the Brook House. He'd some notion of getting her interested in the problem, interested in the boy, even. But he wouldn't bring up the question now. It was hardly the moment. She'd never concentrate on the welfare of Danny when she was so taken up with the present of a peacock.

'Well, Essex calls.'

Alone in the room, she did something that Peter would

never do. She had no scruples but went through the papers on his desk one by one. She could hear him moving about the house, preparing for his journey, and still she read, sorted and read, quite calm. Before her husband had left the house she had picked up the telephone and, much to the guardian's interest, spoken to that infatuated man, suggesting a meeting.

Peter stowed the tools of his trade into the car: wellingtons and tape measures, soil probe and theodolite, camera and papers. He also put a large wicker duck basket in the boot in case he was lucky in locating a peacock. It seemed a rakishly optimistic gesture and made him smile.

Peacocks! The weather was right for a ridiculous quest. It was a pretty morning. A heavy dew lay quietly pearly in the shade and diamond-dazzling where the low morning sun struck orange and violet beams shooting up from the grass.

Turning the car out of the gate and into the High Street, he felt a comfortable belonging to the scene he had known and loved all his life. Never had he stopped looking at it, never found the sight boring or repetitious. Today the almost horizontal rich sunlight lent the ordinary houses a baroque architectural exaggeration. Village vernacular became more imposing, more foreign, when casements were heavily underscored by dark shadow. Doorways were deepened, cream paint warmed to gold, porches acquired cavernous mystery.

He drove past the junky antique shop. This week the window was surreal with shell domes and an antique swingboat. It was nicely painted but you couldn't imagine anyone even thinking of buying it. Peter wondered idly what the Mercer man did for money. Local fence, he supposed. It went with the occupation. Not that he knew him, but Mercer seemed too floppy to be successfully criminal.

He noticed Zanna Eggar emerging from the shop and walking in the direction of the Royal Oak. Lucy's protégée was chewing gum with a sickening rotary motion. He shuddered at the thought of the weekend in Paris; thank God he wasn't joining them. The girl was not in school uniform. Surely it was still term time? Not his business, thank heaven.

Now he was clear of the houses and into the countryside. The sun was warming him through the car window; Peter turned off the fuggy heating and drove on, full of hope.

Peter was right about Zanna Eggar: she certainly ought to have been in school. She'd forged the note from her mother, not for the first time. Truanting in the middle of the High Street held a lovely shiver of risk. She might have picked a safer pub further off, but the Royal Oak was popular, it was noisy, and once you got behind the primly preserved cream-and-beam façade, it was brash. Its careless publican also had an elastic attitude to age.

Soon to be sixteen, she knew she looked well over-age anyhow. Zanna always carried a very exact picture of how she looked at any current moment, like a running video in her head. Half an hour earlier she had been translated from grey Terylene in the cramped and cornerish girls' changing room at school. She could reproduce in colour exactly what the mean little mirror had shown her, could rerun the video. Heavy black hair exactly copied from 'Nicky Clark says Gypsy Queen', and lots of ethnic necklaces to jingle-jangle jazzily.

She paused at the door, looking up from under the fringe. Just in case, you never knew, He might be there. That He who was waiting for her. Every place might be the right place, every now might be the right time. Once they'd met, Pendbury wouldn't see her for dust, she'd be off. Happy endings.

She had a trick of widening her eyes when she was taking fresh things in. She did it now. How she loved this pub clutter: coloured bottles, arcade games machines chattering, rattling, flashing lights, a ram-jam scramble in the dark. Her skin goosefleshed.

There were a few she recognised in the crowd. Nick Mercer would get her a drink, lovestruck Nick Mercer. She started over to him. He was drinking with someone she didn't know, good-looking in a tight, moody sort of way. Her tongue flicked on her lips like a lizard.

'Drink?' Nick said when she'd completed the smouldering masterpiece that was her journey across to the bar.

'G and T. Double, I'm dead.'

Nick had gone to the bar, leaving the two of them alone together, but still the other didn't look at her. She decided it was not a moment to play hard to get. 'I'm Zanna. I'm only here for a minute because I'm going to the Georges Cinq for the weekend.'

She was pleased with the accent. It had come out perfect, French-polished. She'd copied Lucy's pronunciation exactly.

He said nothing. Still his eyes roved the bar, like a mariner searching long horizons.

'Paris, you know. It's the top hotel.'

Nick was back now with the drinks and a new pack of twenty Lucky Strike. Showily he tucked some fivers back into the pocket of his grey school trousers. She noticed he'd changed out of the school uniform shirt into an even more annoying one, Terylene with perfect creases.

'Where'd you get all that money, Nick?' Raught drawled. 'Pinch it off your dad?'

'Don't be silly.'

'Where d'you get it then?'

Silence.

'Must be a bloody idiot your dad, not to keep a count of his money.'

Nick looked confused.

'Yeah,' Raught said, picking up the newly purchased pack of cigarettes and tucking it into his own pocket.

Zanna worshipped Raught with her eyes. 'Can I have a smoke?' She held out her hand.

'Here. Have the whole pack if you like.'

He tossed the cigarettes carelessly down on to the table. She took one and put them back on the furthest side of the table from Nick who had to half get up to reach it and help himself. Nick knew they'd made a fool of him.

Raught's pale eyes settled on Zanna. She felt them as a physical effect.

'What's on at the weekend?' Nick asked. 'Any ideas?'

'Peter Skeffington's taking me to Paris.'

Nick's face changed.

'Skeffington?' Raught repeated. 'Skeffington? That's the old bird with the fur coat. You seen it? She showed it to us when she had us to tea. It's worth a king's ransom. What'd you do, Nick, if you got a king's ransom?'

Nick couldn't think of anything suitably sophisticated to do, so he smoked away at a cigarette that seemed intent on choking him. Any minute now he'd start coughing like a beginner.

'Hey, my sister saw that fur!' Zanna had the start of an idea. 'She was at the tea party. She said it was really soft. She'd never seen anything so gorgeous.'

She turned to look at Nick now, to train her million-watt eyes on him instead of his friend. She tilted her chin down so she was looking up at him from under the heavy fringe. Doe-eyed appeal rolled up on video. 'They say it's really cold in Paris. I'll have to wear my grotty anorak. I think I'd rather have pneumonia. Christ it's a bore being poor.'

'The old bird's ancient,' Raught said. 'Lives all by herself in that far bit of the house. Dangerous really, anything could happen. She could cry out loud and there'd be nobody to hear her. Mind you she's deaf as a post herself. The coat lives in a linen press on the upstairs landing. Third drawer down,' he quoted verbatim.

Nick Mercer fumbled his way to the desired conclusion

and thought it his very own. The plan of action gave him a great confidence in his own manhood. 'There's a Demi Moore on,' he said. 'Shall we go tonight?'

'I'll be safely locked up behind the big fence,' Raught said. 'They've only let me out to do the chores like collect the dreggy music for the dreggy choir.'

'You could get out, climb the fence,' Nick suggested with bravado. Climbing the fence would be no crime compared to what Nick was going to do: break in and nick the old lady's fur. If Raught came with him to the film they could even pinch the fur together.

'I'm not that stuck on Demi Moore.'

'Zanna?'

'Dunno. I might. My mum's nagging on about course-work evenings. Tell you what. I'll try, okay? If I can get away I'll meet you.' She said with no intention at all of being there. 'I'm off up to the Grange now. See ya.'

She got up, automatically checking the mirror over the bar. Yes, she was prettier than anyone else in the pub. She thought Raught might get up and come out with her but he remained seated. Disappointing.

He looked at her retreat, though. 'Juicy little bum on her.'

'She had the hots for me all last year,' Nick boasted.

'Good fuck?'

Nick wanted to get away. At that point balanced between boyhood and manhood, a rush of boy was tugging at him stronger than any fur coats and fucks. He wanted to get out of all this heat and noise, to go up to the reservoir and put a fly over one of those old trout. Above all he did not want Raught to come with him.

'I'm off. See ya.'

Raught was the only one left. It had passed the time, geeing up Nick Mercer about the fur coat, but it wasn't the business he was here for. His restless eyes had been searching all the time for little Ashley Crowther. They were to meet here. Ashley was to bring the sheet music for the choir so that Raught could take it back to the Brook House. Ashley hadn't wanted to come up to the Brook House to do it; he dreaded every meeting with the guardian. Raught had suggested the pub, a suggestion that Ashley had agreed to with some trepidation. Fear of meeting Jimmy Stonor had in the final analysis outweighed the fear that the village might think him a drinker. Raught had suggested the pub not only to get himself out from the walls, but also because there was something special he wanted to talk to Ashley about, something special he wanted the little wanker to do. It'd be easier to accomplish here. The pub would be more private.

Raught leant alone, indifferent, waiting, making his drink last. He had no money to spare on pub prices. Besides, his serpentine mind was far from equating intoxication with sophistication. Even in repose he was watchful, sharp. By habit the blue eyes noted, took in, remembered. When his eye, in its observations, met another it softened not a little bit, but slid on. Raught was unremarked by the usual crowd, he was just another stranger. They'd no idea he was a Brook House boy, because that was not what they expected to see. Like nuns the boys had always been invisible, strictly immured behind those glass-sharded walls.

If Raught was unremarked, Ashley was the opposite. Attention was caught by his very noticeable entrance. This was entirely uncharacteristic. Normally he would come into public places sideways, crab-fashion, hugging a wall and hoping the drab pseudo-clerical grey would melt him into the background like a chameleon. Now he had forgotten his usual caution because he was in mental agony. He was ten minutes late. This was very late for Ashley. Would his new friend have given up waiting and gone home? He ploughed straight through the middle of the public, flushed, panting, and hung about with a string bag which swayed in a wide arc, counterweight to the Quasimodo gait.

'Sorry,' he gasped.

'Okay.' Raught patted the higher shoulder. It was lucky to touch a hunchback.

'Thank you. Such kindness.' The friendly gesture was more than Ashley expected. The string bag was swinging hopelessly round his legs, wanting to tie them together.

'Drink?'

'No, no. Allow me to go.'

Raught allowed him. Sat back and watched. Eventually the little cripple managed the careful journey back. The two glasses were quavering, the liquid spilling, but for once (Raught was surprised) he wasn't apologising. His dark currant eyes were luminous with news. 'You heard? Case number C2091. They're going to prosecute!'

Raught queried with his eyebrows. He was not such an attentive member of the birdwatching club that he could put his finger on every case number just in seconds.

'The intensive poultry farm. Birds bred so heavy they can't even stand. Over a hundred found dead on one visit.'

'Oh yeah. Live birds with maggots up their arses.' Raught remembered the intensive poultry farm. It had quite put him off the Spanish-style chicken that had come up from the Brook House kitchens later that day. 'That's great,' he continued. 'My friend'll be really impressed. He's impressed already by what he knows about you.'

'Friend?' Ashley sat like a well-behaved child: knees together, hands folded on the table in front of him. The incongruity of his posture marked him out, as if he wasn't marked already, from the casual indiscipline of the *habitués* of the smoky parlour. You could see he wasn't used to drink. The untouched half pint sat forgotten beside the neurotic knot of twisted fingers. The sickly pallor of Ashley's complexion goaded Raught; he hated anything

that stank of illness, weakness. The careful cleanliness and
anxious courtesy further fuelled his irritation. It'd be fun to
get the cripple drunk. Raught promised himself that, if this
first scam worked, later he'd give himself the pleasure of
getting Ash boozed up. Light the blue touch paper – zoom!
What a laugh. But not tonight. Tonight there was a job to
do.

'My friend in Animal Lib. Haven't I told you about him?
I thought I had. He's a high-up, a big cheese. When he
heard about you he wanted you specially to have some
papers. Sent them by my hand. Here.'

'Papers?' How puzzling. Ashley couldn't think what they
could be unless . . . ah! Maybe a newsletter? He put the
thought into words and offered to subscribe if the newsletter was not too costly.

'*Newsletter?*' Raught knew it'd be fatal to laugh. Once he
started to laugh during this interview, he'd never be able to
stop. But this was incredible. Where did old Ash live? On
the fucking moon? 'We're talking about illegal acts. Totally
justifiable sabotage of society. Making our point by glass in
baby foods, bombs in shops that sell fur and leather, the
release of laboratory animals. You can't put that sort of
stuff in a newsletter.'

'Of course,' Ashley felt ignorant, naïve and ashamed. 'I
hadn't thought it out.' Animal Lib. Ashley had read about
their doings. They went too far. Hadn't they killed a man
with a bomb in a lab? And now a high-up, a big cheese
unknown to him was sending him papers. Being sent
papers usually meant sending papers back.

'We might exchange relevant information, I suppose.
There might be incidents and cases germane to your
friend's investigations. I could report to your friend as I go
about my duties and inspections.'

Raught didn't bother to reply to this anaemic suggestion. Instead he pulled a scrappy bundle of harmless-
looking photocopied sheets folded in four from the same

breast pocket that Nick Mercer's packet of Lucky Strikes had been stuffed into. The cigarettes fell out on to the floor. Ashley's compulsive courtesy compelled him to bend and scrabble for them. In the violet gloom under the table he gagged on the smell emanating from the frowsty carpet: beer and cigarette ash of generations, but despite his queasy stomach he emerged into the upper air with a shy smile of apology on his face, as though the dropped packet had been his fault. His fumbling fingers made a trembling muddle of posting the spilt contents back into the red and white packet. Raught sat, watching the simple task made ridiculous.

There was something about the motionless figure on the other side of the table, biding his time, waiting until Ashley should be ready, something ostensibly benevolent, undoubtedly brilliant and – the thought opened like a trap-door on infinity – something profoundly unpleasant. Ashley shuddered. Geese walked over his grave. He was shocked by this thought that had come unbidden. Spasms of irrational antipathy were entirely alien to his nature and his principles. Hadn't Our Lord enjoined us to love our neighbours? He sent up an arrow prayer of penitence, 'Forgive me, Lord Jesus, for I have sinned.' Later he would do long acts of penance on his knees.

The remainder of the interview might have gone much better for him had he not been making up for the guilt brought on by that involuntary swerve into sin, that break-ing of the second great Commandment.

'Look, we don't want to draw attention.' Raught still held out the scrappy papers.

'Forgive me.' Ashley took hasty possession.

They came from a couple of sources. Some pages were copies from *The Anarchist's Cookbook*. These dealt with weaponry: how to build small bombs from everyday items, and the construction of rockets on a domestic scale. The other pages, those taken from the ALF manual, dealt with how to accomplish acts of violence, their scope crossing the entire spectrum from massed campaigns to small, sly, single acts of sabotage. Innocently Ashley unfolded the pages and started to read, moving his lips with the words as he always did when concentrating.

'Not here,' Raught was saying urgently.

Not here, certainly not here. Not anywhere. His brain was shipwrecked by the few words he'd read. He was overwhelmed by helplessness and fear. What to do? Utensil, utensil. The papers stuck to his hand as though glued, too heavy a burden to lift or drop or slide or place into any place that Ashley knew of in the world.

'Put them away.' Already this was working better than Raught had dreamt. With a flash of sly glee he leant over the table, took the papers and stuffed them into the string bag among the innocuous sheets of music. Raught's lips were now not far from Ashley's waxen ear. He started to pour out words, staring fixedly at the point where strands of dry hair draggled down from the studiously straight parting as he spoke. Raught willed his words to penetrate through the black hair and greenish skin, through eggshell skull straight into the soft receptive spongy brain.

'What you got there,' Raught imagined himself a hypnotist, 'is some helpful literature along with a shopping list, like. The list's special for you. It's local, tailormade for Ashley Crowther, nobody else. There's factory farms on it, none more than a bus ride away; we want it to be easy, see.' The words fell like glossy inkdrops into Ashley's consciousness, gathering in a great black bottomless pool of terror at the pit of his soul. So persuasive was his voice that Raught found himself half hypnotised by his own soothing stream of words. 'Hunt kennels, if you prefer, or fur stores and animal labs in the area. Supermarkets that sell battery eggs too, but it's specialised stuff injecting eggs with Paraquat. Better start on something simple. Leave out the animal labs for now. They're better guarded. You can always go on to that sort of thing later.'

'Later?' Ashley's voice was a smear, almost extinguished.

'My friend says you're to perform one act on a place in the list and you're to do it in the next week. To show good faith. No need to tell anyone. Even me. If it's a real act it'll get into the papers. I'll keep an eye out. Jimbo leaves his *Telegraph* for me when he's read it. I'll be looking. My friend'll be looking too. And if it's on that list he'll know it's yours and it's been done. See?'

'But . . .'

'But,' Raught sneered in echo. 'The boys said you was just a big mouth, all talk. Good at telling us "do this", "do that", shit-scared to do anything yourself. Other than making lists and writing reports. "Ash is pathetic," they said, "writing reports is all he's good for. Reports won't save fifty-five thousand cows being slaughtered for BSE. Writing up case notes won't get veal calves out of their crates." But I said, "No. Ash is a good bloke. Believes in the Cause."'

Ashley nodded. Certainly he believed. But between believing in the Cause and these acts of violence there was a great gulf fixed. He could not do this. Ashley had no illusions as to his own infinite capacity for cowardice, timidity, and fearfulness. Looking on himself as a man amongst fellow-men he could not but share society's scorn. He was no hero, no doer of deeds, no active engineer of moral ends.

And yet that was not the whole story. There was a shard of iron in Ashley's soul. A shard that went unrecognised by all, including himself. What else could explain the bravery that broached the horrors of Jimmy's kingdom once a week to play the deceiver? It was this shard that circumstance now touched, quite by chance.

It so happened that a drinker who was leaving the pub backed his car in a certain way so that the headlights struck Raught's cheekbones through the window-glass, lighting the planes of the face. Thus lit, the boy's face exactly resembled the face of a particular plumy angel painted by Murillo. Ashley now saw before him the very image of that angel. It was an image most precious to him, one he carried always in his heart. Father Terence had sent the angel as a Christmas card one year they had been apart at the holy season. It had lived in Ashley's concordance as a bookmark ever since.

Ashley gazed on the face in front of him as one who has seen truth revealed.

Angels were messengers from God. They could come in any shape or form. They didn't necessarily have wings. Ashley was enough of a theologian to know that wings were a later addition, an embellishment added by medieval artists to symbolise the messenger's ability to fly from one kingdom to another, thus making possible the intercourse between God and man. In the Bible angels were wingless. As was this angel here before him, this message personified. Here was the direct call to act for his faith. It was being demanded of him that he bring his moral courage to the testing ground.

Ashley's mind struggled and thrashed. Violence in the name of God? It went against his every gentle instinct. St Francis had not used bombs. But then St Francis had been alive in softer times. How to know? Ah, but it was never granted to know absolutely. The whole point of faith was the leap of faith, the leap of love and trust into the unknown. The tender line of light that rimmed Raught's translucent cheek caused Ashley to remember his previous flash of revulsion. Doubly ashamed, he now affirmed his faith.

'I'll do it,' his voice came husky, whispered, 'for Jesus' sake.'

He rose to his feet, gave Raught a little bow and left.

This unexpected and abrupt end to the interview entirely astonished the boy. Victory had come too easily. He frowned. Raught considered himself a good judge of minds under pressure, being something of a specialist in the field. He'd been expecting to apply a lot more before he got results. Indeed he felt cheated. His eyes followed the retreating figure with dislike and if he could have seen into the spongy brain that he had so yearned to reach he would have seen a progression of thought that would seem entirely simple and logical to the believing Christian, and entirely crazy to Raught.

Ashley was asking God's forgiveness for being so tardy in recognising His call. He was wondering at such a direct summons coming to him in a pub. But then Ashley reflected on historical precedent and concluded that it shouldn't have surprised him at all. Strange conjunctions were more often than not part of such sacred summonses: Saul on the road to Tarsus, the infant Samuel. Few recognised the summons straight away. There was some comfort to be had from that. But even as Ashley was acknowledging God's purpose he realised how greatly he was to be tried. Fright was boiling within him. The papers in the string bag brought such a burden of terror, his hands went up to his chest as though to work the struggling bellows of breath. The worst of it was he knew he must undertake this task alone. Dear Terence, who of all people might have shared and eased the burden, must be spared the ghastly weight of knowledge.

Behind him in the gloom Raught sat sullen for a while. The ease of the kill had almost taken the pleasure out of it. But pleasure returned with the happy thought of what the bugger the halfwit dwarf would get up to with those papers. He'd be nicked within the week, if he hadn't blown himself up first. Raught giggled a little, getting up to leave the pub. The big cheese in Animal Lib had been a great invention.

Zanna went back to school where she changed back into

uniform and hung around a bit. She'd get back home bang on the dot.

Up the cinder path she crackled, bored already by the evening ahead, even though it hadn't happened yet. She opened the insubstantial front door and stumbled over a doll with bosoms lying on the doormat.

'Stop kicking dolly Damaris,' Jezebel shrieked. (Even dolls were named from the Bible in the Eggar house.)

Jezebel started to cry with a lot of noise and drama, Salome came toddling along and decided this was a good game; she might as well join in. Little hands flew up to little faces and lattices were made with fingers so the girls could peer out and gauge the exact effect of the tremendous cacophony of their tears.

'What's she done to you, my poor baby?' Martha, sister to Zanna, mother to Jezebel and donor in relation to dolly Damaris, rushed to enfold her nestling in maternal indignation.

Zanna had reached the limits of her tolerance. Now with the growing up of Jez and Sal things were getting out of control. Martha, Jez and Sal were hyperactive when it came to rows, life was lived to a positively latin background of small local melodramas.

She was starting now to get out from under the silent oppression that had been her own girlhood: sparse food, freezing rooms, a Sabbatarian regime, a scared and subdued mother and . . .

No.

She could never get out from the memory of those sessions in the study and the bedroom with her father's disgusting and insistent body. He'd not made her play that game he called Willy and Lily this last year. Her fear of him was lessening. As she read cases in the paper with close attention a realisation was dimly dawning that the lifelong wounds he had incised on her might be used against him in turn. It wasn't very clear in her mind yet but she'd some notion of a realistic vengeance taking the place of the unrealistic fantasies of murdering her father that had been with her as long as she remembered. She could tie her vengeance to getting her own independence away from this noisy house. Somehow. It wasn't something she thought about with the top of her mind because that meant admitting it had happened. But it was in her mind and it was taking shape.

Ignoring the fucking row she took herself off to the kitchen for a dieter's square of cheese and the smallest apple in the fruit bowl, put them on a plate, and had achieved the first few stairs up to her bedroom, plate in hand, when her mother called loud over the brouhaha, 'And where do you think you're going to, miss, without apostrophising to your little nieces?'

'She shouldn't leave her bloody dolls on doormats.' The swearword could easily be denied, it wouldn't be heard clearly against the din.

'You can't aspect a little girl to think of everything. Now say sorry at once.'

Even as she said it, Mary Eggar knew she'd be defeated; Zanna had long been flouting orders. In such circumstances it was wise for the mother to avoid direct confrontation but her control of herself was so small, she couldn't curb her habit of futile command.

'Why can't you have mineral water in the fridge?' Zanna waved the plate, which set her mother worrying for the drugget. 'All that Coke and sugary rubbish for the children, they won't have any teeth left in their hideous heads. I have to live here too, you know; I told you mineral water's the only thing to clear out the impurities. I'll have to drink tapwater and then I'll get furred up like a kettle, and when I die from hardened arteries it'll be all your fault.'

She turned with, she thought, disdainful grace far too good for this rickety staircase, and continued towards her bedroom. 'I'm going to do my homework.' She enjoyed flinging the prim postscript from the height of the top of the stairs.

Her mother's flitting mind had come to rest on the plate in Zanna's hand: 'I hope you're eating sensitively tonight. You've been so pale and brawn lately dear. You can't live on just an ounce of grateful cheese, you know.'

Zanna waved the apple reassuringly. 'If Nick Mercer rings, I can't go with him to the film this evening. I've got to get my prep finished. Moonlight's going to Yorkshire this weekend to be covered and Lucy says I'm the only one who can keep her calm in the box. I can go for the weekend if I get my homework done, can't I, Mum?'

At the word 'homework' Mary gave the Pavlovian response: 'Good girl.'

'*Good girl?*' Martha's shrill turned to shriek. Squatting on the hall floor she clutched her sobbing chick tighter to her breast. 'How can you say that, Mum, after what she did to Damaris?'

The racket of the howling child continued. Zanna shut her bedroom door behind her. It wouldn't help much in this jerry-built house, not like a door at Keythorpe: shut a door there and it'd stop the noise from a whole screaming pack of brats. They'd go to the kitchen now, stuff their faces with sweet things. The noise'd go off soon.

Zanna turned the key in the lock behind her. She had the darling nieces to thank for this new privacy. Jezebel and Salome had their own winsome notions of private property. One day when she was at school, Zanna's room had been fallen on with tiny happy squeals and thoroughly looted. Rich as a dragon hoard it was in bright silks and glittery objects.

'Ooh, the pickles!' the mother had exclaimed and beckoned the grandmother to see how sweetly pretty they looked in their auntie's things.

Zanna achieved her lock.

Despite this first line of defence the schoolgirl still rigged up her books and pens, setting the stage for homework before taking out her magazines, nail varnish, Buf-Puf and eyebrow tweezers. She spun out her little supper, chewing everything twenty-six times because the enzymes in your spit broke things down so they weren't half as fattening if you sent them down to your stomach well chewed. Meanwhile she read an interview with a girl who had managed to become famous just for being.

'. . . a woman has to be very careful of what she eats,' Zanna read. 'I eat no meat, no dairy food, no salt, no sugar, no alcohol and of course no flour. I stick very strictly to vegetables and fruit, the harvest of the earth.'

Zanna lit a Lucky. The slimmer's supper hadn't filled every corner. She rehearsed the lines to Peter's sons this weekend in their Paris hotel. 'A woman has to be very careful of what she eats. I stick very strictly to . . .'

No, it wouldn't do. Part of the point of the Skeffingtons was they taught her what to eat and when, and how, and the names of all the meals. The way they approached food and drink was as different from the Eggars' as a family of Hottentots on a nature programme.

She thought a little of the brothers whom she, like Peter, blurred. One of them would be the way out of home. They both crackled with the spark of interest. She set herself and a brother in a film-set Paris and practised yielding to marriage proposals under the Eiffel Tower.

Zanna's mind spent most of its time in creative fantasy. She was quite incapable of planning. Her grasp on the probable was not yet, and probably never would become, great. Her daydreams had in common that they leapt from the present to the desired state (fame, romance, wifehood, wealthy widowhood) leaving a generous blank for the mechanics of the process. Something would come up this weekend. She'd know the chance when she saw it.

The nails were coming on quite well, Desert Orchid was

a winner. Her mother knocked with fuss and a hot sugary drink. 'Nick Mercer's down the stairs.'

'Oh, Mum. Didn't you say I'm working?'

The boy had taken the unusually bold step of following the mother up the steeply raked staircase. She could see his face above her mother's pinafored shoulder.

'I've brought you,' he indicated a sports bag, 'some stuff for prep.'

'Stuff?' He couldn't have. So quickly? The video ran: herself catwalking Paris boulevards in a seriously slinky fur coat. Martha had said the fur was fantastic.

'Mum, you can leave us now. We've got to do our project together.'

Mary Eggar would never have dreamt of leaving her daughter alone upstairs with a member of the opposite sex if Tom had been in the house, but with him safely away being a Rotary Lion this evening . . .

'Mind you leave the door akimbo, that's all.'

'You okay, Nick?'

He looked awful. He smelt pretty awful too. He plumped down all unheeding on Zanna's bed and it was a mark of his extreme mental fatigue that he didn't even register that he'd arrived at the coil-sprung centre of all his dreams.

He'd spent a fearful evening. First the dismal cold wait outside the provincial fleapit for a film there was no point in seeing alone. Getting cold. Being there early. Feeling foolish hanging about. Increasing self-consciousness under the eyes of the knitting matron all warm and snug and interested in her little glass ticket booth: 'You'll miss the beginning, dear.'

Should he or shouldn't he? Three quid a ticket. No point. They might be late. Or only delayed? He'd look pretty stupid waiting out here if they turned up. Yes, he'd get one. Quarter of an hour, Raught or Zanna might still slip in beside him. Half an hour, it wouldn't happen. It never did to the hanger-on in the gang, the one who was tolerated, did it? Well soon he'd change all that. He'd go and take the thing. Murder the old lady if she got in his way. He got up dully. They weren't coming. They never had been.

Keythorpe had been dark, all watchful windows. The many-eyed house was looking out for him. He stuck to the shadows of the house, only stepping on the green fringe of the drive and avoiding scrunching the gravel. The slow tiptoe creep was a stern test of resolution. Had a dog barked then he would have run, but Lucy was out with the dogs. Even the moon was on Nick's side, wrapped in a blanket of low cloud, lending him invisibility.

There was excitement in standing alone undetected in a dense shadow, measuring drainpipes, anticipating climbs and jumps; me against them.

Honor's door yielded easily to his push (Peter was always talking to her about security). The house was empty. Just when his adrenalin had got him wanting, really wanting to bat the old lady on the head, there was no old lady to bat.

It was like Raught said. There was a drawer to open and something soft to stuff into his games bag. It didn't feel so heroic. Sneaky more like. Deliberately he slammed the door behind him and ran right down the centre of the noisy gravel. All the way down the street to the Eggar house he'd been trying to recover that exaltation, that feeling of criminality that had, for a moment, lifted the deed above the everyday. But all he felt was that he'd been frightened and now he didn't feel a thing.

'Aren't you going to open it?'

Her face was soft and excited as she unzipped the bag. Maybe the coat was leopard; that's what she'd like best, a slinky leopard coat. 'So soft.' Her face was tender. 'Nick, I can't believe you've done this for me. You're incredible.'

She pulled the fur out of the bag and with it came the fug of charity shop. Zanna held it up and her fastidious nose wrinkled, her rigorous eye saw the splits where the skins were starting to perish. The sewn-on fringe of minks' tails, so *dernier cri* in 1950, looked, to her, like a line of dangling dead rats.

'Shit, Nick, you're not expecting me to wear this in Paris, are you? They'd laugh me out of town.'

The stairs were all blurry, but somehow he managed to run down them, several at a time, without breaking his neck.

CHAPTER EIGHT

Drowsy with the fumes of Bacchus, Jimmy Stonor was trying to forget a letter of complaint that had come to him via the board of governors. It had been burying itself gradually lower in the deep litter of his desk. Even receding under a smother of reams and quires, the letter wouldn't die. It was as though the words were written in laser, with the capacity to shine through the vast paper mountain he had built on top of them.

Enough grog and his mind turned easily from this uncongenial timebomb to luxuriate with a pleasant undertow of lechery in the memory of Lucy Skeffington's telephone call earlier this week. She had rung him. The gracious, beautiful, abundant, firm-bosomed lady had rung him to arrange a rendezvous. And even during that exciting telephone call he'd had the wits about him to suggest they meet outside his own kingdom: the Brook House held too many eyes.

It was Saturday morning now and he had all the long weekend to anticipate, to construct scenes of earth-heaving mutual attraction which would be acted out when the two of them met for tea on Monday in the resident's lounge at Wildbeam Park Country Hotel. Jimmy had never been into this, the third great house in the village, but it was firmly fixed in his imagination as second only to the Savoy in terms of elegance, sophistication and expense. There were of course rooms upstairs. He allowed these rooms just to impinge on his consciousness, a tantalising insinuation, a starting point for the sudden wild leap into fellatio that had kept romping into his mind at the oddest moments ever since the delicious afternoon of the measuring up for the cassock.

The telephone rang. He jumped. It was her husband. Terrible possibilities of telepathy. The husband too was seeking a meeting. Might he come over? Now? The guardian paled, but there was not even the hint of pistols at dawn, quite the opposite in fact: the conversation wallowed and made itself comfortable in many small pleasantries; there was an overall tone of conspicuous cordiality. Something about a scholarship scheme sailed past Jimmy's rum-stopped ears. It sounded vaguely like a good thing, distant, disembodied yet benevolent, like a faraway sail bobbing on a pink horizon. With some effort Jimmy heaved himself out of the dereliction of his study and swayed his way so he should be at the porch in plenty of time, with swigs of fresh air taken, before being spotted flatteringly framed in his favourite context when the car drew up.

The guardian was always awed by Peter's car, solid evidence of his power and wealth. Had the guardian's underexercised joints permitted, his unctuous bow would have been almost to the ground.

Threading their way back to the fuggy lair, the two men weaved and swerved to avoid crowds of boys at their Saturday tasks. Stonor might not be a bona fide military man but he honoured the ancient military custom of giving the troops jobs to do with totally inadequate tools. Keeping the boys busy was far more important than getting the job done. Saturday's job was unvarying: the boys cleaned the Brook House till all was shipshape and Bristol fashion. Decks, bulkheads and companionways (the miles of passages, walls and staircases) were swabbed with one bucket of cold water, one grimy cloth, and jars and jars of elbow grease. Window detail was given one worn-out dry toothbrush for the corners and a single sheet of newspaper. As a result, dirt was moved about but never expelled. It gave Jimmy unlimited opportunity to shout, bully, ridicule and punish at whim. If he'd not been drunk, he'd never have let Peter see the hopeless scrubbing horde; even Jimmy knew it was pretty poor PR. Peter was very angry by the time he and the over-friendly guardian had achieved the awful intimacy of the fuggy study. It was an effort not to hit the man. Invited to drop anchor, he sat as far away as he could from fumes of the rum-swept breath.

'An educational scholarship is, I agree, unprecedented in an establishment of this kind, but your governors have indicated they are not against it in principle. Quite the contrary. However, they're very properly reluctant to give me an answer without first having consulted yourself. The matter of the detailed future of the Brook House is of course in your hands. You're in charge.'

Jimmy smiled. He liked being in charge.

'They don't seem averse to the notion of a boy being sponsored, rehabilitated by a local family, a kind of halfway house.'

This had got clotted in Jimmy's ears; he hadn't quite yet twigged what was being talked about.

'So when I have the scheme prepared you would not stand in the way of my sponsoring Danny's future, finding him a school? It was made quite plain that as principal of the corrective establishment where the boy has been placed by the courts and social services, your consent would be absolutely necessary.'

So many long words. Jimmy nodded sleepily.

Ever since this morning had dawned, Peter had hoped against hope that he might get the boy out from the Brook House just for a few hours so the two of them might make a start on planting the avenue together. There was something optimistic and forward-looking about such an enterprise. Faith in the future made visible: the tree, symbol of life and of eternal renewal, planted in orderly lines stretching out and up to a far horizon.

Danny was located among the passage-scrubbers. He took his seat in the grand car with a docile and bewildered air. His fellow inmates watched.

'What's that?' Danny was deciphering the dash.

'A cigarette lighter. You push it in.'

'D'you smoke then?'

'No. It's just in case.'

During the journey Peter realised how many just-in-cases were built into his life.

The car drove up to Keythorpe's imposing façade with Danny stiffening in his seat.

'Here we are then.'

It was all Danny could do to get out. His terror of the large house, echo of his own asylum, made him awkward, clumsy, and quite deaf to Peter's emollient flow of words. Peter tried to soothe him with hands and voice as he'd soothe a green horse or nervous dog. Danny tripped getting out of the car.

'Let's get some boots. Plimsolls are no good, they'll be soaking in five minutes.'

The Keythorpe gumbooterie housed a comprehensive armoury against weather, built up over the generations. Never was a boot or jacket thrown away when there was a shred of wear left in it to provide protection against mud or rain at a later date. Danny thought he'd come to another cloakroom in another place of hordes of boys. He thought each garment had a present owner and concluded that he'd been brought here merely to swell a different workforce. The car journey had been an interval between one hopeless Saturday job and another.

He didn't feel disappointment because he had not been expecting anything, but he did wish he hadn't been singled out to come. Till now Mr Skeffington had been a sort of comfort in his mind; the two of them talked and there was nobody else with them. Now he accepted that Mr Skeffington was like Mr Stonor, lived in a house like him, had his Saturday workforce. He understood now that this was how men were. He was wrong to have thought anything else, but it made him want to stop living really.

'Come on, we've trees to plant.'

This was a Saturday job Danny had never done. He never even realised trees were planted by people, thought they just came in the ground. He would be humiliated by unfamiliar tools and instructions. The boy put his mind into the fugue state where nothing could touch him. Chin down, jaw clenched stubbornly, he followed Peter. Large and small feet made dark trails through the daylong dewpearls of the moisture-laden autumn day.

Last night's clouds (so helpful to Nick Mercer) still hung about in remnants. The sky was one low canopy of mist, with cloud-land reaching down to settle, here and there, on earth. Roundabout the limit of the view, grey bunchy cumulus blurred with the great undefined masses of oak, creating a floating and uncertain perimeter.

When Peter planted anything, he made sure that history would know its origin. Under the roots he would tuck a coin bearing the date of the year when the planting took place. Ever he had an eye to the decades and centuries ahead, but he didn't trust to perishable paper, still less to fallible memory, human or computer. Metal endured.

Peter had been to the bank and got forty new-minted pound coins. He gave the heavy canvas bank bag to Danny in a gesture of trust that served to make the boy suspicious.

Looking about for crowds, Danny saw only the gardener, a silent and efficient man. He was here to dig the holes. He slid the diamond-shaped turfing iron under the grass and brought up the growing layer neat and flat as a square of green carpet. Then he put down his turfing iron, took his spade and dug with short strokes; effective as a badger, as silent and as quick. Then it was the turn of man and boy.

'Choose a tree.' Peter pointed to the bundle of grey-barked saplings, each no thicker than a man's thumb, with their roots like powdery grey wires pointing round in a stiff circle. Danny knew he'd choose the wrong tree. He gave them the same look he would have given a bundle of adders.

'This one'll do, it doesn't matter which.' Peter shook out the nearest one. He held the roots down in the prepared hole.

'Now you take that stick and lay it on the ground so it's lying across the hole. That's fine. We've got the hole the right depth so all the roots will be covered with soil when we put it back. The next thing to do is this: I take out the tree, and you put one of the coins from the bag into the bottom of the hole. It doesn't matter which. Now I'll tell you why we're doing this: it's so that when the tree falls down or somebody cuts it down, they'll find the coin and know exactly how old the tree is.'

'But . . .' Silence.

'Yes?'

'But I thought you said about counting rings?'

'Well remembered. This is making sure. A belt and braces job. Sometimes a tree will get diseased and rot away from the inside. Then there are no rings to count.'

A little later Danny said, 'I think you know everything.'

They worked on, the boy holding each sapling steady until the depth of hole was judged exactly right, when Peter would take over the holding and Danny lay a coin, always monarch up, between the spread of roots, and Peter would pile back the soil. Soon he noticed that the boy was breathing oddly, blowing out the vaporous air in little puffs like a steam train.

'Playing dragons?'

'No, sir. You told me plants breathe carbon dioxide in and we breathe it out. That's right, isn't it?'

'So you're giving them a flying start.'

Like two zephyrs in the corner of a map, Peter and the boy inflated their lungs and blew on each new planting. Peter had forgotten the untainted smell of a child's breath. They fell into the routine of the repetitive task.

The quality of light was changing now. The mist, instead of lending luminosity, was leeching it out of the atmosphere. Starlings were gathering for the night, crowding on the ridge tiles of the house and farm buildings. The large flock massed and chattered, settled for the night, then wheeled again, mysteriously well-organised, to settle in exactly the same place, a Sandhurst-perfect and totally pointless manoeuvre.

Peter's watch had travelled through the small segment of the boy's freedom.

'Time to take you back now, I'm afraid.'

The boy was silent in the car. Remembering that Sunday-night-and-back-to-school feeling, Peter was hardly surprised to see the eyes and nose start to run. He looked for small words of comfort, couldn't say the large, it wouldn't be fair. Until he could be sure of his fairy-godfather role it would be worse to rouse the boy's expectations.

'I'll never finish the avenue,' Danny gave as excuse for his tears.

'You started it. Starting's the most important. Like we show our faith in the future when we plant our trees, you've got to have faith in your own future. You won't be at the Brook House forever, Danny, and when you come out I promise I'll be there to help you.'

It was one of the hardest things Peter ever did, dropping

the dejected boy at the door of the Brook House and standing under that miserable benighted porch while the door shut in his face. 'Dammit.' His eyes blurred. All the way home he had to keep telling himself that there was only one way to do this: the proper way. Proceeding by procedure. The car felt very empty without the little passenger.

Uncertainty was one of Raught's best weapons. He made it a speciality that people could never foretell when, or from what direction, he would appear. He liked to induce a perpetual tension of expectancy.

Danny was allowed all the evening for long drawn-out apprehension. All evening he expected the punishment. It didn't come, not even in the washroom. Bedtime came closer. Maybe he could relax. For some unfathomable reason he was being let off. He put his head under the bedclothes and dwelt on the day past with happiness. He saw the colours: gold coins on brown shiny earth and very pink earthworms with orange saddles. He remembered how the moneybag had got lighter in his hand, and he thought about the white labels tied to the trees and saying 'Cedrus libanii' which he had memorised with no notion how to pronounce. Under the private shroud of inadequate blanket he blew out carbon dioxide in happy little exhalations.

There was a certain damp outhouse where bats found it congenial to hang through the winter months. Raught had, earlier in the day, dispatched a little team of followers who with a skilful quickness had managed to capture one. An hour after bedtime, when authority was fast asleep, they collected round Danny's bed and took the bat out of its box. Some held the boy and some held the bat and stretched its wings out so they could tack them to the floor with drawing pins. The little furry creature flapped its impaled wings in a futile frenzy to escape, but only managed to tear its tissues further.

125

'Tell us. Tell us what he did. Tell us what he said.'

A boy lit the match and started singeing the fur.

'Tell.'

'You his gay boy then?'

The bat was frenzied now, the thin membranes tore and streamed. Danny's nostrils filled with the ferrous smell of blood.

'We planted trees,' he said and wished he hadn't told.

CHAPTER NINE

Peter avoided looking at the line of infant trees from the window the following morning. Over a heavy-hearted breakfast he took the precaution of looking up the minor French race in the back pages of his Sunday newspaper and discovered without surprise that his wife would not be coming home rejoicing. No need to prepare a panegyric on Muckraker, Lucy would be in greater need of a stiff drink.

Her entrance before he'd finished breakfast was astonishing. Breaking the custom of a lifetime, she was early by hours. The dining room came to life: flurries of new hot coffee, encores of scrambled eggs, croissants demanded with a reverberation of rolling French r's. She was in a brilliant mood. He liked to see her eating and happy.

'Losing races obviously suits you, darling.'

'I've a dreadful confession to make but I know I did the right thing, so don't be cross.' She looked girlish and excited. 'I left the Eggar girl in Paris.'

'Cross? It's a brilliant notion. The Froggies'll love her. Can't think why I didn't ship the little *numéro* over the Channel years ago. Her father might mind a little, I suppose. Dust might be raised chez Eggar.'

'He won't. He can't.' She told him the things Zanna had told her about her home life during the intimacy of the trip, and how the solution had seemed so simple: leave the girl out of reach of her ghastly family while she sorted herself out. Lucy had given her some money and, more importantly, fixed her up with a job in a racing stable over there. With her skills as a horsewoman she was more than capable of doing the job.

'And,' Lucy added brightly, making him want to kiss her, 'there's an added extra. Her French'll get awfully good. Tell me I'm clever.'

'Brilliant. But you'll be even cleverer after you've managed to pacify old Eggar. Incest. How revolting.' He shuddered. 'Paedophile incest. It doesn't seem possible.' He took hope. 'You're sure she didn't make it up?'

'Pretty sure. I can tell when she's lying. And there were details she couldn't have made up . . .'

'Don't, I couldn't take the detail.'

'But actually the thing is it doesn't matter even if she was lying. She's turned sixteen now. She can do exactly as she wants. Parental consent is a thing of the past, isn't it?'

'Just be here to shield me from the old Bible-banger when he gets on the telephone, will you?'

'You won't need shielding. I've words from the horse's mouth to make him blench.'

She asked excitedly about the peacock, whom she had decided to call Zoroaster, thinking the name would please him. She admired the avenue through the window and asked about its planting. How had it gone?

The time had come to tell her about the Brook House. Surely there'd be no better time with her in such an excellent mood. He wanted to fill her in, so he started by painting the whole picture. He started with generalities, his misgivings about the place and how they had been growing with every weekly visit. How he felt the boys were being brutalised by the existing regime. How helpless he felt in the face of the Brook House's anonymous authority when he'd no grounds to go on but an overabundance of instinct and foreboding. The brutalities he witnessed up there remained within the letter of the law, though time and again they far outstepped the spirit. She waited for him to mention the specific boy she'd read about in the letter on his desk but he took too long. By the time he got round to mentioning Danny she had already decided he was being dishonest with her, masking his real concern, keeping her away from his real feelings because he felt she was too shallow to understand. She was jealous of the warmth in his voice as he told her about Danny's help with planting the avenue. Her soul was stabbed by the tenderness with which he described how Danny had breathed little bursts of carbon dioxide on the saplings.

So that was why he wouldn't come to Paris! He'd wanted to stay here and plant trees with the boy. His voice never softened like this when he talked about his own sons. It wasn't fair. It wasn't a crime not to be interested in trees.

'God, you're so naïve, Peter.' She heard the shrill note in her voice, and hated it. 'You think he's a genius just because he takes an interest in your boring trees. He's taken you in. Can't you see? You don't need an adoptive son. You've got two already, if you remember. You might try paying them the same kind of attention.'

'I wasn't suggesting we adopt him as a son, merely that we might sponsor a scheme . . .'

She couldn't take it. The Eggar thing had been a strain. The girl's story to be evaluated, the decision to be taken on her future. It had been a huge and lonely burden. She'd come home for peace, for cosy times and confirmation of her radical solution. Peter instead was making a new and unwelcome complication. She felt indignant on her sons' behalf.

'I do wish you wouldn't harp on. I've done my childhood bit. If he's as sweet as you say, sponsors will be queueing. I'm going to unpack.'

She left the room. Peter sat down with his head in his hands.

She sat down too, upstairs at her dressing table. The

quarrel had horrified her. It cut lines. It made steps leading towards a different, darker future. Oh, she had been conscious all these years of the slow, frustrating process of drifting out of frequency. She had been just as puzzled as Peter but the difference was she'd found consolation in the boys, home-based consolation, the one growing as the other dwindled. Peter had looked outside. A clandestine relationship hidden from her, a cheat, like taking a lover. That was what had prompted the unprecedented scene. Until today there had always been politeness between them. Understatement and humour had been preserved, whatever the circumstances. Never before had such words been said. She looked at herself in the mirror and did not like herself at all.

The rest of Sunday until teatime she spent among the horses and he spent among his file cards. Each, absorbed in their own preoccupation, almost managed to forget the other. They lunched separately. This was not difficult: Mrs Occhi had been given the day off. A cold lunch was left in the kitchen.

Four o'clock found her once more at her dressing table, a nineteenth-century boulle bureau not quite up to downstairs quality. On it sat a truth-telling triple Venetian mirror. 'Efficient, that's the watchword,' she told the top half of mirror-Lucy, and tucked some frivolous tendrils, suggestive of inefficiency, into the body of the dignified coiffure. There was work to be done. The next job was the meeting with Jimmy Stonor; make a success of that and she'd have knocked this whole boy scheme on the head without having to have another quarrel with Peter.

Lucy knew she placed too much importance on her appearance but always gained great confidence from knowing she looked well. She couldn't help it. Any small discord about her appearance, any hiccup in the laundry leading to a mismatch in the colour of stockings, say, or the missing of a shirt button – even in an out-of-the-way place where no eye could possibly see the lack – would make her unhappy and unsettled; her concentration would evaporate and the small imperfection would grow and swell in her brain like a cancer, blotting out the greater perfection of the whole effect.

Today she felt calm and well-prepared. She knew there was no tiny traitor, no incipient ladder in the tights biding its time, plotting to split and multiply, split and multiply, extend, expand, and finally explode her world.

Pinkly cashmered and softly tweeded, Lucy felt well prepared to defeat her husband's intention. In the hours that had passed since their quarrel a warm feeling had grown that her physical perfection was bulked and made solid by the reasonableness of her purpose. She'd set up this meeting before she went to Paris and after she'd gone through Peter's desk. Its purpose now, as then, was to find out every single detail she could about the boy Danny – this wedge that had been driven between Peter, herself and her sons. Once armed with this information she must find good enough cause why he was far too dangerous to be allowed anywhere near herself and Keythorpe Grange. After all, there must be a perfectly good reason why he was shut up in the Brook House. They didn't just shut up ordinary boys in there.

She entered the country house hotel almost convinced that she was saving Peter from himself. Plenty of her friends' husbands went a little odd after twenty years of marriage, it was par for the course. Usually the oddness took the shape of blondes, or motorbikes far too young for them. She had only an overenthusiastic rush of philanthropy to cope with. Well, if she couldn't get the better of that . . . Lucy put her chin up to go into battle.

The country hotel was a sea of soothing pastel hospitality. Lucy and her host were by no means the only ones taking tea here expensively when they might have got it cheap and just as good at a hundred other places. All about them groups of twos and fours spoke quietly across stiff-starched ivory damask.

She could have wished for less exotic cakes. The guardian had chosen a rum baba. His eyes lit up at the dumpy glistering round. 'Yum,' he said archly. The eyes opened theatrically wide behind the grotesquely magnifying lenses. Eyes big as saucers. First bite. The sticky syrup from the cake trickled down his skewbald beard. Appalled and fascinated, she watched the golden globule's bumpy journey down the repugnant pipe-foul fleece. Giggles suddenly jumped and jiggled in her throat. She could only sit still, fix her eyes on a florist's perfect triangle of stiff scarlet flowers, and battle to subdue the inward squall.

Jimmy, equally, was speechless. Ever since she'd come into the resident's lounge and he had stood up without knocking over the teetering tea table, he had been as in a dream. Words had not entered his head. It was quite sufficient to be sitting silent, gazing hard at her profile with the concentrated attention of the silhouettist about to wield the scissors.

His eyes had never been so close to the back of her neck before. (Lucy had turned her face three quarters away so he might not see the twitching mouth.) His tongue came out a little way as he looked: such white sun-shielded skin, and the clouding fine blonde filaments too short and downy to be included in the twisted crown of gold that crowned the queen of Jimmy's heart.

He was oblivious to the stretching silence.

'What a pretty room.' Lucy was recovering.

'A gracious setting,' but his courage failed him, and he could not complete the rehearsed, 'for a gracious lady.'

He beamed at her, leaving another heavy silence.

'I wanted to talk about the boy,' she launched determinedly.

Now that she had started on the serious business, the giggling fit melted as though it had never been. In its place came an impatience for this stupid tea to be drunk so she could be out of this tiresome man's company.

'The boy,' he repeated, still distracted. The standard lamp was shining through her exposed earlobe; he was mesmerised with longing for the tiny mouthful of flesh plumped and flushed with minuscule capillaries.

'Danny, I understand he's called Danny. Peter, my husband, wants, I believe, to adopt or sponsor him in some way.'

'Of course, dear lady, of course. Anything you want.'

'I don't want.'

The guardian's mind moved with the speed of a becalmed yacht.

'I don't agree with my husband on this issue,' she explained. 'I need to know if you can stop this ludicrous idea of his.'

'Ah.'

Still he gazed at her, steadily, idiotically, and she felt quite certain he'd taken on board neither word nor meaning.

'Do you determine the future of the boys when they leave the Brook House?' she insisted.

'I suppose I do.'

'Suppose? Isn't it written down?' She longed to shake him.

'Oh that would be in the deeds.'

'And they?'

Passive incomprehension.

'Where would the deeds be?'

'Somewhere about my study, I suppose. I'd have to look them out.'

'And the inmates' case notes. They'd be there too?'

He cast his mind back to his doubtful filing system but answered with a blithe untruthfulness, 'Of course.'

'I should like to see them. Might we go up there now? It's a matter I'd like to be clear on sooner rather than later.'

First he must finish every last paid-for cakelet. He was ages spearing every runaway crumb on the dainty three-pronged forklet inadequately designed for the purpose. She thought she might scream, watching him labour on with his finger crook'd politely. Instead of screaming she did the useful thing: small-talked for fifteen whole minutes on the go without asking him a single question, thus ensuring his jaws weren't distracted for a single minute from the vital business of chewing.

At last she could get up. Lucy felt his eyes adhering to her as she navigated this washy, indeterminate room ahead of him. She walked with some vigour, lest his yearning eyes fix her forever like a ship in a bottle.

After the usual ceremonial courtesies they eventually got as far as the guardian's study. There was a certain amount of fuss and commotion as she chose to sit in the chair which, he noticed rather late, was the one with the girlie magazine peeping out from the side of the cushion.

'No!' he roared in anguish. 'Sit here, dear lady, here.' Wrenching her out of one brown leather seat he guided her to its twin, commending it warmly for its greater comfort and view down the garden. Lucy accepted identical clammy discomfort and a splendid close-up rectangle of fog.

'It seems to be closing in.'

Jimmy was in trouble with his filing. It had grown and oozed and bulged into drawers and cupboards which were always waiting for tomorrow for their final discipline. He delved about helplessly, hopelessly.

To draw his audience's attention from the patent muddle, he embarked on a wave of words explaining the exact nature of his role at the Brook House, but anything concrete remained as fugitive from his mind as it did from his fingers. His clarification to Lucy was everything but clear; a sinuous, circuitous spiral of words, a long master-piece of incoherence. For some reason he started telling her about the life cycle of the anchovy as it made its remarkable migrations round the Mediterranean, found itself pickled in barrels, and finally justified its whole exis-tence spread on teatime toast from porcelain pots.

All that long, confused fishy journey, metal drawers slid and stuck on their runners, folders were lifted out, pieces of paper slipped here and there and feathered to the floor. Lucy saw it was no good and joined in the hunt herself. Soon they were both on all fours on the carpet, retrieving and re-sorting. It was ridiculous.

Once more the guardian found his eyes in close and informal proximity to all sorts of delicious parts of the body of his adored. While she scanned the floor, his hand hovered over the lovely globe that was her mohair tweed bottom. His mouth fell open a little and behind the thick curved glass his eyes took on a dreamy vacancy.

Lucy, unaware of the yearning hand poised so neatly over her rear end, peered closer at the papers, thinking the fog must be getting terminal, there seemed such a sudden judgment-day conclusion to the light. Still on all fours, she lifted her head and saw the reason for the sudden drastic obscurity: pressed against the window (the one with the recommended view) Tom Eggar's face was peering in. There was a short intense interocular shock between Tom and Lucy before his face was withdrawn. In that instant she saw him with ridiculous detailed clarity: the fraying on the turned-and-mended collar, the waistcoat buttoned under the jacket. She could count each grey-white bristle on the smooth pink chin, follow the curve and hollow of each childish rounded cheek. She saw it and it was gone. Such an unlikely vision, Cheshire Cat-like, disembodied.

Tom Eggar had no business here. She wrote it off as hal-lucination, product of the overanxious moment. Head down again, Lucy went back to the undisciplined papers.

They found them last, the two things they were looking for: Danny's case notes and the original deed, enshrining Jimmy Stonor's momentous appointment as guardian. Danny's case notes proved nothing to her advantage. He had, so far as she could see, been vaguely implicated in a house robbery by the prime mover, an older boy. Danny's guilt in this matter was never proved to anyone's satisfaction. His main crime appeared to be vagrancy through lack of a home. He was a boy who'd fallen through the net, and he'd had the bad luck to fall into the Brook House.

This was not the damning evidence of sordid guilt that she had wished to find. She must think a little.

She had time to think a lot, for Jimmy Stonor had found the deeds of his appointment. He was standing clearing his throat prior to taking the great pleasure in reading the document aloud to her. He started reading, solemnly circumnavigating the clauses, subclauses and heretofores of his awesomely worded contract with all the odd timing of one not bosom friend to the written word.

Lucy let him run on. She felt the prickle of eyes upon her and, scolding herself for a stupid imagination, raised her eyes again to the window. Almost she expected a curtain call from a spectral Tom Eggar; his ghost would come back mother-naked in a rude and revolting encore, just to confirm that he'd never been there in the first place.

Fog still flattened the rectangle behind the glass, ambiguity blurred foreground, background. This time she saw against and among it something quite different, indistinct, maybe there and maybe not, impossible to tell through miasmic, milky swirls. She thought she saw Raught but this sight was not like the other. That small close fragment of Tom Eggar had been an epitome of the man, condensed, summarised in one square foot. This fugitive vision of Raught was an insubstantial wisp, out of range before she could register the vague physical shape. Lucy's eye and mind took in the patterns, the conjunctions that, synthesised, made the confirmation implying Raught. No particular made itself plain; it was as unlike as it could possibly be from Tom Eggar's earlier microscopic clarity at the same window. For all its insubstantiality this second vision roused a spinal shiver.

'. . . signed and sealed by the chairman of the board in the presence of the bursar and dated the third day of—'

'Marvellous,' she interrupted. 'You know, I have been thinking that I might be able to help you.'

Jimmy simpered expectation.

'You've been so understanding in the matter of the boy. It means a good deal to know I can count on your solid support.'

He made a declaration of solidarity in return. The Rock of Gibraltar was insubstantial, dear lady, compared to the support he promised fervently and sincerely.

'I should like to do a small something in return for you.' She'd got herself into his study, now she was thinking how on earth to get herself out. 'I've been thinking. With this great choir of yours, guardian . . . '

(Was this the moment? Did he dare ask her to call him Jimmy?)

'. . . There must be a lot of laundry. All that white cotton.' Raught's phantasm had conjured the robes, dormant in her mind since measuring day.

'I thought if you would like me to take care of it, you could send the robes down to the Grange once a week for washing?'

'Mm . . . more than kind.'

When she had left he retired to his study. Heedless of the many unclothed females he scrumpled beneath him, Jimmy Stonor sat down to a new dream of love once a week among the laundry.

On Monday things must be seen to be normal in the Skeffington household. It must be as though there had been no quarrel between Peter and Lucy, as though those words had never been said.

Mrs Occhi was back on duty. Six-thirty found Lucy and Peter at their customary whisky and soda. Lucy was at her softest, most feminine, most pliable, taking a wifely interest in the details of the week to come.

'Why don't we have your mother to dinner one evening? Maybe we should make a fixed thing of it every week, like having her to lunch every Sunday. Would you like me to ask Honor which night of the week would suit her?'

The telephone rang.

'Ah!' she said. 'That might be her now. Or the boys. I've not heard a word since they got back from Paris. You take it, darling.'

He did.

'Mr Skeffington? Tom Eggar here. I was wondering when my Zanna would be back. I do believe she has been spending the days – and the nights,' on the word 'nights' the rustic voice rose shrill and hysterical, 'with your son, sir, and your wife, sir. You think she is your wife, sir, and yours alone, but I know different. I have been following her with the eye of righteousness. On Sunday afternoon, the Lord's very day, I saw her on the floor among the papers with that fanciful Adonis.'

'Adonis?'

'Her fancy man, that guardian, her lover, sir, in his study, making an exhibition, crawling on her belly like a serpent. I saw it all and now I want my Zanna made an honest woman of, a ring on my Zanna's finger and the deeds to Gasson's Spinney in my hand, those are my terms, sir, the ownership of the land to be made over directly into my own name and no money spent out.'

Peter put his hand over the receiver. 'It's Eggar,' he mouthed to Lucy. 'Banging on about Zanna. Raving. Gasson's Spinney comes into it too, for some reason. The man's away with the fairies.'

'I'll cope.'

Taking the receiver calmly from his hand, she coped. She was succinct and serious, pitiless as the avenging angel. She gave no quarter, used no euphemisms, and she did not disguise her disgust at the old man's crime. When he, in roundabout rambling defence, banged on biblical, she charged him with the ultimate sin, the sin against the Holy Ghost: the corruption of innocence. That was the pivotal moment after which the tenor of the exchange changed entirely. The man cracked. He was annihilated.

When she put down the telephone Lucy was spent. Her profile against the white light showed translucent, drained of colour. Her hands were trembling. Peter wanted nothing so much as to take those hands in his and warm the shock out of them, to console her body and her mind. But first there was one thing he must do.

The phone call had thrown up one shadow of suspicion that he must settle: 'I saw her on the floor *among the papers.*' If he failed to deal with this shadow immediately, it would add its new presence to the gallery of shadows in the marriage, the numerous misunderstandings whose presences crowded the silences between them.

There was nothing he hated more than confrontation, but now he must confront. He must break through the skin of politeness that lay like smooth oil on the surface waters between them, submerging and concealing the jagged edges of truth.

'I don't think much of you going up to the Brook House, Luce,' he said heavily.

His face was full of nothing. It was the empty face she'd come to associate with stark occasions as his system took sudden shocks. Good God! Did he think she was making love to Jimmy Stonor?

'You can't believe I'm having it off with that foul old guardian on the floor of his study!'

'Not for a minute.' He responded to her lightness with a

toneless, corpselike calm that frightened her. 'But I think I know what you were doing there. Oh, Lucy, how could you? I told you there would be nothing done about the boy that you might find difficult.'

'I can't think what you're going on about. It was nothing to do with the boy. I told you. That matter's closed and I don't want to speak about it again. You can arrange whatever scheme you want to get the Brook House into better order and the boys better looked after. I won't stop you. Jimmy Stonor's obviously impossible. Get him booted out, I'm with you all the way. The day he leaves Pendbury I'll dust off the bunting.'

She'd lied about the boy on impulse. Maybe it had been stupid doing what she'd done in Jimmy Stonor's study but on the other hand what other course of action was there open? She'd needed to find out about the boy before Peter got further embroiled. If there was a history of viciousness it was her duty to uncover it. In the final analysis she was the only one who could protect Peter from his own kindliness. Lucy took a deep breath for a last self-preserving fling.

'If you really want to know what I was doing up there I'll tell you. I went to offer Mrs Occhi's services to launder the choir robes. It struck me the Brook House machines might be overstretched. So you might be rather pleased with me, don't you think? Not gruff and grim. Let's be friends.' She hardly dared put her hand out to this stern, judicial husband. 'Please? I didn't like it when we had that row. It frightened me horribly. I was trying to make it up to you with the choir robes, in my own small way. *Pax?*'

Peter frowned. Laundry help could be offered over the telephone. There was no reason to visit, and there was certainly no excuse at all for crawling around on the floor as Tom had described, surrounded by papers. That was the noose, the hanging detail. Papers were too reasonless for Tom to have made them up. Peter could think of all sorts of circumstantial details that Tom might have mentioned in his cack-handed attempt at blackmail: whips, corsets, whatever. But papers? That was so unlikely as to be true. Lucy, his efficient Lucy, he could see her in his mind's eye, getting down on the floor, sorting the notorious muddle that was the guardian's paperwork. She would have found what she needed and then she would have organised Stonor into signing the right form so that Danny would be transferred, whisked away from the Brook House to some other interchangeable asylum. The boy would disappear without trace. Easy to lose one small boy in the endless reshuffling of the indigent and unwanted. Peter experienced a stab of panic, and confronted the truth. He'd come to rely on the boy. Without Danny he would leave the world echoless. His own sons, Dom and Ben, might inherit the acres, the worldly goods, but Danny was the one to whom he might give the important legacy, the revelatory view of the world beside which genes and acres paled into insipidity. Danny had been thrust in his path, the perfect pupil; it would be terrible to lose him now.

Lucy and her schemes. And yet how could he blame Lucy? She had not changed since their marriage, rather she had stayed exactly the same; hardened a little, become what he thought of as more trivial, monotonous, unalterable, but he had known the character of his wife right from the start. He'd dealt the hand of cards himself. What if the triviality, monotony and seeming rigidity of her personality were down to him? What if he'd driven her into the arms of silly novels and decorating magazines? These facets might have grown only in response to his unbending attitudes. Right from the start of the marriage every clause had been accompanied by a secret footnote in his head, an unvoiced expectation that marriage to him would change Lucy. The unwritten contract had been that his own perception of values would, by everyday proximity, seep into her personality osmotically, changing it without any direct effort made by himself.

Change had never been part of the marriage contract.

What if she, too, had married with the same mental foot-notes? What if she'd assumed that contiguity would change him? Maybe he should blame himself for never compromising, never taking the smallest intellectual step in her direction. He'd been rigid at the start; then later he'd withdrawn. How destructive to the marriage had been his private dream?

Peter's eyes shifted focus. He'd been standing with his back to the room, looking out of the window and seeing nothing of the milky landscape it presented. He turned, wanting to say the start of a very long *'pax'*, wanting to embark on some explanation, however faltering and ill thought out, of all these things that had been going through his mind. But when he turned he found the room empty.

She'd gone upstairs. The bath was already running. Lucy was tearful and slightly hysterical. She'd not liked that dip into the darkness of things downstairs: first Tom and then Peter, it had been like falling through a black bottomless hole. Up here in the bathroom she used her calming trick: she lined up things and got them organised.

Her bathroom was a good place. It was coloured aquamarine like under a sunny sea. She'd made the spaces unresolvable. Things on glass shelves seemed to float in blue air. Mirrors melted into water. Everywhere glittered, as shells do, freshly harvested from the sea. Lucy never could pass a rock or a cave or a beach without filling her pockets with magpie accretions. Strange petrifactions came back to her bathroom. Glittering felspar swam on her shelves, with nubbles of fool's gold, bright, sharp-edged blue john, spiky-edged coral and gnarled leprous growths. Amorous oysters, thick-layered like contour lines, scallops and conches, blue mussels, green jades. Whorled chambered ammonites, coiled snakes petrified, belemnites, jelly-like thunderstone cones. Black-and-white tiger shells striped and shadowed, echoing patterns of sandbar seas. Dolphin shells frivolous, twisted and fluted, as pink and as white and as fleshy as ears. Spotted snails, garden snails, *helix aspera*, left-handed *sinistra*, perfectly curled. Soft warm colours in the heart of the spiral, cool, hard surfaces, glassy to touch.

A shelf of silvery slate patterned like salmon's scales ran round the rim of the bath. It was here that Lucy lined up the calming paraphernalia: the long-handled back-brush, the shampoo, the flannel, the half-dozen cotton buds, neat in a row.

She would scrub the very echo of Tom Eggar from every inch of her body. She would wash her hair and clean every whorl of her ears. Not the smallest wisp of his corruptions and insinuations should cling to any part of her. She stepped into rainbow bubbleland.

Downstairs Peter contemplated the empty room. Well, he concluded bleakly, at least she didn't give the impression of an unhappy wife. There was some satisfaction to be gained from that. Keythorpe outweighed himself, perhaps? Perhaps. If so, he'd honoured his part of the bargain. The marriage was honourable, he supposed ruefully, but it didn't alter the fact that just at the moment the world felt as uncertain as jelly beneath him. It wasn't a feeling he was used to.

Chapter Ten

'The rod and reproof give wisdom.' Tom Eggar had given the rod and the reproof in plenty; generous measures even unto overflowing, but where was Zanna's wisdom?

Lucy had no idea what changes she had caused to the local balance of power when she had decided to believe the girl, equip her with the means for independent flight, and lock horns with the father.

'Correct thy son and he shall give thee rest; yea he shall give delight unto thy soul.' Tom felt let down by his Bible. Rest and delight were not very abundant. Sharper than the serpent's tooth, his daughter was, and yet unaccountably she was also flourishing as the green bay tree. It was not meant to be thus.

Authority waning, rejected (as he saw it) by his God, Tom became more noticeably mad. He was almost silent now in company, and several degrees more unreasonable at home. Sarcasm was lavished only intermittently on his dolt of a son-in-law. He'd even forget to ask if Arthur had money to burn whenever he lit a cigarette. Towards his women the patriarch had used to be inflexible and oppressive. Now the real steely autocracy had gone. There remained only brooding silence and feeble unpredictability. The real yardstick of change was his unprecedented forgetting to say the lengthy food-cooling grace before meat.

This, more than anything else, brought home to his family that Tom was no longer the man he had been.

Two women had worsted Tom Eggar. It preyed on his mind, came to monopolise his thought and action. The careful daily care of his garage slipped his attention, and a previously minor sideline was prompted to an obsessional task. Tom took to shadowing two women obsessively: Lucy Skeffington and the daughter he had lost but thought he saw in all sorts of females. All day he followed women. He might by chance start by following the real Lucy but then a different girl would walk by his eyes and he would see Zanna, or another Lucy, in the girl's eyes or hair or elbows so then he'd pad about after this new female. After a time he might realise his mistake. Then he'd catch sight of someone else whose ears or knees or shoes reminded him . . .

All day until it was dark he padded Indianwise, slipping into doorways, hugging hedgerows, not cracking twigs, focusing binoculars; following women. He listened, he watched, he sought, he sniffed the spoor. Sooner or later the daughter of sin was bound to drop a valuable fumet.

An unplanned result of Tom's monomaniacal distraction was the growing-up and flourishing of Arthur. Somebody had to man the garage. Tom's long time-eating stalks left lengthy gaps at the vital customer contact point. Arthur was not slow to exchange oily overalls for a salesman's suit and a salesman's patter. Customers who had been used to Tom going through an incredibly tiresome and conscientious naming of parts under an open bonnet were now asked much sexier questions: 'How did the body feel under them? Wouldn't they like to stroke the curves?' Sales went up.

Tom had gone mad on Sunday. By Tuesday Arthur had taken advantage of terms just-too-good to refuse, to change from hand-pumped petrol to phallic revolvers that squirted. The field was to be cleared of rusty wreckage, cars wheelarch-deep in nettles were to be uprooted and

Eggar's garage to be upgraded. Soon there would be talk between Arthur and his mother-in-law of power of attorney. Arthur had already got hold of the keys and gone through the desk in that awful private room Tom had called his snuggery. Soon Tom's land deeds would be discovered; Tom's wife and Tom's son-in-law would be locked in mortal combat over possession of the valuable documents. There would be a titanic struggle over who got power of attorney. But that was a little way away into the future.

Meanwhile the household was in chaos. Pandemonium was well groomed, a highly organised place compared to the Eggar house in the first week of Tom's madness. The family hardly noticed the appearance of a strange young man they'd never seen before turning up one evening and saying he was a schoolfriend of Zanna's and he'd lent her some things and she hadn't returned them and now he needed them for school. Please? If it wasn't a nuisance?

The strange young man spent ten minutes in her room before he left swinging a sports bag. He'd obviously found what he needed.

Raught had needed, and got, the fur. He was getting impatient. Things were going nicely but not quickly enough for his taste. There were things to move along. He'd a meeting arranged with Ashley, but it wouldn't matter turning up late for that, he'd stretch the little hunchback's nervous wait by not going first to the vicarage. First he'd take a little risk. The Grange, Keythorpe Grange, was his target as he walked beneath the beauty of the night. Six o'clock in late October and a nail-paring moon was transforming the winter landscape into a tender bluish-grey pastoral. Raught didn't notice. Nor did he pay attention to how particularly well the stars were performing in the thin and frosty atmosphere.

He reached the Grange and saw with satisfaction that the two family cars were not parked on the gravel. Double-checking, he went quite carefully round to where he knew the garage was.

Good. No cars, no people. Luck was with him. It was with him again at the door. He couldn't believe these idiots who never locked their doors.

He had been some little time alone scrutinising the papers on Peter's desk before Mrs Occhi came upon him on her mission to draw the curtains. She'd left it rather later than usual, not expecting the family home for a bit.

A strange young man at Mr Skeffington's desk where all his private papers were. She jumped, and her heart got in the way of the breath in her throat. His hand was on the surface of the desk. Snooping maybe, or stealing something. This was Mrs Occhi's great fantasy dread. She had never yet had to test out how brave she might have to be on behalf of her employers.

'I rang the bell. Maybe it's not working.'

The young man sounded relaxed.

'Are you expected? Mrs Skeffington always lets me know.'

He smiled, just like any ordinary visitor, except that most ordinary visitors would give her an ordinary, six-out-of-ten smile. This smile that now was turned on her was exceptional, it warmed unused emotions, spoke direct. The good-looking youth extended his hand and gave her his name, and flattered her when she introduced herself as the housekeeper. Surely not? She must be a Skeffington daughter or a sister.

He'd brought these things – and now she noticed the great billowing bundle of linen by his feet – on Mrs Skeffington's say-so but if this just meant a whole load more washing for Mrs Occhi, he didn't see why he shouldn't take them down to the launderette and do them there. He could see she already had more than enough to do if she really was who she said, and kept this whole great house running by herself.

Mrs Occhi's life was thin of people with time to sit in the kitchen over coffee and cake. The boy's appetite was gratifying, and he was interested in everything she had to tell him. She found herself running on about all sorts of things, the family, the house. Soon she forgot that she had ever been frightened of him, or suspicious. Anyone could get lost in this rambling place. And there were times, she must admit, when she failed to hear the doorbell.

Raught left behind him a fervent hope in the housekeeper's heart that the boys would get their cottas so dirty they'd need laundering after every single Sunday outing. She'd bake her special walnut cake next week. The young man had said he was very fond of walnut cake.

When Lucy got home later, nothing suspicious was reported because Mrs Occhi had forgotten she'd felt anything so inappropriate. Lucy had been putting off breaking to her housekeeper the news that she was in for a huge volume increase in the weekly wash. Now, conveniently, a problem left alone for long enough and solved itself. There was no reason for Lucy to bother asking herself why the housekeeper was embracing the extra task with such sunny acceptance.

Time now for Raught to make his way to the vicarage.

Father Terence had been on corrosively good form all day. This was not usual. It was more like him to wake in a state of sluggish mental and physical constipation, and drag the costive mood about with him till evening, but this morning Father Terence had woken in sunny mood, a mood further reinforced by the post. God was giving his waking eyes a preview of all good things in envelopes on his breakfast table. The bills, of course, were there in the morning mail. Like the poor, brown envelopes were always with us. Requests and dunnings for the corporeal and the supernal.

'Bills, bills! Altar wine and candles. They ought to fall free like manna from heaven, prettily drifting down. Don't you agree, Ash?' he asked skittishly. 'It seems somehow rather wrong to put a price tag on these sacred things. Ah well, not my will but Thine. And Thine seems to be that pounds, shillings and pence are expended upon them!'

But all was not bills and dunnings. There were among the brown envelopes a high proportion of interesting pleas: a special collection for the mission to convert the inner cities, an African parish desiring to be twinned, a request for the hall to be used for a meeting of the Clumber fanciers club. And . . . and hallelujah, the letter from the diocese giving him permission to get the jewelled cup out of the bank and use it at communion on the occasion of the inauguration of the choir. The augmented numbers warranted the use, even if the insurance cost was dreadfully steep.

'So many people needing my services. It is a full life, but a happy one.' Terence touched his dog collar. 'It would be difficult, in spite of my constant worries about my own inadequacies, not to feel fulfilled. Of course I have my worries and my personal disappointments, but set against the real joy of serving the Lord they can give me no real cause for complaint.'

Ashley was torn. Before Raught arrived tonight he had to ask Terence a difficult question. Always sensitive to his friend's moods, the last thing Ashley wanted to do was to spoil Terence's happy day.

Since the terrible day those papers had changed hands in the pub Ashley had not come across Raught. Every day since he had dreaded accidental meeting. He had been given a deadline. It had been exceeded. He lived in a torment of dread.

He had known in the Royal Oak, or thought he had known, that Raught was God's instrument calling him to the great affirmative work in his life. He had felt the great warm rush of certainty. And then he had got home and read those papers in detail, those astonishing hate-filled manifestos. Panic-stricken, he had stuffed the blurry photocopied bundle underneath his folded vests in a drawer where nobody but himself would ever go. Their presence there had ever since been seething and growing like a living thing. The heavy presence of Raught's terrorist cookbook pressed upon Ashley's mind during his every waking hour, and it greatly disturbed his sleep. The lists came before his eyes: the shops said to trade in cruel animal goods, the farms that dealt in torture, the experimental laboratories, the local hunts, and shoots. Then there were the recommendations and calls to action. They terrified him with their imperatives to violence: to bomb and burn and kill. Deprived of sleep, Ashley found himself more uncertain than ever of his own judgement. Burningly, he needed the answer to this vital question: his instinctive revulsion. Was it mere craven cowardice? Or was it a proper revulsion against violence?

This was the question he needed to discuss with Father Terence today before Raught came. He could not discuss it directly, of course, being obliged to respect the secrecy laid on him. What he wanted to ask the priest was this: when you got the call (which the priest of course had also had or he wouldn't be a priest), did it just come the once or did it keep at you? Was there such a thing as a false call? Or did God regularly call just the once and then make things really difficult simply to test your resolution? If Terence said the last was true, then Ashley must not ignore his sacred calling. If not, he needed his friend's considered opinion solidly behind him before he dared tell Raught that he'd changed his mind and wasn't going to do it.

All day Ashley waited for the perfect moment. All day the priest gleamed and beamed with unusual happiness. It wouldn't be right to bring it up during the communion round to the housebound parishioners. It wouldn't be right during the tea, sandwiches, cakes and ceaseless happy chatter of the Mother's Union coffee morning. Nor opening the tins at midday, nor when they popped into the Legion of Mary. By teatime Ashley's eyes were drowning in worry and Terence was if anything even more cheerful.

'I . . .' How could he introduce a problem into their beautiful day together? 'I wonder if we might have a go at painting in the spring?'

Ashley's crisis had turned his mind yearningly back to their first days moving into the Pendbury vicarage. Those days for Ashley had been the happiest in all their happy years together. Days with the feeling that the two of them were embarking on a partnership, setting up the vicarage together. Ashley had felt enfranchised, glimpsing at last an end to his own feudatory role. It had not lasted, this liberation, but he knew it would have done if only there had not been the tiresomeness over the order of service. Terence had needed to fight the good fight against the parish as only he could do it, alone, and somehow Ashley's manumission had been sacrificed, a casualty of the tensions engendered by the Prayer Book War.

Surely the bringing back of those happy days together would help Terence's mind tune into his own and then the question about the nature of a calling could be asked with ease.

'It could do with freshening up. Look.'

'Mm.' Responsive to the general principle of refurbishment, Father Terence wasn't going to object if Ash felt energetic enough to do it.

Encouraged at not meeting with rejection outright, Ashley went on to make himself absurd by shuffling along the skirting board pointing out cracks, scuff marks and little imperfections. His case hardly needed proving. Change and decay were all around, but the sight of the awkward little jack-in-the-box springing up to stab at the picture rail, then crouching down to point at a cracking floorboard, goaded the holy man to fury. Even now new doors were opening on gracious vistas of gentrification. The time really had come, for instance, to have his new friend, the guardian, to dinner, return some of that rum-oiled hospitality he'd met under the azure eye of Nelson. How could he possibly give a civilised dinner party with Ashley around? You just couldn't be sure of what he'd do next.

'What do you think about colour?' Ashley looked up from his latest crouch with those imploring spaniel eyes.

'Jimmy's done his study a good tobacco brown.'

Flinching eyes. Crouching spaniel kicked.

It was on this that Raught pushed open the study door. The boy's eyelids were at half-mast, but they took in everything, including a high charge of emotion in the room.

'I rang the bell; maybe it's not working.'

Terence didn't know that Raught was expected. The priest was suddenly a little breathless. Blood surged to the skin tight across the cheekbones. 'Bless you, what a treat. I am only sorry that I cannot stay to entertain you. I'm afraid I must leave that to my curate.' (He occasionally upgraded Ashley, to impress.) 'I have a marriage couple to prepare for their important day! So I must just tootle next door to do my sacred duty but if you can bear the company till then, do stay and share a bite at our humble board.'

Terence whisked through the door with a stylish inky swing of cassock.

'Does he always talk like that?' Raught declined into the recently vacated comfortable seat.

'Men of God do, you know.'

'You called a meeting.'

'It's those, er, things you gave me.'

'What about them?'

Ashley stood up. He poked the anthracite eggs which waterfalled and smoked some more. 'I'm not a brave man,' he muttered at the fire.

Odd to see this magnetic youth in the chair where he had never seen anyone but his friend. Raught's hands were far down in his pockets; his eyes were on the feeble fire; his face held none of the expected anger.

'Bit of a problem that,' he said in a most reasonable voice. 'You see, once you take on a commission you set the machine in motion. Unstoppable really. I was talking to the big man, the organiser, about your timetable a few days ago. You were scheduled in for action but overdue. Tell you what I did. Just for you. Nicked this fur here, see? From a shop. Told him you'd done it. Proof you're one of us now.'

Ashley's body was trembling, every bone had turned to water. 'I can't do such things. I know that now.'

'Pity you didn't know it before. I told you the terms.'

Raught left a little silence. 'Look. Do something, okay? You don't have to go straight into the big league, the strychnine and baby food lark. There's plenty of smaller things. One positive act. For the animals' sake? Think of those poor tortured rabbits with shampoo dripped in their eyes. You'd so something to help them, wouldn't you?'

Ashley nodded.

'Swear.'

Back at the Brook House the boys were always swearing blood brothers oaths in to-the-death secret societies. The oaths seemed to exert some superstitious binding compulsion.

'Swear by St Francis that you'll help the animals.'

Terence bounced back from an unusually concise pre-nuptial peptalk. Raught had left, taking with him the stolen fur.

'I can't think why he didn't stay. He knew I wouldn't be long. I've so much to talk to him about, his role in the service. It's the choir's inaugural next week.'

Ashley hardly needed reminding. Terence was obsessed by preparations, his nervous anticipation of the first enlarged service switch backed hourly from the highly exalted to the deeply pessimistic.

'I suppose I shall just have to pop up to the Brook House

one evening and organise it from there. Never done, never done. What did he find to talk to you about while he was here?'

'Animals.'

'Oh, that. Well, I've got plenty to do even if you haven't. Something on a tray would be a kindness.'

The next few days of Ashley's life were more distraught than usual. He had given his word to St Francis, his favourite saint. It *must* be a calling. If it was not a calling he would be breaking his sacred oath to the saint. There was no point in asking Terence now. If only he had not been so timid. Promising action made action no easier. He muddled times, dates and jobs more than usual. The priest let him know that he was very little practical help at this crucial pre-choir time. Ashley turned up at the Brook House for choir practice on the wrong day when the boys were somewhere quite else. He had his music with him and there was no one around, so he sat down at the tinny piano in the damply muggy passage, to find some calm in scales and arpeggios.

Music had power over Ashley. In private and when he was absolutely certain that he had no audience, he could play well, even with a degree of that direct connection to the music that makes for inspiration.

Alone, uninhibited, in one of the Brook House's green-linoed passages, he made sublime music on an old wreck of a metal-framed upright, with a dull thud where B flat ought to be, and an all-pervasive echo as though the notes were coming from inside a biscuit box. His voice had always been small – how else would one expect such a puny pair of lungs to terminate but in a gusty wheeze? – but, carried away, he sang merrily to the infectious jollity of Bach's 'Magnificat'. The notes missing in the old box were supplied by the singer. The small heavily knuckled fingers meandered fluidly, took themal material and developed it flexibly, swooping and swerving round the melodic line. The small voice stuck rock steady to the tune. The world was forgotten until he reached the final amen. He sat for a moment with shining post-performance eyes, then he gathered together his pieces of music and went back to the vicarage; and the nearer he got to home, the more pronounced was his limp with every dragging step.

Chapter Eleven

Guthlac, St. (?673–714), hermit. Of royal blood, he was a monk at Repton; he later migrated to an island in the fens where he lived a life of severe asceticism.
The Concise Oxford Dictionary of the Christian Church.

Much was expected from the choir's inauguration. Nothing was ruled out: heavenly warblings, mass demonstrations, banana skins.

Peter, reasonable man, went to church with reasonable expectations, merely anticipating augmented sound. His walk to church past the Pendbury pond was often a quietening influence, a small interval useful for measuring the week's circumstances against a Christian ideal. Peter walked briskly under a sky of langorous clouds, undecided yet what weather they should bring. In the fields the dye-splashed sheep were calm; there was an air of Sunday suspension, marking time.

At this time of year the muddy, less than exotic village pond had called the potshards and tufted duck all the way across the North Sea to join the scruffy natives on the small expanse of domestic water.

'I am as the duck,' Peter told himself, recalling the ancient psalmist, 'a speck of infinitude in the universe.'

Hard as he tried to put his own life into its proper place

beside the larger issues of mystery and duck migration, it was, he knew, himself and not the psalmist who must find the answers to the immediate conflicts in his life.

Tom Eggar, treading the same path with the same purpose, was more ambitious than Peter in his requirements of the day. During the next hour Tom confidently expected the roof of St Guthlac's to be cloven in twain. God wouldn't tolerate His pews being packed with junior robbers and blasphemers. Tom was looking forward to a mighty clap of thunder prior to the wrath of God descending with all its accompanying detail of grisly tortures. His heart skipped as a young ram at the thought. St Peter, ping pong bats in hands, wouldn't have to think twice before waving Tom off to the right. Then he could watch from on high as all these sinners who were going to occupy the east end of the church on the pretence of singing were waved down into the pit. And their Sodom and Gomorrah of a priest with them. After the Almighty had dealt with the abominable sinners in church He would stretch out His long arm along the High Street of Paris, which in Tom's mind looked much like Pendbury High Street with a sprinkling of tarts and poodles, pluck out his sinning daughter and add her to the pile of writhing bodies goaded by toasting forks.

Tom blurred the muscle that exposed the long yellow teeth; his wife beside him recognised this as a smile. Trotting with smaller steps to make up, she welcomed the smile. Any smile from Tom was welcome. This one confused her, but then many things confused Mary Eggar. Why should Tom smile? Hadn't he been ramping on before they started off for the service about Zanna's wicked sin, and the scandal of juvenile deletions in the choir stalls?

At last her anxious eyes left his face to turn towards her other preoccupation, the little granddaughters. Her eye could never dwell on them without her mind dipping into her store cupboard. She reviewed the packets of chocolate chips, slithered almonds, dedicated coconut. After church she'd make them a surprise cake for this afternoon. Her bovine face softened. She caught her favourite daughter's eye.

'The family that prays together strays together,' Mary mouthed lovingly, and Martha nodded.

The family crocodile was splendidly turned out. Their feet might be treading the road to worship but beneath four heads of groomed-to-the-hilt hair, their thoughts were on other things. The collective cortexes and medullas of the Eggar family were not bothered about priest and choir, mostly they were revelling in their freedom from Tom and their splendid new clothes. Arthur was delighted with his new blazer with the garage logo buttons, and Martha was wondering whether the rest of the village would appreciate that Jezebel and Salome were dressed exactly like the little princesses Eugenie and Beatrice in last week's *Hello!*

The priest and his assistant had arrived extra early this morning to make sure of everything. Ashley cracked his knuckles loudly. He wished he could feel confident about the Mussorgsky.

'Pity it's not a special feast. We should have waited till we were out of the dreary after-Pentecosts.' Terence was slipping into the green brocade cassock that signified a Sunday with no particular feast to celebrate. 'I look much better in white,' he fretted.

'You know I always like you in green.' Ashley brushed a colourless hair from the brocade shoulder.

'Oh do stop touching me.'

Ashley knew it was his privilege to be the target of his friend's first-night nerves.

'Pity we can't do better than golden rod.' The priest frowned. 'Surely it's a bit early for glycerined leaves. We've all the winter for them.'

'I love the subtle autumn colours.' Being cheerful to the point of idiocy only got Ashley's head snapped off again.

Danny had been excited during the swinging walk to church in his blue cassock. The choir stepped through the gate as a body, and crossed that invisible line from a world he was allowed to see to one he was not. The procession filled the narrow lane, its high banks untrimmed, with long grass the colour of hay, and so many things to stop and see if they had been allowed. Stronger than the want to stop was the community compulsion, the music making them go on. 'We're like water being poured down a narrow thing,' he thought, 'running down faster and faster, all blue drops together. How does water feel, rushing like this? I might ask Mr Skeffington next time. Oh. No.' He didn't ask Mr Skeffington anything any more. He didn't go to meet him on the drive now. He never had since that day . . .

It would be good to try the wild strawberry that still clung to the autumn-fading plant, break step and look at those queer toadstooly things with slugs sliming along their caps and the busy black beetles with twiggy pincers. All these things he saw in the Brook House grounds, but there they were part of his prison, he would never look at them there to study. These red and white toadstools, tall-stalked and spotted, were the same as the ones under the pine trees where the snakes lay in hot weather. The place where you were gay if you didn't go. He was gay all the time since he'd been out that once. Better not to go out, it made you more alone inside. Those red and white ones were poison like the snakes. Raught said if they put one down your throat while you were asleep you'd die in agony and it'd be unde-tectable. Lots of murders had been done with them. You couldn't stay awake all night, you always went off some-time. And then you'd die poisoned. Sometimes it made him cry.

The Brook House marched on its showy way towards the

lych gate. They'd not yet got up the marching band, so Jimmy, at the head, had a tape recorder under his arm. Stirring stuff from the band of the Coldstream Guards: 'See the conquering hero comes'. The little crowd of Eggars were forced into the recess of a porch but they didn't mind. Not for such a show. Jimmy Stonor bowed to acknowledge the courtesy. Martha bridled, gummily coy. Jimmy and the boys flowed on, white ruffs foaming, blue cassocks billowing, an undulating sea.

Pom pom pom pom tiddle pom tiddle pom. At last the church was settling down. What a turnout! More like harvest than a mere green Sunday. Ashley risked a glance up from 'Pictures at an Exhibition'. During the bits that were not too difficult he could catch up with the body of the church without having to move his head, the angled mirror lending the organist a detached lack of curiosity which was quite misleading. Reflected round the vestry jamb, Raught's duplicate appeared. His eyes met Ashley's in the square of glass. 'Soon,' said the falcon glare, 'soon.'

Ashley's fingers stumbled. He looked for comfort: 'Utensil, utensil,' but still his fingers tied themselves in knots around the unambitious piece.

Raught showed himself openly at the vestry door to ring the little silverplated bell that had been such a bone of contention when introduced by Father Terence. At its fairy tinkle today the congregation rose, today obedient as milky lambs.

In the front pew, Peter leant over towards Honor. 'Going to behave, Mother?'

Her smile was the dignified minimum from one accustomed to hobnobbing with crowned heads.

'Be subject for the Lord's sake to every human institution.' The priest read the introductory sentence.

'The Lord be with you,' wished the pallid priest.

'And also with you,' Honor and all the village wished him back in one voice quivering with evangelical sincerity.

160

Pendbury had closed ranks against the Brook House boys. Civil obedience was restored. Heaven had come down to earth for Father Terence.

Danny had never been in a church before. He was unprepared for the thin, pale light, the calm of floating motes against jewel-coloured glass. His nose, accustomed as it was to the mingled smog of institutional cooking and adolescents' bodies, had never met the cold stone smell of unused air. The sound of the organ was to the cranky Brook House piano as full and rich as a river is to a dripping tap. It was a sound to fill this space so full, the church might take off with it and float into the sky. Lacking clear Christian instruction, Danny was not certain that St Guthlac's was not heaven, the priest was not the Lord. A place and a person you visited once a week and then, when you died, it was here you stayed. He was too awed to sing the first hymn.

The congregation rose. Father Terence was moving smoothly into place, gliding to the crossing past choir stalls miraculously inhabited by row upon row of handsome lost sheep, hair curling into the smooth napes of young necks. He must relax, must have faith; Jimmy Stonor swore they'd had hitchless rehearsals.

Ashley wanted to cry. He needed all his magic incantations to keep control. The service so far had been bitter to him. Wormwood and gall. Musical control had been taken out of his hands entirely. He had been powerless from the moment of Raught's imperious ringing of the starting bell to Jimmy Stonor's bossy back view. The guardian had settled himself solidly exactly between organist and choir, so that he entirely blocked Ashley's vision of everything going on at the chancel end. The organist could not see Terence at all. He tried to peer round the huge white cotton back but the angle was wrong. How would he know what the priest wanted if they couldn't exchange their normal little signals? Jimmy Stonor ignored Ashley's tentative whispers and got right behind the flamboyant business of conducting, cassock billowing like a pillowcase on a line. Worse, Jimmy raised his arms to start each hymn without even the courtesy of a turn and a glance to alert the organist. It made for ragged beginnings and flustery catch-up dashes all the way through. Ashley fretted about not being sufficiently pumped up for these surprise starts, so he overinflated the organ which wheezed and farted. Jimmy was not entirely sound on timing either. He took 'For the Beauty' at an impossible gallop. Ashley's tummy was starting to play up. How could he discharge his duties when he was muffled blind like a parrot under a sheet?

The Ministry of the Word. At last Jimmy Stonor moved out of Ashley's way so he could see his friend moving to the symbolic centre of the church, to read the words so special that only the priest could read them and all the congregation must stand up to show respect. How kind of Jimmy to shift over so Ashley could see. But Jimmy was not shifting, he was walking. Treading the deck with steady sea legs in case it should start to heave, Jimmy Stonor, smart as paint in sandals with special cassock-matching socks, walked up to the east end, collected the cross and took up pole position behind the priest in the very centre of the church. A crucifer, and Terence hadn't told him. Ashley bit his lip.

There was more to it than merely Jimmy Stonor. They made a tableau, the four of them, focus of all eyes. The father reading the Holy Gospel, the guardian hovering behind him so the words should be read under a slightly *tremens* cross. Either side of the priest, decorative in spotless white, a matched pair of choirboys, Raught and another chosen for height and for handsomeness. Each boy held a new wax candle to light the Word. This was a novelty, a piece of theatre that appealed to the Pendbury congregation. Eyes misted at the beauty of the male foursome.

Only Ashley grieved: crucifer and altar boys; he might at least have told me.

The priest rolled out the appointed text: Romans 13. "'Since all government comes from God, the civil authorities were appointed by God, and so anyone who resists authority is rebelling against God's decision, and such an act is bound to be punished.'"

Standing behind the priest, Jimmy's face showed on top of Terence's, as though the top of the priest's head had opened up to grow a second.

"'If you break the law however, you may well fear: the bearing of the sword has its significance.'"

A ripple of satisfaction flowed through Jimmy's beard. Raught and his approximate doppelgänger, militarily erect and flatteringly lit behind their candles, flanked these promises of eternal damnation.

Peter was furious. What an idiot thing to do, read hellfire and damnation. He had been watching Danny off and on since the service began. The boy was placed so Peter could easily see him from his front pew, and he had been taking pleasure in the emotions that could be read so easily on the little face. Awe and curiosity had passed across that transparent canvas, and a response to beauty. Now he saw a profoundly sad resignation as Danny heard the New Testament and Gospel readings. Peter was filled with indignation, and a longing to console.

But Peter was mistaken, it was not the tub-thumping harshness of the words that spread the melancholy in his little boy's heart. Danny was not listening to St Paul's vengeful threats, he would never imagine that he was meant to hear and apply to his own small self the meaning of these importantly delivered words. Insomuch as he was listening at all, his musical ear had tuned into the general rhythms and inflections of the readings, the soundtrack to the larger composite sensory picture that was this unfamiliar place, church.

Danny had seen Raught ring the bell in church as he rang the rising bell up at the Brook House. Now Stonor's deputy took up the candle as Mr Stonor took up the cross. Peter Skeffington and all the village stood up in their pews and bowed to them standing at the top and reading from the book. Wherever you went in the world, Danny saw, with no surprise but a resigned, even expected acceptance, you could not get away from Raught's control, and Mr Stonor.

That was the cause of the dismay that Peter was misinterpreting on his little boy's face.

The priest picked up Paul's stern words and ran with them. His sermon was thunderously extravagant and greatly pleasing to Tom Eggar, who was on the edge of his seat with his eyes rolled up towards the roof so he shouldn't miss a minute when the chiliastic chaos broke out above.

Father Terence also pleased the boys' guardian. By the end of the grim sermon the old sea dog realised that he had made not only an astonishing musical debut, but also a really useful ally. The man of God and the boys' keeper finished the service well pleased with themselves and each other.

Terence always wore a frown to process down the aisle. It was fitting. Today the frown was directed specifically at Ashley. Everything had been perfect this morning, it had been the service of his dreams: the jewelled cup, the ornamental choir, the old woman saying the right words, the obedient flock. All heavenly! But Ashley's music – that had originated in the Other Place. His organ playing had never been worse, he was doing it on purpose to spoil Terence's special day. Listen to it now: the Preobrajensky taken at the pace of a funeral march. How could the boys possibly step out smart to this?

After their priest the villagers poured down the aisle in one consenting stream, not even a tiny faction branched off

towards the side door. They were in the business of showing the Brook House how joyful life could be if you
belonged to a pleasant law-abiding community.

'Well, Mother?' Peter queried as they stood among the
good-humoured villagers queueing and smiling and
jostling.

She gave him a look. 'They'll soon get bored.'

He was about to say she had a point when he was
pushed in the back by Tom Eggar who was passing through
the congregation in a daze, his neck skewed, his pupils
dilated, and his eyes darting upward in quest of the dooms-
day clouds that he still had not despaired of, the heaven
that he still believed must split open. Mary supported him
out of the church, apologising profusely to left and right:
there was something extraurinary about her Tom today.

'What about a little celebration?' At the end of a satisfac-
torily full receiving line, Jimmy Stonor.

The priest accepted the impromptu invitation, and
stepped out to the rousing sound of the tape recorder side
by side with his new friend, coeval heads of the odd little
quasi-military display. Oh the grand old Duke of York! A
pavement procession quite like Rogation, really. Up the
hill and out of the village marched the new alliance. Up to
the Brook House for a drink. It might become a weekly
ritual.

The big, quiet church was empty now. Everybody had gone.
Only Ashley was still there, solitary. The memory of the
past hour hung like ectoplasm round the gothic shadows. It
was some time before he could find the will to unfurl from
his dull-eyed slump over the keyboard. Mechanically he
set about all the little jobs they always did together, the
valedictory housework. Sliding the card numbers out of
the hymnboards, locking up the Host in the little wall safe
behind the fringed brocaded curtain. These were the chores

they always shared. It was one of the best moments of the week, the quiet aftermath, pottering about taking care of the details in God's house. An intimate time of small jokes, observations compared, mulling over the service and people just gone.

Ritually each week, he and Terence would wait until they had made St Guthlac's spick and span, cleansed from it all signs of the recent invasion by an untidy congregation; then they would take the pair of conical snuffers to the two watchful flames that burnt either side of the altar. They would bow simultaneously, straighten up, take two paces forward, and extinguish the two flames at exactly the same moment. Putting the week to bed together, beginning the new one in unison.

Ashley went about these jobs alone today but he went about them every whit as conscientiously and thoroughly as though he were doing it with his friend. Every hassock was hooked, every hymn book ranked; nothing should be left undone, though the altar candles broke his heart, and all the time his head carried a vivid picture of the gaily coloured procession in motion with the guardian and Father Terence at the head thumping up the village street, up the village street.

He had no more work to do. Twelve more hours of Sunday stretched before him. The little man locked the church carefully, turned his back on it and went out into the world with his childish limping trot. He'd go and do it now. Suffused and excoriated by pain the little man went directly to his secret place.

There they were, typed and stapled, the pages that the big cheese had sent to him, and him alone. Sitting on his narrow bed he shivered as he revised the tremendous explosions you could make from weedkiller and acid, scanned ghastly pictures of damage wreaked by the combination of petrol, a milk bottle and an anonymous comrade's good bowling arm.

Bombs and such were not for him, not even in post-Eucharist extremis, but he read again, in confirmation, the typefuzzed amateur printjob telling him that liberating laboratory animals and sabotaging hunt kennels both qualified as fighting the good fight.

Ashley got to work with his little curved nail scissors, the backstack of the *Church Times*, and glue. It was awkward cutting out in rubber gloves but the pamphlet was admonitory on fingerprints.

A steady silent plod through ankle-high winter keep, wet with November mizzle, had him wishing he'd taken the tarmac way. He might have risked the road today. Every Sunday lunchtime Pendbury High Street took on a *Marie-Celeste* quiet, while the population concentrated exclusively on the inner man. But even houses at belly-worship had windows, and this way across the fields was the less likely to be overlooked.

The grass was alive with leatherjackets. Today was their day in all the year to crowd the ground with their exuberant hopping wormy bodies. In a day or two they'd all be dead but meanwhile they milled and swarmed crooklegged in the long grass with sudden staggering springs. Hundreds of awkward bodies insanely stiff of purpose, crashing into each other, then climbing up one grassy tussock pointlessly only to blunder down into the next. Each foot Ashley put down brought a great cloud springing and swerving about his ankles. However carefully he trod, he could not avoid crushing the helpless things. The soles of his shoes obsessed his mind: they must be jammed with dead and half-dead bodies, some wriggling in the last death of their nerves, some already still. His feet, sensitised by his appalled mind, could feel the cushion of squelchy softness under each step. He was conscious of a mounting phobia, and called on St Francis to pity himself, these poor insects, the world.

It was one thing to be an animal terrorist in the safety of

your frowsty bedroom, another when you were at the gate-
way of the hunt kennels, and the moment now or never.
Ashley had thought he could feel no worse in life than
wading through those poor helpless daddy-longlegs, knowing that he was cutting off the proper leisure of their death
dance. Now he knew that he could feel worse. This fear
was unlike anything. He was very cold, and the sweat was
running from his armpits down his ribs.

He reached the point where the path forked, and hesi-
tated to take the path towards the kennels. His mind and
body were now at the final crossroads of decision. Still he
might put his hand in his pocket, scrumple the patchwork
letter, and walk on – himself free, though the hounds
remained imprisoned. On the other hand . . . Ashley
remembered Raught, he remembered the grog-huddle that
would be going on even now in Stonor's study. He remembered his promise to the saint.

He opened the gate and took the lefthand path. He didn't
even need to deviate: the path went right alongside the
kennel buildings. He looked round quick, and saw only an
emptiness, only a beautiful windy silvery landscape with
crows hang-gliding leisurely on fluid currents of air.

The gate had no padlock. Slipping it was merely a
matter of leaning over a little to reach the latch. The noise
of the dogs was shattering. Twenty-two and a half couple
bayed and brayed and snapped and snarled and whined
and whimpered at the passing human footstep with its
implication of delicious bloody meat. He wanted to go
back to the gate, refasten the latch he had loosed, slip in to
retrieve the anonymous letter he had dropped over the
fence, but that meant hanging about. Stronger than his will
to undo the deed was the desire to get away quick. He
stumbled on up the footpath, round the corner, out of
sight, panic-blind and panting. Brambles threw out their
hooked runners to snare him, bracken made deep, ravelled
traps, and all the time he listened for the hue and cry: the

hounds of Pendbury seeking him down the labyrinthine ways.

The kennelman lay in his large chair before the television. Made sleepy by the monotonous screen and heavy lunch, he grunted and shifted his belly. Those hounds would fire up sudden at a passing rabbit, magpie, anything.

It was some time, too, before the hounds themselves discovered their freedom. Ashley was far away by the time the first brown leather nose coincided with the gate, and shoved it open.

Instinctively Ashley found his way back to the refuge of his church. He spent a terrible hour at damp stone sanctuary, his thoughts too incoherent to know how to pray. The place that had been so rich in sound was quiet now and empty. Empty it seemed of God as well, for him. He heard his own tears hitting the stone floor. Long and painfully he knelt, thin bone on stone because a hassock would have been less penitent. A random church visitor would not have noticed the small shadow huddled into the imperishable splendour of the gilded organ.

After a long time he rose and took a duster from the vestry cupboard. Keeping the orange prop in his hand, he climbed on pews with the excuse of dusting windowsills. Only after peering out to north, south, east and west, ascertaining the emptiness of landscape in every direction of lych and churchyard, did he dare slip out of church to shuffle home.

Ashley made vegetable soup for them both that night. They always had a simple Sunday supper, often something-and-toast. He pared and chopped, swept by a sense of loss, a longing for the peace he'd once possessed before this cataclysmic day.

Over the soup Father Terence, magnanimous in popularity, showed a peculiar patience, almost tenderness, towards his clumsy friend. He referred at first tentatively to the innovations he had made in the day's service, and then, when Ashley offered no reproach, relayed kindly, word for word, all the complimentary things Jimmy Stonor had said.

'He said he'd never seen greater authority at the altar. I thought you'd like to know, Ash. Not in the spirit of false pride – God forbid I should be guilty of that sin – but I know how you take pleasure when my career is justly appreciated. Young Raught's a clever lad. Jimmy's right hand. He had one or two suggestions for improving the choir that, frankly, I wish I'd thought of for myself.'

Ashley became quite passive in the days following. He had never before kept a secret from his friend. Inwardly he had always thought of the two of them as twin souls. It weighed heavy on him that he was the one who had cracked his own note in the harmonious double peal that was his life and Terence's taken together. Ashley had bad dreams and a bad conscience. He felt ill and dirty, his honour and his candour smudged.

The obvious depressed inertia of his friend inspired a playful capriciousness in Father Terence. The priest put the little man's sudden disintegration down to jealousy, and told himself that a little mortification was thoroughly good for Ashley's soul. Ash had had his own way too long; if Father Terence was to grow in the ways of the Lord he must have a wide and balanced circle of advisers and Ashley must just face up to the fact.

'Today's the day for your choir rehearsal. Aren't you going up to the Brook House, Ash? Oh well, you stay here then. I'll just pop up. I've a few things to talk over about the coming Sundays. Maybe I shall stay to lunch. Shall I tell the guardian you are not feeling well enough? Have you seen this?' He waved the local paper at Ashley. 'It will be of interest to you. Animal liberators they call themselves. I don't think much of people who liberate hounds so that several can run into a pensioner's garden, tear her cat to pieces, and then run off on to the road and get themselves run over, do you? It will do them a power of good to see the real consequences of their actions. I shall go and visit the old lady who owned the cat. I shall provide consolation in her time of loss. Maybe you could find one of your waifs and strays in need of a home. I should like to take her a new pussycat when I call to console her.'

After that Ashley's inaction became positively existential. He drifted helpless, useless, in the wake of the priest, annoying him and perpetually inviting his abuse.

'Answer the telephone, won't you? It might be the Brook House. I'm only home if it's Jimmy or Raught.'

Telephones and doorbells. Long moments of paralysis anticipating nemesis, police uniforms.

'Ashley Crowther? The name's Puddephat.' The telephone brought a stranger, one who was not asking to speak to the priest. The stranger had a warm and friendly voice. 'Raught told me about you,' said the person. 'I believe you have a story for me? Young Raught tells me you've done a brave and daring deed. Am I right? He also tells me there's an excellent hostelry not too far from your village. We could meet there and you could tell me all about yourself and your cause and your beliefs in congenial surroundings.'

The relaxed one-sided chat went on for some time in this vein. It wound up with: '. . . my readers look forward to hearing all about you, and myself to meeting you.'

Ashley felt warm for the first time in weeks. He went to his corner and sat down, trying to make up his mind if the voice was Scottish or American; either way he liked its warmth and the old-fashioned courtesy of the phrases.

The priest looked across, full of curiosity, and saw his friend's face unfrozen for the first time in days.

Normally, after taking a telephone call, Ashley would set Terence's nerves jangling by reporting verbatim every 'hello' and 'how are you' and what sort of weather the caller was enjoying. Petty revenge, the priest supposed,

Ashley not telling now; but still Father Terence went on wondering who on earth it could have been on the other end of the line. Rare the occasions he couldn't have a good guess.

Ashley's underlying mood was changed by the short talk with the journalist. The innermost spaces into which he had withdrawn these last days had been bleak and heavy. A ray now relieved this leaden landscape, and as time drew away from the telephone call and towards its physical fruition, the little ray touched further and further corners until Ashley had convinced himself that he might after all not have set himself utterly beyond the reach of God and man. He could even convince himself that these last few days might have been his final testing, his three days of darkness before the blinding light of transfiguration by newsprint.

The maybe American, maybe Scottish voice grew kindlier and more sympathetic with each time he remembered it. He would put all his jumbled good intentions before this professional man, hold nothing back. Then Mr Puddephat, he, whose job it was, could tell the story clear to the world, plain and right and true as it was in Ashley's head. After that, even if hounds and cat had been killed as it said in the paper, people would understand.

Ashley put on the rubber overshoes. The weather had been changeable all week, and it was time for his bicycle ride to the rendezvous. For all it was a dark evening, and the sky above him inconsistent with the scudding of clouds and sudden blatters of rain, Ashley's heart was bathed in a warm and slumbrous light. He cycled with a billowing waterproof cape under an intermittent moon, certainty growing that he was riding towards his own redemption. Bump bump, the file cards safe under his waterproof knocked against his ribs to the chance rhythms of the road surface.

He was early, of course. The meeting was for six so he'd

decided he must set off at half past five to allow for any unforeseen emergencies, punctures and so forth. With twenty minutes to kill and shy of drinking alone in a strange place, he made himself thoroughly cold in the car park looking at his watch, getting cold feet in both senses, and rehearsing phrases. By the time he entered the pub he was frozen, pink, dripping, and muddled.

The journalist had no difficulty in recognising him from Raught's concise description: 'pale-skinned, black-eyed and hunchbacked, probably wearing a polo neck because he likes to pretend he's a priest'.

'Hello, I'm Puddephat. Bugger of a night out there. What can I get you to drink?'

'How do you do?' Ashley took his hand shyly. 'Might I have a coffee?'

Puddephat went to the bar. He was a large man, not gigantically tall, not vastly fat, but his presence dominated. The journalist's suit looked as if he'd grown both a bit taller and a bit fatter since putting it on. Lots of grey hair sprang energetically from a pink-fleshed face with skin open-pored and shiny as though it'd been oiled. A red and white bandana handkerchief often came out of his pocket for mopping the beaded brow, and more colour was added by the billowing cravat whose purple and cerise stripes probably told an important old-school fact, but those facts were not the sort that Ashley knew.

'Here we are then.' The journalist negotiated the body-packed bar without a drop overboard. 'Cheers.'

'Cheers. What delicious coffee.'

'I put a drop of brandy in it. You look starved with cold.'

The journalist's concern touched Ashley, he found it encouraging.

Puddephat exhaled, 'Ah, Scottish water!' He always said that when he began a glass of whisky, so he said it many times a day.

The large man settled back on the bench as if it were

comfy as anything and gave Ashley the first of many wholeheartedly chummy smiles, the one that made his eyes disappear completely behind crinkles of irresistible friendliness. 'Tell me all about it then, Ashley.'

Ashley wanted to, but pub tables being too small for a properly organised layout, the file cards were soon all over the place and Ashley was bending under the little table to retrieve runaways. It was hopeless, he wasn't going to make a good showing. The cards were jumbled beyond his control, out of sequence, noodles in alphabet soup.

'Tell you what, my friend.' Puddephat spread his large pink hands with their sort-of gold, sort-of signet ring on to the table. The splayed fingers covered the scattered disorder of cards. Leaning forward, he smiled shinily at Ashley. 'Look, my friend, forget about case numbers and such, just tell me in your own words, right?'

Eventually, after many stumbles, Ashley did find some of his own words. Sparse and jerky at first, they became a little smoother. Every time he looked up there was this friendly face nodding encouragement. It was such a relief to tell the whole story to someone. He unfolded towards Puddephat's genial face.

The invaluable work he did for the RSPCA led on in a more or less straight line to the hunt kennels incident. He also told the journalist about spreading the gospel at the Brook House but then he remembered that he really shouldn't have talked about that, so while Puddephat was up at the bar getting another of those very warming coffees, he backpedalled a bit and dared, after Puddephat's second 'Ah, Scottish water!', to say, 'Maybe you could not write that about the boys? It's not what I'm supposed to be there for.'

Puddephat knew all about the Brook House sessions already. He knew a lot of other things about Ashley as well, and about the village of Pendbury. Raught could never have lured this reporter from a national down here merely on a no-news story about the number of cats and dogs in this world being reduced by a few.

'Look, I'll tell you what I'll do, my friend. I'll remember that you said it and bear it in mind about the boys, okay?'

Greatly encouraged, Ashley felt it would be a betrayal of their new friendship and implying a lack of trust if he put into words what he himself felt to be understood, that they were just chatting as friends, off the cuff.

The journalist was evidently tuned to his thoughts.

'Well, that's work over!' he said cheerily. 'Let's have a last one for the road before I have to get back to London.'

'Let me get this one.'

'Don't you even think about it, my friend.' The pink slab of a hand came heavily down on to his shoulder with the double purpose of keeping the little man in his place and steadying the journalist as he got up. 'One of the bonuses of this job, the rag pays me to drink with new friends, I'll stick you on expenses.'

'Tell me about yourself, Ashley,' he asked with the third Scottish water. 'You live in the village, do you, in Pendbury? D'you have a house or what?'

So Ashley told this friendly man all about himself and how lucky he was to share in the life of the vicarage.

In no time at all it was eight-thirty and time to pedal back for the nine o'clock All Soul's vigil at St Guthlac's. The journalist motored off, fast and warm, and fervently benisoned by his new friend.

Ashley hardly noticed that the rain had really set in. Hood up, handy packable cape streaming, he bicycled buoyantly.

'See you around,' Puddephat had said. Not goodbye.

'See you around.' Ashley said the unfamiliar phrase to his handlebars, practising. 'See you around.'

He must try to keep this secret that came bursting out into smiles and song. He must not tell Terence until he wandered nonchalantly into the study with the newspaper under his arm and put it casually down in front of his friend with the story just happening to be on top.

That night at the All Souls service Ashley had a great success in church with the 'Dance of the Blessed Spirits'. Never before had he managed such a dignified yet animated musical tribute to the souls of the faithful departed. Terence even congratulated him.

CHAPTER TWELVE

They were not strict Sabbatarians up at the vicarage. Six days shalt thou labour . . . How was a vicar expected to rest on the seventh?

If it was a busy day for the man of God, it was quite frantic for Ashley with all his unrecognised aide-de-camp duties. He was the one who opened and closed the church, he went up early before the services to unlock, and he returned late, having locked. He was the one who got the priest's vestments out of the cupboard, and unveiled the altar, which had spent the week under plastic sheeting because birds would fly in through holes in the roof and mess on it. It fell to him to trim the candles and get the brass and silver out of the wall safe. There were a thousand little jobs. These apart, he had his own recognised job of playing the organ.

Between these sacred duties, Father Terence gave his friend innumerable opportunities for 'drudgery divine' at the vicarage: Ashley cooked the meat lunch of the week, and cleaned busily . . . 'Who sweeps a room as for Thy laws/Makes that and th' action fine'.

Speaking to the priest you might get quite a different impression of Sundays at the vicarage. He liked to paint his Sabbaths as a kind of sacred blank. Ask Father Terence if he had read an article in one of the Sunday papers? He would frown and administer a courteous but firm crushing of the heathen: 'Sunday paper?' he would say. 'No. I certainly would not have seen that article. I do not take a Sunday paper.'

In truth it was economy, not principle, that kept the vicarage uninformed on the seventh day.

Since Ashley's interview with the journalist Puddephat, he had been wondering how he was going to manage to run up to the newsagent's on a Sunday and get hold of Puddephat's paper. It would take more deceit than he was capable of planning. Towards the end of the week he found himself running out of custard powder and as a result spent Friday and Saturday in a tussle with his conscience. Knowing the tin was empty, it had come into his mind, quite frankly, to deceive Father Terence by not replacing it until Sunday.

All week the Sunday paper had been in his mind. His heart had kept up a gallop of nervous excitement. Sleep was a kind of subsiding into a treacly calm overlaying the knowledge that was with him every minute, daytime and nighttime. Puddephat's words came back to him, and his own words, and certain promises Puddephat had made.

'The world will know the name of Ashley Crowther.'

He was not a man for fantasy or imagination. Never desiring fame or greater fortune than he had, he was not attracted by the starburst glory that a newspaper article might bring. He did not dream, as others might, of consequences: of photographs and chat shows, or imagine any pleasures of celebrity. Nevertheless he looked forward to the article for his own reasons.

All the hundreds of dogs and cats and pigs and poultry that Ashley had quietly and often secretly saved from one thing or another had been an end in themselves. But now that solid past had been invalidated by one act: the release of the hounds with its dreadful consequence. Ashley could not understand how the release of the hounds could be seen as a good act at all, but Puddephat obviously could.

The journalist had seemed to admire the act greatly, spoke highly of it, praising it to the skies. Ashley concluded that when he read the article he would at last understand the goodness of the act. He would be all right in his mind again. He would be able once more to pray to his God. It was a great pain to him that ever since inadvertently causing the death of fellow-creatures, the path to prayer had been barred to him. He was too deeply ashamed before his suffering God to be able to kneel before him.

God must have missed Ashley's prayers for Ashley was good at praying. The priest's companion had never in all his life presumed to bother God with a personal request. He remembered being made as a boy at school to pray for the football team every time it played a match. Ashley had bowed his head in unison with the other boys; it was cowardly, he knew, concealing the fact that he was not praying, but it seemed to him a worse sin to pray than not to pray. It was surely insolent and inappropriate to expect the Deity to keep an eye on goalscoring? So now as a grown man he would not allow himself to pray that Puddephat's article would appear in this week's paper but oh, how desperately he hoped.

'We've run out of custard powder,' he said after early Eucharist and before the family service at ten. 'I'll just nip out and get some. Treacle tart needs it.'

(How white, how little, was a little white lie?)

Bicycling up the street, his small viaticum jingling in his pocket, he picked up and paid for a copy off the pile.

Outside the shop he stood on the pavement beside his propped-up bike, opening page after page, and found himself famous. His legs went suddenly from under him and he had to sit down on the pavement. He was genuinely astonished.

'GAY VICAR'S LOVER ANIMAL RIGHTS TERRORIST.' The sensational story spilled over several columns, and there was a colour photograph of the two of them emerging from the vicarage for a walk, from what it said was their torrid love nest.

The page blurred and danced. The first shock was physical and completely debilitating. It was as if a hand had squeezed his heart. He wheezed and gasped and struggled for breath, and sat down on hard tarmac as his legs went from under him.

When, much later, he could get up again, he could not mount the bicycle but walked like an automaton, wheeling the machine along. He could not think. He was completely overtaken with a blind misery and a kind of creeping acceptance. This was how his life was and always had been. Last week's exhilaration, all those possibilities, had been an illusion. He ought to have known right away in the pub that Raught was a messenger not from God but from the Tempter. Oh! Had he only been clear-sighted enough to resist. Of course it had not been a call from God. When had God's hand ever led to the death of an innocent creature?

Ashley's eyes followed the stroboscopic repetitions of the bicycle's wire wheels as the tyres went round. The spokes, physically there yet insubstantial to the point of transparency in motion, were a parable for his own life.

The street would widen soon round the next bend, and there the village pond would be. The painted pub sign would be where it had always been, and the clustering houses, and the grey spire of his beloved St Guthlac's would be pointing to heaven.

He could not face the church in his shame. Terence. No, he could not think about Terence, it made his mind swerve hectically.

Before the church and vicarage could come into view, he had cut away sharply from the road up the path towards the reservoir. Instinct was turning him towards the place where he had last been happy together with Terence. It was a fixed place, their quiet water of the mind. If he could get there, he might find coherence.

He struggled and blundered up the hill. At some moment the bicycle became too much trouble, and he opened his hands to let it fall into the scrub beside the path. It was raining now. Large drops falling iron-hard from an implacable sky. Collared doves were calling roundabout, far and near, fugitive as corpse candles. Thunder was rolling in blue-black tors.

He was panting by the time he'd gained the water at the top of the hill. And then he heard the voice of Raught, of all voices: 'Hey, Ashley. What you doing? Looking for a lost hound?'

After that he was rudderless, he did not know the way. Without intention he followed one of the tracks, a clear path on which to set one foot before the other. Small animals fled his noisy progress. Squirrels threw down their beechmast, jays screamed and a cloud of rooks rose from the soft remains of a decomposing rabbit.

Without intention, Ashley was following the last path taken by the village's unwanted debris. Old fridges got dragged down here, defunct televisions, stained and bursting mattresses. Tipped in a tumble down a steep bank, they ended resting hugger-mugger heaped on an orphaned piece of land disowned by both the council and the railway company whose track ran past the bottom of the stinking pile. His uneven legs were taking him downhill faster as the ground sloped steeper. Down through ragged, rusty tins, mouldering rags, unidentifiable splashes of disorganised matter. At the bottom of the bank a couple of strands of barbed wire was the nominal barrier shutting off the railway line.

Ashley's downhill propulsion brought him to rest hard against the double wire. He was stopped but not cut, because the barbs were muffled by a scruffy brown fur caught on the top strand as though it had been flung in a very wide arc from the top of the bank. He took a hold of the fur as he stooped to duck in between the upper and the lower strand of wire, and he kept it in his hand as he walked on to the railway line.

Who would be injured by his departing? Terence would only benefit. When he lay down on the cold iron, the fur helped to pillow his head. He took the end of the soft, musty-smelling thing and wrapped it round his eyes so he should not see. Then he curled his knees up to his chin and lay still, waiting for the train. High in the stormy air above him, black specks gathered and converged. Swirling and swaying in the air, a pattern of wind made visible, the whirling vortex was centred on the still body. The glistening crows cried raucously against the storm. They were warning off rivals, keeping away the other carrion-feeders, making sure they would have Ashley all to themselves.

Chapter Thirteen

The bishop was in no doubt what to do. 'He'll have to be put on an enforced retreat. Somewhere very old-fashioned.' He looked puzzled. 'Is there anywhere that still observes the greater silence? D'you have a list?'

'I think they're all Roman these days, but I'll look and see,' said the bishop's chaplain who had been appointed for his Machiavellian mind, thus allowing the bishop to preserve his own sprightly twinkling innocence. 'I hear he's High,' said the useful subordinate. 'If he converted he might save us some embarrassment.'

The chaplain was dispatched immediately to press Father Terence into the dusty episcopal Ford. The uncomprehending cleric was driven to an isolated community of Holy White Friars who lived by the primitive rule far away in the Pembrokeshire hills where they abstained from most things in their extreme asceticism.

'My lord feels sure you must need a small time of retreat and spiritual renewal. The death of your friend, the shock.'

'But it was nothing to do with me,' blustered Terence, 'Ash . . . Mr Crowther was only a kindness, a charity case. I took him in out of Christian duty and gave him a home. It was like having a dog. You must know that.' In the aftermath of his friend's death it was as if Terence had assumed Ashley's twittering ineffectualness. 'Surely if I could be allowed to put my case, clear my name.'

'In time, in time. His lordship is wise in the ways of the world.'

'But how long must I stay here?' Father Terence rolled his eyes round in despair at the idealistic discomforts. It was a place that promised strict observance and severe forms of penance.

'The holy friars will judge when the time is right for you to leave. Meanwhile you might with profit spend the time in meditation upon your vocation. Might you have been mistaken in thinking you had been called?'

'Never. No, certainly not that.'

The chaplain reported back: 'He's not going to go willingly.'

'Hm.'

'I gave the matter a certain amount of thought in the car, my lord.'

'It was, of course, my mistake to put him in a country parish.'

'Your propensity, my lord, for expecting goodness. One forgets how far back the rural population has fallen. They're like some sleeping beauty who closed her eyes in the fifties and missed out entirely on the new moral enlightenment. How did today's church pass them by with its message that no one is guilty? The English villager remains homophobic to a man despite our best efforts. I'd like to send Pendbury a woman priest but we'd best play safe.'

'We'll find somebody quiet for Pendbury,' said his lordship. 'But what of Father Terence? What of his future?'

'When the fuss has died down we might pop him back into an inner-city living. He'd be perfectly at home in one of the great conurbations, Manchester, say, or outer London. Let us think of possible parishes.'

The bishop's chaplain riffled through the handy private index he kept in the back portion of his Filofax. God forbid it should ever fall into hostile hands but in times like this it was a godsend. He'd start at A. A for Apologetic. No. C for Convulsive (shakers and quakers). No. But between them B, blessed B! That stood for Bent – one way or another.

'Outer Croydon!' He waved the Filofax triumphantly and might have cried eureka, had he been given to extravagant utterances. 'Gay for Jesus and with a flourishing donkey sanctuary in the glebe land.'

Neither the bishop nor his chaplain having a complete grasp of detail on the Ashley/Terence story, they thought both men were equally fanatical about animals.

'The donkeys will be a great consolation for the loss of his partner.'

The suicide thrilled the Brook House. In the long shadow cast by Ashley's death the place was very scary, more so than usual. Morbid preoccupations, never far from the boys' thoughts and conversations, hardened into something more substantial and more menacing than the habitual, almost mechanically recited horror stories. The customary after-lights slash 'n' terror tales had always revelled in competition for the more frightening thrill: the gorier meat, the huger explosion of green pus. Now the atmosphere was differently charged. Grisly fictions had become an inadequate plaything. Some thin fluctuating line between the imagined and the nastily possible had been crossed.

It had to do with having their very own corpse. Ashley wasn't just some smudgy black-and-white picture on a newspaper page or screen, he wasn't some freak who'd been built up in some special effects studio. He was little A-A-Ashley who they'd all known intimately because Ashley-watching was a sport. You could compete for laughs in your parody of the walk, the twitch, the hands, the s-st-stutter. They were intimate with the body they were talking about.

Discussion of Ashley's decaying corpse introduced a sustained tension of excitement that, with the days, was growing and rising like a noxious gaseous bubble to the surface of the Brook House's thick violent atmosphere. They never tired of their repeated journeys over the known territory of the little cripple's cadaver.

Boys pontificated on exactly how the twenty-two-and-a-half-ounce brain had sprayed all over the engine of the train in a beige-and-blood splatter like porridge and ketchup. They were precise about the detail of how the bones had crunched and the brown-irised eyeballs had scrunched when they burst. Every inch of flesh was described in detail at the very moment the train hit it, and when there was no novelty left in describing the moment of death, the boys moved on to the thrills of progressive necrosis.

'He'll be smelling now of skunk and rotten cabbage and very old cheese. Fancy a bit of cheese, Danny? Say, pass Danny the cheese.'

In reality Ashley was spending his pre-crem wait decently tidied up, deodorised and sanitised behind the dark satin curtains of Alf N. Sure Funerals. Alf's boys were rather proud of the good job they made; disappointing no one came to view one of their more challenging and, dare they venture to suggest, more successful reconstructions.

'On the third day he goes purple again and hard.'

'No, it's slime-white, greeny.'

Fights broke out over the colour sequence.

Then there was the jellifying to be described, and the bloating. There were lots of good details in the countdown to zero. Five, four, three, two, one, POW! SHAZZAM!! Atomic explosion! The gases blew up, the body bust open, and the guts slammed all over the place.

Several boys were great authorities on mortuaries. Been there dozens of times, spent half their life there to listen to them; and they were all agreed that it was nothing like the tidy chests-of-drawers on the telly with luggage labels on the toes. These mortuary lurkers spoke of charnel houses of great horror, skulls grinning out of disgusting degrees of maggoty liquefying flesh. Among the corpses, they all agreed, you always found a few just living, taken there by mistake but left unclaimed, their weakening cries heard but unheeded by a robotic and sadistic army of indifferent technicians.

There was one boy who had made a study of the after-death specialists. He could tell you about the fly that came at eight days, the worm that fed exclusively on dead brains and which would even now be burrowing up whatever was left of Ashley's nostrils to get at what remained in the shattered skull.

Since the incident of the bat, Danny had been the boys' first sport. Now they were focusing on him more intensely. He was granted no remission day or night. Until this time it had been understood that the system in the establishment depended for its success on leaving the target physically unmarked. Now there was a psychic signal out: violence would soon be okay. The line would soon be crossed. The victim heard the signal loud as his oppressors. Bloodlust hung tangible, a red curtain in the air.

At any time Danny would find himself suddenly surrounded. They'd make a ring round him, chant cheerful playground chants adapted to the violence of the moment.

Danny developed a new means of dealing with them. It wasn't enough now to look to Peter's soft world of ideas for consolation, to put his head under the bedclothes and think about the evaporation of rain or the mechanics of wind, or the magic way history was embedded in the landscape for millions of years and could be read like a book by means of stratigraphy and palaeontology. Once it had been enough to be the only boy in the Brook House who knew these great and important truths. They were his armour against the world. But now this armour was far too weak and abstract to protect him from his newly lawless atmosphere.

The boy assumed a fugue state, staying very still

physically, day and night, trying to shut down his mind, to eradicate himself. He tried to leave nothing living on the surface of his body, as if the outside shell had died.

It was felt appropriate that the choir should sing an anthem at the funeral. A local organist was good enough to step in to rehearse the boys. Raught, who had been keeping an eye on Danny's distintegration, made sure he had a chance to talk to the boy after practice.

'You don't want to believe all they say about mortuaries and all that stuff.'

Danny came a small way out of his autistic detachment. His eyelids moved a little.

'Think about it,' Raught went on, 'they don't just let in tourists, you know. Wouldn't be respectful. Or hygienic. Believe me, I know. Those places are just like Sainsbury's in this day and age. Think of it as a chill cabinet.'

Danny was standing still, and his eyes for once were here, not someplace else. Raught could see he was really getting to him.

''Course if it's like Ashley, not natural causes, the patho has a go at you with the Stanley knife but he puts you together again so you're decent for the funeral. Real artists with the superglue and make-up they are. We won't have to worry when we kiss the body.'

'Kiss the body?'

'Yeah, of course. It's what the choir do. Never been to a funeral before then?'

A negative flop of the no-colour hair.

'He's in the coffin in the church, see, with the lid off while we do the service. He's in the middle up by the stalls we're in. We do our singing and then at the end, when we all go out in couples as usual, following the crucifer (that's me), we bend over one by one and kiss the body on the lips, and it's only when we've all done that, all the choir, that they'll put the lid on.'

'Are you sure? Nobody's said.'

''Course I'm sure. I've been to dozens of buryings. Stonor's probably keeping it quiet so they don't all do a bunk and run away.'

'You've done it? Does it smell?'

'Stinks. That's what all the flowers are for. Ever wondered why they have flowers at a funeral?'

'And what about the colour?' Danny must know the worst. To kiss green jelly flesh.

'Depends.' Raught shrugged.

After that he only needed watch the boy carefully.

Danny's escape plan had nothing sophisticated about it. Escape from the Brook House could be achieved without great difficulty, all the boys knew that. But they also knew that punishment for running away was one week in solitary and extra time, unspecified, added to their incarceration. It was a punishment that served Jimmy Stonor well as a deterrent.

Raught had bet on the milkman, and he was right. The older boy took up position in the upstairs window with the clear view of the drive and the gate. From the window he watched Danny's furtive sporadic little dashes from cover to cover up the drive until the running boy reached the great clump of evergreen subjungle under the big holly nearest the gate. There he burrowed down. If he'd not been watching, Raught would never have known there was anyone in the solid billow of rhododendron.

Raught knew it was time to go and fetch Jimmy Stonor but first he allowed himself a good long moment. The thin boy leant against the wall of the bare attic room and closed his eyes. His cheeks, normally a pale impersonal ivory, flushed warm red. Raught was imagining himself inside Danny's body. Raught's nostrils flared to take in the smell of the damp earth in the twiggy cave. His back could feel the discomfort of trying to stay totally motionless in the crouch that made him as small and as invisible as possible. Raught could feel the proxy cold, the stiffness of the hunched spine. Having recreated for himself the exact physical blend, now he wanted to feel the boy's fear. Against his closed eyelids he measured the right weight of terror against excitement, the precise degree of apprehension. Danny would be saying his prayers now. He'd be bribing God. Inside him he'd be calling for his mother.

The sound of the rattling milk float's arrival snapped Raught's eyes open. It was starting up the long drive on the way to make its delivery. This was the time to get old Stonor to join him at the window.

Side by side they watched the silent show, the slow vehicle bumping its way back from its delivery and stopping at the gate for the whitecapped dairyman to show his plastic card up to the camera, and behind him the half-crouch of the small terrified figure.

Jimmy nudged Raught and whispered, as though they could be overheard by the faraway pantomime, 'He's climbing on now, look.'

The guardian pressed his button. He had an electronic override on the gate.

The responsibility for the funeral arrangements fell by default on Peter Skeffington. There was no one else to do it. Besides, he wanted to do something for Ashley. Peter was much affected by the sad small thing that had been Ashley's life. He found himself, to his own great surprise, exhibiting all the exhausting symptoms of bereavement that he remembered from deaths much closer to himself.

No one else would touch the funeral with a bargepole. They really hated Ashley now he was dead. The sidesmen were most awfully sorry but they'd be too busy to do the hymn books. The wardens simply couldn't manage to get out of the office . . . any other day . . . Only Peter's longstanding reputation as village benefactor stood between the village and a public protest against any sort of church service at all.

Peter decided that after the funeral he would construct a goad for the village, a permanent reminder. He turned over in his mind which part of the village green was prominent enough to be planted as a Gethsemane garden, with a little plaque 'In memory of'. He'd fill it with hyssop and bitter herbs, a vine for the vinegar on the sponge, and worm-wood. And he'd find out if gall was a plant or just a state of mind. Meanwhile he'd go it alone, making sure that Ashley had a fine funeral.

'Have you made a list?' Lucy asked him. Invariably every occasion in Lucy's life started with a list: shopping, tele-phoning, partying, and now burying.

'Move over,' she told him and brought a second chair to join him at his desk. 'Make me some room.

'What have you done about flowers?' she asked him.

'Nothing. I always thought flowers just did themselves. But of course you're right.'

'I'll organise that if you like.'

'I don't expect you to do anything, Lu.'

'The village is very anti-flower. Anti the whole service. You're not making any friends over this.'

'It wasn't my first purpose.'

'They don't want his bones to rest anywhere near their blameless forefathers in the churchyard.'

'Quite right. The dead are so vulnerable. You can't be too careful what they might catch. Christ! I find it difficult to love this village at times.'

'Well, it's a lot for them to cope with. Both queer and a suicide. Enough in itself but what with the hounds, and being the *vicar*'s boyfriend.'

'And what do you think, Luce?'

'Me? I never thought about Ashley much when he was here and now I rather regret it. I wish I'd bothered to know him. Not for the usual morbid "now he's gone" reasons, but he must have been more interesting than I realised. To go out in such style. Wrapping a fur round himself. That was

191

theatre, that was choreographed. Far more telling than some gauche note. Do you know, suicides often sign their notes with their full name and then cross out the name. Isn't that creepy? I heard a programme on Radio Four.' Lucy sat forward again to the desk and picked up her pen. The list wasn't nearly long enough yet.

'"All Things Bright and Beautiful".' she nodded. 'Good. Can you think of any other animal hymns? Let's print a few hundred really smart service sheets. We'll make it An Event. Do you know, I've always longed for one of those Victorian plumed hearses. Four jet-black stallions really on their mettle. Remember it if I predecease you, darling, won't you? Do you think you could manage to nobble the bish for Ashley?'

She'd made him smile. The first time for days. 'Aren't you getting a bit state funeralish? I get the feeling I hear the trundle of gun carriages.'

'Why not? the press'll be swarming. Give 'em an eyeful. We might as well be splendid as drab. May I have the run of the orchids?'

'Royaler and royaler.'

'Why not? I'll whip in Honor. It's a full hat and pearls job as far as I'm concerned.'

'Darling, you're wonderful.'

Their eyes met. Ages since an impulse to love before bedtime had hit them simultaneously; he'd thought it never would again. He started to get up from his chair beside her at the desk but then she dropped her eyes, deliberately transferring her attention back to the papers under her hand. She was remembering her subterfuges at this very desk. Her stupid politicking with the guardian; she knew at the time it had been foolish, overkill. There were quieter ways to deal with such things. She'd known all along of course that it wasn't, at heart, only about the boy but about getting back at Peter for an accumulation unresolved over the years.

She poised her pen. 'And we'll process out to the Maccabees?'

As soon as Honor was told the anthem she had great pleasure in spreading it abroad, flinging in the grandly casual aside that it had, of course, been sung with great effect at the late King's funeral.

This musical titbit from the high table was the latest to be devoured by the insatiably curious village, which was watching with fascination.

Eyes followed Lucy to the printers. Ears heard that twenty of the fattest beeswax candles had been sent down from Harrods. Righteous dignity was engorged. Soon it choked on the bootful of white and purple orchids that took Lucy Skeffington three journeys to carry into the church from her parked car.

It would have been more apt to go for a quiet service at a difficult time of day, considering. Surely there was to be no question of hallowed ground?

Mary Eggar was a loud as anyone in the village against all this pomp and circumcision. She had at last seized the point that her Tom was now permanently catastrophic and that he would never, ever, come back from his living trance to boss her. A new life was beginning. Seizing the moment, she found her voice. Moral leadership was not going to slip out of Eggar family hands, not for all the trees in China. As for the funeral, she'd not go, not over her dead body. Despite this unambiguous declaration she was seen to visit Country Casuals where her investment in a black ensemble was noted. Later the same day she was observed to make a journey to the Oxfam shop where she bountifully bestowed on them a lifetime's supply of flowered pinnies.

During the past week Peter had realised just how much, in practical terms, Ashley used to do about the parish. He was struck that they'd never paid him anything. If any family showed up he'd see what could be done about a pension.

Peter blessed Lucy's customary efficiency in the domestic department. She was a good wife. She'd been marvellous this week over the funeral business, too: funny and compassionate at once. He wished – but there was no use wishing.

She produced delicious sole and crème brûlée for the pre-funeral lunch. Honor approved: meatless but not altogether penitential. Some pleasures could only be enjoyed here on earth. Heaven would be too late, Honor suspected, for crème brûlée.

The church looked solemn, appropriate, stone shoulders hunched against a sombre sky. Ashley arrived, not in the horse-drawn contrivance of Lucy's desire, but in a normal hearse. The coffin was covered with more of Lucy's orchids. Peter squeezed his wife's hand. He was surprised to find his mother's black kid glove nudging on his other side. The three of them walked hand in hand together past the dreadful press of cameramen crouching round the coffin and exploding their flashguns. Honor's fierce old face puckered as she fought back the tears; Peter was moved and astonished. It was not Honor's way to cry at funerals.

He had beautiful eyes, the old lady was thinking, and he was intelligent and courteous and kind, and we were friends and I did badly by him. I was not always kind about him in conversation with other people. Honor had long planned to be buried in her wedding dress with the train cut off. Lucy had been told and was under instruction to organise it when the time came. It had seemed important to Honor, but now it only seemed important to be buried among friends who cared and not among these flesh-devouring carrion here for the notoriety. None of them had loved Ashley or even liked him. Many had never met him. A lot of them had hated and despised him and yet a lot of people were sobbing and making a great deal of show into handkerchiefs. Mass hysteria, thought the old woman, sticking up the chin of a tougher breed and stopping up her tears. *Noblesse oblige*, even if it was the saddest funeral she had ever attended.

Lucy, who had been the least close to Ashley in life, suffered less from remorse, general or personal. The general principle of gays in the vicarage, such an abomination for Peter and Honor, neither offended Lucy nor delighted her. It left her neutral. On the personal front she felt neutral too. Ashley the man had been to lunch a couple of times. She'd been polite; there was no reason to reproach herself. Unless she wanted to delve into that imprecise concept: the sin of omission, and that was as long as a piece of string. Be bothered by the sin of omission and you would never, she opined, be able to sleep at night again. But Lucy's armour was, against her inclinations, pierced to the heart by the tragedy itself, the story. It seemed dreadful that a harmless little fellow should kill himself for the sake of a page of newsprint, whether true or untrue. She was also affected by Peter. For some reason she couldn't fathom, this death had incised some strong emotion she couldn't name deeply on Peter's soul.

Like Honor she was repelled by the keening and mewling of the *hoi polloi* in church. Her technique for staving off any incipient liptrembling weakness was to take pleasure in the beautiful, suitable picture she had made with her fat beeswax candles marching up the choir stalls. She had made the inside of the church match the outside: solemn and appropriate. She wondered why orchids were not used more at funerals? They were spot-on with their mourning colours and their winged implications of angels.

People were standing at the back. A favourable impression was made on the visiting vicar on this, his first visit. Indeed he was finding it the very model of an old-fashioned country parish. Bless me, you could almost say the twentieth century had passed Pendbury by. The gentry in the front pew, the humbler folk – so many of them! –

195

ranked behind. Redolent of Hardy, really. Thank heaven Pendbury had progressed beyond those rustic violin bands in the gallery; they must have been a sore trial. This organist was really very good, for the country – of course he'd had better in his last London parish. A goodly choir, and young; they'd not drop off their perches yet awhile.

They processed out to the churchyard.

Finding time to look about him during the committal, the visiting vicar checked out the fabric of the church and registered it as satisfactory as the human element.

'God . . .' cue to swivel his eyes Godward: roof in very good repair, gutters unclogged, fishscale tiles all present and correct, '. . . will show us the path of life.' Path between graves well drained. Evenly dressed with gravel. Smartly cut grass edges razor-sharp, wouldn't disgrace a royal park.

'In his presence is the fullness of joy . . .' Joy indeed. A wealthy, stable parish, to run to year-round upkeep. Beyond his black toecaps was a grave to rejoice in. The neat mathematical excavation brought to mind diagrams in elementary geography from the faraway days of his prep school: topsoil crayonned brown and enlivened with squiggly pink worms, subsoil of Wealden clay hatched orange. Beside the open grave greensprouting turves were neatly stacked for the replacement. Sensibly the grave had been covered with a tarpaulin until the very last minute, providing protection from frost and passing rain. Happy the parish in possession of such good old-fashioned sextonship!

He was sick of inner-city burials. Came a moment when you were too old to trawl the local building sites to bribe a navvy to bodge a hole so the coffin should somehow be jammed between service pipes and builders' rubble.

'And at His right hand . . .' The view to his right hand was absolutely glorious. It might have been taken off a picture calendar: the quiet village nestling sweet under gold-rimmed opaline clouds. 'There is pleasure for ever more.'

The bishop had told him the living was vacant. To be next vicar of Pendbury. To subside gently into this small uneventful place. To be a stranger to stress and crisis, with nothing more important to think about than jams and jellies among these dear simple folk. So long as you were careful crossing the busy road. And the railway line. Oh dear me yes, you must be careful crossing the railway line! He sprinkled the symbolic handful. Even the earth here was wholesome and uncomplicated: brown and crumbly and fragrant as pipe tobacco.

'Amen.'

The vicar signalled the dispersal and made himself aggressively agreeable to everybody he could see. Without fear or favour he went about pumping every hand.

Peter, oblivious to the clerical hand stretched out to him, pushed through the crowd much quicker than was decent. He had been worried throughout the service because Danny was not there. Nor was the guardian. The party from the Brook House seemed to be led by the boy Raught, who performed with his usual matchless beauty and what Peter thought of as sinister grace.

'Where's Danny? And why's the guardian not leading the choir today?'

'There's a governors' meeting up at the Brook House,' Raught told him. 'Mr Stonor had to stay up for that.'

'And Danny?'

Raught had never smirked in his life. He'd rather twist his own finger round till it hung useless. 'I believe Danny's ill,' Raught said, but the smirk leaked out. And then he added (never be caught in a lie), 'Or in detention.'

'I'm going to the Brook House,' Peter told his wife. 'Mother will give you a lift.'

'No.' Lucy's responsibility nagged. 'If it's about Danny, I'll come with you. You might need me.'

Peter was puzzled but too troubled about the boy to wonder. Raught watched their hurrying a moment before turning his attention to the doddery old woman they'd left alone.

Honor was cross with herself. Stick out her chin and glare as hard as she could, still she felt vulnerable, mortal and tentative, three things she was not used to feeling. For a forceful old lady, this was a debilitating and ageing mood to be in. She had missed the mink when it had been stolen but she'd never got around to reporting it. Partly because she'd talked the article up so very far from the truth, partly because she knew she was becoming awfully forgetful. Sometimes she put things in a different place, and often she'd come down in the morning to find she'd left the door unlocked all night. Her son nagged her constantly over security, and she didn't like to give him such very obvious proof. He'd want to put in a minder and she couldn't bear to have someone live with her.

Now the wrap had turned up in this discreditable suicide. She'd no doubt at all it was hers. Odd of the little man to steal it. Those animal people were passionate about fur, she knew, but she knew him better than that and she really couldn't see him doing anything quite so pointless. She would say nothing. It would be too tiresome to be connected: the police, the papers.

All this was what led to the clouded bewilderment on the dowager's normally decisive face. For once she looked like a pathetic old lady. Head down, she tottered along the gravelled path, swept along in the darkly dressed column of homegoing mourners, yet separated from them by the space the crowd grant one who is not totally of them in years, wealth or health. Had she now, at this moment, lifted her careful gaze from the path and looked straight up in front of her, the quavery blue uncertain eyes, swimming on their teary rim, would have locked straight into Raught's speculative assessment.

'Here,' he said to one of his fellow choristers, 'take this,' and lobbed the cross at him.

He hurried up to Honor. 'May I help you, madam? The path's a bit slippery here.'

'Thank you.' She allowed her elbow to be taken. Surprising to find good manners; she'd never thought the Brook House ran to Eton conduct.

'I come up to Mr Skeffington's house once a week,' he said. 'If you like I could run in and wash the car for you.' He ran an elegant thin white finger down the doorframe and showed it to her, grimy.

'I don't know.' She looked doubtful from behind her steering wheel.

'I wouldn't want paying. It's not allowed while I'm still up there.' His eyes slid towards the general direction of his asylum.

'Well, why not then?'

'I get bored, see, there's not enough for me to do and I like to keep busy. Maybe I could chop your firewood, dig the garden. Little jobs like that. If you ever needed something doing?'

He was not leaning against the car but standing respectfully away without touching it.

She smiled up at him, summoning up an echo of that lively and flirtatious smile she'd given the sex all her life.

'I could start this week if you wanted, madam.'

'You must have been sent from heaven. I shall call you God's gift.' She laughed and waved, and drove home feeling much younger. 'Goodbye, God's gift!'

Raught stood still and lifted a hand somewhere approximate to a salute at the retreating car. He'd be odd-job boy at first; and then, a little later, when she had become frightened by odd noises at night, things coming, going, moving, she'd want him there more. He'd be watchman to protect her from the terrors of the dark. Raught had no doubt he could wedge himself firmly into the structure of the wealthy Skeffington household in a very little time. Then he'd have as long as he wanted to delve deeper into the equation of need measured against dependence and suffering.

Up at the Brook House the solemn juggernaut that was the governors' meeting was rolling slowly and wordily through the preordained agenda. Jimmy Stonor was sitting facing the might potentates. The guardian was rubbing his hands as one who has made a valuable acquisition. It was a pleasure to have nothing but a catalogue of triumphs to recite: the choir, the organic vegetables, the proposed scholarship, first of its kind. The past months had been a time of movement, expansion, unqualified success. He could afford to spread his words, coil and twist and wind them into a good thick hempen rope such as would moor him to the job for many years to come.

It was on this static tableau of placid mutual congratulation that Peter opened the door and demanded to see Danny. The guardian's eyes flinched at the name. He'd quite forgotten the boy, who would just now have completed his first twenty-four hours in solitary.

How had Peter found out? All the building was empty but for the governing body down here and Danny in the dark room upstairs. Might he yet recoup and reform things by bluff? First he would bluster a bit.

'This is a most irregular interruption, nothing like it has ever . . .' but Peter cut him off with a most reasonable appeal to the board.

Here was an obviously respectable person known to the board by name and reputation. Was he not indeed the man offering a valuable scholarship? Here he was appealing to them in the most conciliatory language. The governors, those not entirely in their dotage, were sufficiently perspicacious to discern that it was not usual for an obviously respectable sane outsider to invade a board meeting and engage the guardian in war to the knife over the health and whereabouts of a little boy in his care.

Scenting excitement, trouble and drama they elected to join Peter, Lucy, and the reluctant guardian up the monumental staircase of imitation marble.

At the second bend in the staircase, even sham marble petered out. Dilapidations got worse the higher they rose through the giddy heights originally allotted to the lower orders: dusty decayed upper landings, pitchpine planks and a smell of mouse. With the increasingly shabby surroundings the party was becoming apprehensive. There was a sniff of shame in the air. They were under the eaves now, and Jimmy seemed to have some difficulty in remembering exactly which room the sick bay was. Hard pressed, he eventually reached the limits of invention, the place where he could prevaricate no further.

The governors were now bitterly regretting their first bold decision to get to the bottom of things. They were shuffling and embarrassed, trailing reluctantly behind Lucy and Peter, whose suspicion and anger was growing with every new sign of Jimmy Stonor's dissembling. The crowd stopped at a small door leading to what must, long ago, have been the room of the humblest in the hierarchy of domestics. Beside the door was an old-fashioned domed brass lightswitch, brown under years of dim tarnish. Jimmy snapped down the nippled switch and, with the look of a hopeless man, turned the key to unlock the door.

Blind as a mole emerging from the darkness, Danny had flung his forearm up against his blinking eyes. The other hand went down quickly in modesty. His thin body's flesh was uniformly pallid with an almost bluish tinge except where he was dirty. There was a window in the attic room but it was solidly boarded up with nailed planks. There was no tap or basin, no heating in the room, no light other than the central bulb controlled from the passage outside. In the corner was a chamber pot.

All of the men tried to step backwards at once, they shambled and muddled against each other in the narrow doorway, their eyes sliding anywhere but in the direction of the boy. Only Lucy stepped forward with authority. Forgetting for once to be graceful, she ran across the room to him, taking off her black funeral coat as she ran. The naked boy didn't move; he stood quite still and docile while she wrapped him in the coat and, unconscious of his weight, swung him up into her arms.

'I'll take him home,' she said as she glared across the room at the ashamed men.

It was some hours before Peter could come back home. There were formalities. The police took time.

'She's asleep,' Mrs Occhi told him.

He went quietly up the stairs. He sat down on his side of the bed and looked down at Lucy on the pillow. Her face was soft in sleep. The thin skin under her eyes was smudged with black. She must have gone to bed without cleaning off her make-up. This touched him, indicating as it did a deep disruption of Lucy's world. He reached out to trace her face.

'Have you sorted it out?' she asked him in a quiet voice.

He took the hand that lay outside the covers. 'I think so. You look tired.'

'I can remember less exhausting days.'

The dreaminess went out of her voice, as she came further out of her sleep. She sat up on one elbow, her face turned towards him and he saw the features taking up the pattern of composure with which she faced the world. Some of the aggression that had been in her when she swept Danny so magnificently away returned to her voice.

'He'll have to stay here. I'll look after him; Mrs Occhi can help. We'll need a nanny. I've planned it all. We'll make it just like the old days with the boys.'

Oh God. Not a third Polypheman.

'No, Luce, no. He won't need a nanny,' he said.

'But I can't look after him all by myself. What when you

go off? You'll be leaving on your journey soon, the Silk Route.'

'If Danny's staying here we'll do this thing together, me and you. The Silk Route's been there a thousand years, it'll wait for us. Maybe one day I'll take him with me. One day. It's the sort of thing he's interested in.'

'Don't make me feel worse. Why didn't you tell me?' She was crying. 'Why did you make me seem so hard?'

He folded his arms round her shoulders.

'They hadn't even given him any loo paper,' she whispered.

'Hush.'

She lay back on the pillow, and closed her eyes, controlling her tears. 'Do you remember when you were a child, Peter? How impossible it was to tell about the really terrible things because you didn't know the rules? You had no way of knowing what really meant any thing at all to an adult.'

'I never knew unhappiness even touched your childhood, Lucy.'

'Oh, I don't mean unhappiness. I don't mean terrible things like we saw today. I just mean being shut out from reality and fobbed off with Winnie-the-Pooh instead. Being kept in a special place where I had to be sunny and pretty and carefree all the time or I was a disappointment and not doing it right. And all the time it was like living on the brink of some awful abyss. As if the adult world dealt with reality and reality was horrible and pressing at the doors and windows, like a monster waiting to get me when I'd stopped being a child but till then I was to pretend I couldn't glimpse it. I was allowed to weep buckets over *Heidi* and *Black Beauty* and the dogs but there wasn't allowed to be any weeping when Mummy got cancer, and if I hadn't overheard it on the telephone I'd never have been told about it at all. Just life as normal and an even stronger feeling about the brink and the abyss. That's what

I meant about childhood being terrible. That's why I tried to make things different for the boys. I'm not sure I succeeded, though. It doesn't seem to have gone as right as it should.'

'Oh, Lucy.'

He looked down at the hand which he had not let go. The rings he had given her held the light. They were the only ones she wore.

'It may be difficult. Have you thought? It may be a long time before he's ready to be happy. But we'll try doing it together this time, see if we can make a better fist of it?'

'I put him in your dressing room, so he's close for night fears.'

'You won't have to mind the sight of me taking off my socks then.'

Peter was starting to undress. In the formality of their marriage she had for years only seen him disappear behind one door dressed in day clothes and emerge from it, abracadabra, fully dressed for the night. He was self-conscious in front of her; it wasn't easy to get out of your things with grace once you started thinking about it.

She moved softly in the bed, releasing a waft of her own particular mixture of perfumes.

They would always make love in the dark. For years it had been a lonely, cancerous business. Tonight their bedroom was lit. It looked different. A triangular slice of light pointed in from the door which she had left open to reassure the boy. Familiar furniture became unfamiliar sketched in shades of amber and mauve. The bedclothes mounded softly round her body, rising and falling into mysterious plum-coloured hollows.

By the light shining into the room, Peter wondered at her eyes. Half-undressed, entirely unconscious of what he was doing, he sat down on the bed to look at her eyes: prismatic, mobile, transparent as the winter sea. He could never melt and pass through that glasslike lens. He must rest content at the surface.

He'd no idea how much time passed before he became aware of his half-dressed state, his body hair, his socks, all the details that might extinguish the anticipation of desire. He got into bed, preserving the polite space between them, and lay with his eyes open. The shadows shifted; he felt her tentative hand stroking his hair and moving to trace the lines of his face with fingers that communicated a touching impression of shyness. He turned towards her to reciprocate the gentle generous gesture, ran his fingers through her hair, freeing and spreading the golden veil, over her shoulders, her breasts, and found himself overtaken by a kind of desperate irritation. His whole body was quivering. Regardless of manners, politeness or delicacy, he gave in to the frenzies that came of their own accord, plunging desperately to get through the barriers that separated them, past the surfaces, beyond the envelope of each other's flesh. They wrestled with the different moods that swept them. Sometimes it felt more like fighting than loving: pushing and clawing and chasing and subduing. There was sadness, too, a terrible sadness which came with the knowing that always the moment came of finishing, unjoining, becoming two again.

Eventually they rolled back from each other exhausted, sweaty. They lay on their sides, supporting their weight on their elbows, looking at each other.

She threw back her head and he thought she was going to start to talk but she laughed instead, drew her finger down his cock grown small again, looked up at him flirtatiously, rolled forward heavy and sensuous against him and they tumbled into a different loving: humorous, candid, lecherous, uncomplicated, the sort of loving that led her straight to sleep.

He heard her breath come heavy and sweet and contented, he saw the dewpearl sweat glint in her hair. He wanted to stay awake all night watching her, watching over her. Lucy was his again. He lay back to keep watch. He was content, smiling, warm with the happy testosterone glow. He felt a brotherhood with rutting stags barking on heather moors and heavy bollock-swinging bulls in fields. If he dropped his eyes and looked down his body it was quite possible he'd find he'd grown a fleece covering the whole of it like a satyr . . . Before he had time to look he too was asleep, curled up like a comma against Lucy's blissful body.

CHAPTER FOURTEEN

Ten months later an invitation card appeared at the foot of the glistening cachepot in the drawing room. The stiff rectangle was deckle-edged, mightily gilded and encrusted; altogether worthy in every respect of the pot it was propped against. September was the month for the most exotic plant in Lucy's annual march of the flowers: a Mexican datura whose huge golden trumpets hung heavy, scenting half the house with a narcotic perfume redolent of harems, houris and hubble-bubble oblivion. Warmer climes wafted on the Sussex air, conjuring exotic possibilities in Peter's mind. Lucy watched, her face taking on the etchings of strain as his fingers traced the petals and his eyes lit with the spontaneous lyricism she knew of old. She knew herself excluded from the path his thoughts were taking and accepted with a doll-like fatalism that there was nothing she could do to bring him back; he must come back of his own accord or not at all.

Peter's thoughts were in Mexico with the man who'd collected the plant and brought it back to Europe: Humboldt – he of the famous current. Peter's face had taken on the look of a sleepwalker as his mind became occupied and overtaken by the paunchy little German adventurer of extraordinary courage and tenacity. Humboldt couldn't swim yet he explored miles and miles of crocodile-infested Orinoco by canoe, making some painful but instructive experiments with electric eels on the way. Physically unimpressive, yet he'd a mania for climbing active volcanoes and managed in 1801 to reach the greatest height ever attained by man at the time. Poor Humboldt, adventure simply would not leave him alone. Peter smiled, remembering how the stout explorer had stopped for the harmless purpose of observing an eclipse of the moon and promptly been set upon by a band of negro slaves who thought he'd caused the moon to vanish and were determined to wreak revenge. And here, here in the drawing room of Keythorpe Grange, was the daughter-plant whose parent had so enraptured Humboldt that he'd 'run round like a fool afraid he should lose his senses if this state of ecstasy were to continue . . .'

Peter could see it all vividly. The man warranted a whole box file subsection to himself . . . Peter shook his head. He wasn't going to think about these things any more. No longer were history's ghosts to be allowed to run in his mind like a continuous alternative. He knew the damaging consequences of trying to live in isolation and spiritual solitude. Things were only going to work if he put away the thoughts and preoccupations of yesterday, kept his plant connections under control and prevented them from impinging. It was not as though his invisible world would have to be excluded altogether; it would be allowed to take its proper place. He would work at it in the time allotted at his desk, and when he was not at his desk he would give the here and now its proper due, making sure to remain always most conscious of the present and visible, which, at this moment, was pressingly encapsulated in Honor's invitation card.

He studied it closely, recentring his mind. The stiff pasteboard was yellowing. It must have been knocking around in her desk for decades. Surely even Smythson's didn't still produce such fabulous thick toreutics these days?

Honor, the card informed, would be *At Home* this after-noon at three o'clock. The bottom right-hand corner that usually described the expected form of dress for the occa-sion housed a scrawl of blue-black ink: *Full tenue* and then on an afterthought she'd crammed more words into a space too small: *& gumboots.*

'Outdoors then?' he cocked an eyebrow.

'Presumably.'

Peter and Lucy caught a flash of flowered pinny whisk-ing out through the front door: Martha the messenger retreating. They hailed her but she pretended not to hear for she was operating under strict instruction. Honor wanted it to be as though the card had arrived by means of some entirely ephemeral agency. She had told Martha to be as silent and invisible as Ariel, a puzzling instruction con-sidering Ariel was a washing powder.

Full tenue. Peter contemplated his cupboard. He must confess to feeling sartorially stumped.

'Hoist black tie?' he asked Lucy.

'And tuck the trou inside the wellies? Bizarre.'

He ended up in predictable tidy tweed but then decided he looked dull and unadventurous. This was hardly full tenue. Nipping out he found a full-blown scarlet rose which he cut and tucked into his buttonhole. ¡*Viva fiesta!*

Lucy had a new hacking jacket that she'd been dying to wear. Danny asked if he might wear Peter's old Barbour jacket. The Barbour had been a garment of great mystical significance for the boy ever since Peter had placed it round his shoulders on one of their first walks together. The wind had been cold that day, and Peter anxious the boy should keep warm. The boy had plunged his icy hands into its pockets and discovered the curious hoard Peter kept piling into them. For years the pockets had served him most usefully as a kind of mobile desk, bulging with all the outward and visible scraps of Peter's inward preoc-cupations. There were notes written to himself on odd pieces of paper as he went about his jobs and journeys, abrupt vegetable connections on pink file cards, a begadgeted penknife useful in all sorts of ways, a handful of acorns gathered from the oldest extant strain in England in the medieval forest at Hatfield; he'd been planning to plant them out for months, soon they'd be starting to sprout. Another pocket held the warm soft pile of Zoroaster's first feather moult that Peter had picked up and was intending to give to Lucy but always forgetting. The garment had come to play an important part between the man and the boy, the sort of part a teddy bear might play in a more straightforward relationship between father and child – that is to say a shared object of affection and a means of communication.

Peter was very happy that Danny should wear his coat. In the very early days, before their relationship had developed depths and complexities, he had tried to give it to the boy, but there persisted in Danny the old resistance to gifts of any kind. Instead they wore the jacket turn and turn about, a kind of interchangeable skin. It was an important day when Danny started to contribute to the pockets. Peter had been very happy to find the boy's first small treasures in among his own: conkers, snailshells, a flint. It was sometime later that the first note was discovered jumbled in among Peter's oddments. 'When will I have to go?' it said.

Months later, as the child was gaining confidence, a second note asked: 'What do I call your mother?' and later still, 'Please no more rhubarb.' The Barbour had become an excellent channel of communication for the questions and emotions Danny found difficult.

Peter, Lucy and Danny had no idea what to expect when they knocked on Honor's door punctually at three. It was a warm afternoon with the sun still well up in the sky. Gumboots seemed pessimistic.

Honor herself was in spanking *tenue*, though rather surprising to look at, being more theatrically got up than was her custom. Her dress had a touch of the lady explorer about the edges: a capacious khaki cloak covered the customary London-cut tweeds and was fastened in place by the mourning brooch of the late King Alfonso's plaited moustache hairs, an object that had always held great fascination for Peter as a child. She was shod not in wellingtons but in stylish pointy-toed fur-topped boots that hadn't seen daylight since they'd done duty for Aladdin in the village hall. Her dashing hat was ornamented with the stick pin presented to her by Queen Maud of Norway. From her ears swung seed pearl earrings, a gift from Princess Helen of Romania, according to legend.

'Mother, you look magnificent.'

'Don't you ever wash your boots?' She glowered at her son, after which she forgot to be fierce for she was mightily cockered up by the surprise she'd prepared.

'We will proceed overland,' she said grandly, as though there were an alternative.

Instructing the others to pick up the many baskets, flasks and bundles she'd stacked in the hall, she watched with satisfaction as they gradually became festooned and hung about, rattling with odd ornaments: a kettle here, a sandwich packet there, like tinkers at a fair while her own hands remained free, one to grasp her son's arm and one for her trusty swan-necked stick. A prudent move: Aladdin's boots had slippy leather soles.

Lucy and Danny followed on, listening to the conversation in front of them and smiling at each other or widening their eyes at strategic moments in the conversation.

Beyond the lawns and garden Honor led them up the incline of the new cedar avenue. From the top of the little hill they could see across to the village green where ducks, geese, cows, sheep, the car boot sale and even the Saturday bus appeared Lilliputian in scale, and very busy. In the fields the crops looked beautifully symmetrical. Fat white clouds bobbed in a blue sky over the now-empty Brook

House whose elaborate chimneys stuck up like a question mark through the dark fir trees.

Honor couldn't see why they'd had to close it down altogether. No good overdoing it. An official reprimand would have done. And of course the bogus old admiral fellow had to be given the sack; he was a little on the queer side. But the rest could surely have stayed the same: Sundays were a great deal duller these days. The Brook House choir was a loss; not to mention that charming boy with the beautiful eyes who had offered to do odd jobs. He reminded her of a leprechaun, and now he'd be doing them for somebody else wherever they'd all gone to. Vexing. Rumour was the Brook House was going to be turned into a health hydro. Well, that was about a hundred years too late as far as Honor was concerned. The traffic in the village would be appalling. Pop stars' wives in BMWs whizzing about the lanes far too fast in gym clothes. It didn't bear thinking about. Maybe Peter could be pressed into action.

'Step out,' she chivvied her son, 'we're not there yet.'

The rest of the party would have been quite happy to unpack their weird appendages and stay here having tea on the knoll with its magnificent view, but this was not Honor's plan. She allowed them only the shortest of pauses before urging them on. Down a mossy path freckled with lichens they clattered unwieldily, down into an overgrown Victorian dell originally planned as a wilderness heavily influenced by the fashion for gothic gloom. A hundred years had turned the planned wilderness into a real one, transformed it into a kind of knitted jungle of shrubs festooned with shaggy garlands of clematis, purple-leaved vine and scarlet-berried nightshade. Wild fruits and honeysuckles draped against the dark canopy of trailing woodland evergreens. A path of sorts had been kept open, winding and consciously picturesque. Rocks were mounded up in mossy outcrops. Clusters of cypress trees pointed admonishing fingers to the skies. A mourning willow wept as it hung over, almost extinguishing a bench that sat beside a foetid, green-glazed pool guaranteed to infect the sitter with one of those damp, fatal old-fashioned diseases: TB perhaps, or galloping consumption.

Honor pressed on. Peter and Lucy realised where they were going. Peter glanced backwards with a slight frown of concern. He'd purposely avoided this place on his daily walks with Danny. The boy wasn't ready. Seeing his frown, Lucy rearranged her burdens to free an arm which she put around the boy's shoulders.

'Come.' Honor was full of confidence. She summoned Lucy and the boy to join the front rank. Too late for Peter to cancel his mother's surprise. His face was looking strained as they rounded the sudden bend in the path that would reveal the drama, the animal graveyard, strange period piece, crumbling landscape of death and of memory.

Danny's eyes and mouth made three Os of delight. His mind had not been trained to be depressed by the intellectual theatre of death, so he saw only exotica in the small valley furnished with all the requisites of melancholy. There was fascination in the abandoned stones, funerary urns, chaste veiled marble maidens, skulls designed to hold floral tributes, and in the setting: gloomiest shades contrived to pleasing wretchedness and expressly designed to inspire thoroughgoing morbid meditation on mortality.

It was here two years ago that Honor had met Ashley Crowther for the very first time, quite unexpectedly. As they threaded their slow way through the *memento mori*, Honor with her stick, Ashley with his limp, she had not at first connected the waxen-skinned stranger with the billowing back view she saw at the organ in church every Sunday. Their talk had the candour that perhaps only a chance meeting with a stranger can release. Maybe the limbo landscape also had some influence. However it was, there had been none of that formal aloofness of normal intercourse. They'd touched on death and memory, on

213

expectations and disappointments, and the passing of everything. A strong bond of understanding had been formed between the bright-eyed Christian and the proud fierce independent old *femme du monde*. She recalled his voice, husky as a shadow, his tenderness and terror before God; he had a faith to envy, speaking of this God with compassion and devoted admiration that she only hoped for his sake his God returned. A child, she'd thought him, to keep his heart so open and defenceless; his absence of self-worth an abyss into which others about him might drop their indifference soundless and without trace. She remembered his vulnerability to this day, with pain, his eventual fate lending an aura of horror to what had only seemed naïve until taken in that awful context. Who would have thought that he, so young, would die first of the two of them, and in the end of his own overflowing compassion?

Honor sighed. She paused a moment, leaning on her stick, the shadows filling her head.

'Are you all right, Mother?'

She straightened her back and clapped her hands, calling out to draw Peter and Lucy's attention to a serviceable trestle table that she had caused the invisible Martha to place here earlier in the day. 'Put the tea things here,' she cried imperiously.

The three of them took far too long according to the old lady's notions. She fidgeted and fussed impatiently. Lucy and the boy took forever setting the table. Peter was being impossibly clumsy and slow as he fought the good fight with the unfolding chairs, remorseless pinchers of fingers. At last the table was set with what could only be described as a fine commodious tea. Splendid as it was, the tea was hardly the main event. Honor was dying for them to notice the real point of this safari to the outer reaches. At last she could stand the wait no longer.

'Look.' She pointed with her swan-necked cane down the poetical path to where a yew thicket was tangled about with a thick grapevine and half-smothered in ivy. Through the funerary greens poked the top of a new white obelisk.

Danny was first down to read the incised inscription. 'Ashley,' it read, 'The Animals' Friend.'

No man had been commemorated here before. Now that she was showing it to her family it struck Honor for the first time that Peter might think it inappropriate.

'I thought we should do something,' she said firmly. 'I enquired about the ashes, you see. Nobody had claimed them. Have you ever heard anything so ghastly? Imagine languishing on some funeral director's shelf. D'you know, apparently they have hundreds unclaimed? I've never heard anything so pathetic in all my life. If you leave me on a shelf, Peter, I'll come back to haunt you most unpleasantly, I promise. I had them delivered and put them in a cupboard and they hung around: too reproachful. So then I thought of here.'

Lucy and Danny had immediately gone further and now they were scrambling about the rocks and bushes hand in hand, reading the inscriptions and sentimental verses about faithful cows and heroic Pekinese. The best ones they shouted back cheerfully to Peter, who'd gone back with Honor to sit at the table.

This new regime suits my son well, thought the old lady, who in her day had been so keen on bloodlines she would never have tolerated a pedigree-less mongrel child like Danny as houseguest for a day, let alone an unspecified stretch of years.

'I always thought your Gethsemane garden was a rotten idea,' she told Peter, 'revoltingly morbid.'

'So did I,' he smiled. 'That's why I never got round to it.'

Some time later the four of them sat becalmed round Martha's trestle table, lulled into inactivity by boiled egg and crumpet, anchovy toast and tiny biscuits. Peter and Lucy were in quiet mood. Danny had been slowed to a stop by his vast intake of tea. Only Honor, basking in the surprise she had so successfully manufactured, was pink-cheeked, lively-eyed and restless with further thoughts of the future that stretched so much shorter for her than for the others and was, consequently, so much more urgent.

'I have been thinking,' she said relentlessly. 'If you really are planning to journey the Silk Route like you said and it's not all just empty talk, then we should go next summer during Danny's school holiday. *Anno domini, anno domini*, I haven't a year to waste. I have been reading up that part of the world but my books are rather out of date. I cannot believe we will need so much expensive and bizarre equipment as they list. I daresay the Royal Geographical Society will have a more up-to-date opinion. I have noticed that the books are all agreed on one thing: the women in those parts have the reputation of being sluttish, accommodating and extremely handsome. That is something that will not have changed. Lucy and I will come with you and Danny of course. We women will certainly ride. One can ride mules but it seems excessively authentic. I believe that royalty in those parts use the white camel as their favoured form of transport.'

The tea had shrunk to crusts and crumbs. The baskets, flasks and hampers were much lighter to carry on the journey home.

Honor and Lucy led the way, deep in detailed discussion of the *tenue* suitable for exotic parts. Behind them Peter and Danny heard odd snatches: hats, veils against sun and sand, the merits of mosquito creams, citronella candles and the vexed question of footwear. Danny started to dawdle and fall behind as he stopped listening and moved into his own world. Peter had learnt about the boy's pace slowing as his mind made journeys; on these occasions he always fell in behind the boy, assuming the role of reassuring backstop. Danny's past still impinged, and then the small boy's freckled face would take on the dogged look of unconcern which meant he was back in a hostile land that not even

Peter could reach. But sometimes lately there had been rare gleams when Danny had spoken to Peter of his own accord with sudden strong bursts of feeling.

Danny stopped, waiting for Peter to catch up. Under a pale and lustrous sky the swallows were dipping. Distance had dwindled the two women's voices to a murmur. The boy's face was gentle and preoccupied, entirely without the look of closed unsureness he had worn unremittingly for so many months. Peter took his time catching up. Nothing must be hurried, nothing forced.

Danny was frowning and the tip of his tongue had crept out of the corner of his mouth. Peter knew this as a sure sign. Danny had thought of one of those questions he couldn't find an answer to; one of those big fundamental puzzles of life that he used to ask about as they walked up the drive of the Brook House on Peter's Sunday visits: 'Where does the wind come from?' or 'How do you make more blood?' What was the boy thinking now? What surprising question had the enquiring mind thrown up?

Impatient of waiting, the boy started to run back the last short distance between them. He wanted to ask Peter about all the new words he had heard Honor and Lucy use. He was puzzled by so many strange words all at once, but not unhappy. Caravanserai, citronella, silkworm, mirage, Mongolia; each word a fragment of a new kaleidoscope. How did the new words fit with the other new words he'd heard today: obelisk, necropolis, mausoleum, redemption? The words belonged to different places in the world, but he bet Peter could make them all come together and be connected. Peter could make everything in the whole world belong together and be connected. He could do anything.

The words jumbled and swirled through his mind; they flew through his thoughts and landed like butterflies on a great white obelisk shining against a cloud castle in a silver sky. Peter was beside him telling him their meanings as they walked side by side along a road that spiralled and spun like a brightly coloured silk ribbon floating through dazzlingly fine and changing light. Green dragons drowsed in fruit-heavy thickets on either side of the disembodied road, spotted leopards draped themselves over vast shiny magnolia trees. Lucy and Honor towered above him in huge white hats on huge white camels. Their kind, familiar faces shone down, smiling at him through the shimmering light.

The imprint of this strange enchanted world swam in his eyes even after Peter had caught up and they had fallen into step, climbing the rutted mossy track together at an easy pace.

'Please,' Danny could contain the question no longer, he had to know. 'Please can you tell me? How do you walk on a road made of silk? Is it difficult?'